UNWILLINGLY HIS

GILDED DECADENCE
BOOK FIVE

ZOE BLAKE
ALTA HENSLEY

Published by Stormy Night Publications and Design, LLC.
Blake, Zoe
Hensley, Alta
Unwillingly His

Digital Cover Graphics: Korey Mae Johnson
Photographer: Emma Jane
Model: David Wills
Original Custom Paperback Illustration: Yozart
Paperback Graphics: Deranged Doctor

INTRODUCING

**The sinfully decadent dream project
of best friends and USA TODAY Bestselling authors,
Zoe Blake and Alta Hensley.**

Alta Hensley, renowned for her hot, dark, and dirty romances,
showcases her distinctive blend of alpha heroes, captivating love
stories, and scorching eroticism.

Meanwhile, Zoe Blake brings a touch of darkness and glamour
to the series, featuring her signature style of possessive
billionaires, taboo scenes, and unexpected twists.

Together they combine their storytelling prowess to deliver
"Twice the Darkness," promising sordid scandals, hidden secrets,
and forbidden desires of New York's jaded high society in their
new series,
Gilded Decadence.

THE GILDED DECADENCE SERIES

A seductively dark tale of privilege and passion.

Ripping off the gilded veneer of elite privilege exposes the sordid scandals, dark secrets, and taboo desires of New York's jaded high society. Where the corrupt game is a seductive power struggle of old money, social prestige, and fragile fortunes... only the most ruthless survive.

Ruthlessly His
Book One
#arrangedmarriage

Savagely His
Book Two
#kidnapped/capture

Brutally His
Book Three
#officeromance

Reluctantly His
Book Four
#bodyguard

Unwillingly His
Book Five
#agegap

Sinfully His
Book Six
#taboopriest
(comingsoon)

CONTENTS

Chapter 1	1
Chapter 2	3
Chapter 3	9
Chapter 4	13
Chapter 5	19
Chapter 6	23
Chapter 7	27
Chapter 8	31
Chapter 9	41
Chapter 10	49
Chapter 11	55
Chapter 12	61
Chapter 13	69
Chapter 14	77
Chapter 15	81
Chapter 16	87
Chapter 17	95
Chapter 18	103
Chapter 19	111
Chapter 20	117
Chapter 21	127
Chapter 22	133
Chapter 23	143
Chapter 24	155
Chapter 25	165
Chapter 26	173
Chapter 27	179
Chapter 28	187
Chapter 29	199
Chapter 30	207
Chapter 31	215
Chapter 32	223
Chapter 33	231
Chapter 34	237

Chapter 35   243
Chapter 36   249
Chapter 37   255
Chapter 38   261
Chapter 39   267
Epilogue   271

The Gilded Decadence Series   273
About Zoe Blake   279
Also By Zoe Blake   281
About Alta Hensley   293
Also By Alta Hensley   295
Thank you   303

CHAPTER 1

STELLA

I stormed across the courtroom and slapped Lucian Manwarring across the face.

Unlike in the movies, there were no shocked gasps, no outraged cries, no laughter.

Definitely no laughter.

There wasn't even the repeated frenzied slam of a gavel as a red-faced judge screamed, 'Order! Order in the court!'.

There was only silence.

Tense, repressive, ominous… silence.

After all, I had just slapped a vengeful god.

At least that was what everyone was thinking around me. I could *literally feel* their mortal terror. It radiated off the assembled courtroom like a wave of heat after a bomb blast.

Lucian Manwarring was the foreboding patriarch of the powerful and rich Manwarring family. His exploits in business were famous… or rather infamous. There were few people in New York who weren't terrified of this man.

When crossed, he didn't get angry, he got even. Scorched

earth even. His billion-dollar whiskey empire was built on the charred remains of countless other businesses and men.

He was feared, respected, reviled, and envied.

My father had hated him with a burning, white-hot passion.

Which was why it made no sense. Why would he name Lucian Manwarring the trustee over my inheritance in the event of his death?

A sharp pain pierced my chest.

They were gone. Both of them. My parents had been taken from me in an instant.

A vision of twisted car metal, the smell of blood, and my mother's moans as snowflakes gently drifted down on me from the opening in the torn roof floated across my inner eye. I shook the disturbing image away.

I needed to focus.

If I didn't do something, Lucian would succeed in not only stealing my entire inheritance, but in having complete control over my life until I turned twenty-nine. That was three years from now!

The very idea of being under this man's thumb for that long was untenable.

My right palm stung, but I resisted the urge to rub it against my thigh.

I didn't want to give the bastard the satisfaction of knowing he had hurt me.

Trying to match his glare, my eyes watered as I refused to blink.

Or were they tears?

Through clenched teeth, I threatened, "You won't get away with this."

The corner of his mouth lifted. "Little one, I already have."

CHAPTER 2

LUCIAN

*H*ow amusing.

Stella Deiderich had struck me.

In public, no less.

Of course, now I would need to teach her a lesson.

She'd need to learn what happened to bad little girls the hard way.

The easy way never seemed to stick.

Rising slowly, I raised my hand to the judge to signal he was not to interfere.

I circled the plaintiff's desk as I buttoned my suit jacket before stepping up to her.

In business, I used every advantage, no matter how trivial, to get the upper hand.

One such advantage was my superior height.

Usually taller than the average man in the room, I completely towered over Stella's slight frame.

She really was uncommonly beautiful, despite her age. With more maturity and life experience, I could see her becoming an absolutely stunning woman. At the moment, she was a little too thin, perhaps from her sudden grief. And her eyes held the wild, unguarded emotions of youth, rather than the calculated intelligence of a woman who knew her place in the world.

Recent events had shown me I needed to make some changes to my life.

Marriage, for one.

This wasn't about love or any superfluous need for affection, but more about preservation.

My children had shown an admirable, if inconvenient, rebellious and stubborn nature as of late. It had become clear: if my vision for the future of my company was to be realized, I would need more offspring. And for that, I needed a wife.

The idea of searching for one was as distasteful as it would have been inconvenient.

Fortunately, the perfect prospect had practically fallen into my lap.

Stella.

Her father, that moron Wallace Oliver Deiderich, had decided to travel in an ice storm several months ago. He'd managed to kill himself, his wife, and the driver in a terrible crash. He had also very nearly killed his daughter.

It was chilling to recall. I had held her in my arms not moments before when she'd accidentally bumped into me on the sidewalk that night after slipping on the ice.

If I had known...

I recalled being intrigued not only by her beauty... but by her obvious hatred—of me.

Clearly her father had been distasteful enough to share his business woes with his wife and child. I imagine they were regaled over the dinner table with tales of my evil manipulations as I'd divested him of numerous companies and investments, significantly reducing not only his fortune but his influence.

I wouldn't apologize for it.

Wallace was an idiot who had run those companies into the ground.

While the world and my peers may have perceived my actions as the worst of corporate greed, I knew the truth.

Over five thousand people, close to thirty-five hundred families, and four entire towns in the Midwest would have been eviscerated with unemployment, bankruptcy, and debt when his factories eventually closed from mismanagement—had I not stepped in.

Still, it served my purposes for the public to think the worst.

In business, no one liked to cross the devil in a corporate boardroom.

True to his bumbling nature, Wallace had neglected to update his will.

The foolish man had me listed as the executor of his estate and trustee to his precious daughter's fortune, a leftover detail from an early friendship from our college days that had long been relegated to the trash bin.

Well, one man's stupid fuck up was another man's opportunity.

Aware of the suspended silence in the courtroom, I pinched her chin between my fingers and leaned in, whispering close to her ear so we were not overheard by the keenly interested crowd, "You'll pay for that."

Her back stiffened.

Before she could pull away, I wrapped a firm hand around her upper arm and spun her in the direction of the exit.

The courtroom erupted in excited chatter and camera phone clicks.

Dammit.

I loathed public spectacles. As of late, it had been my errant children's romantic exploits keeping our family name in the tabloids. Now it would be mine.

"Mr. Manwarring," the judge called, stopping me.

"Yes, your honor?" Even though he worked for me, I kept my tone light and polite. This was still his courtroom, and I needed to keep up appearances.

"Did you want to press charges for assault? Or I can hold her in contempt of court? Maybe a few days in a cell will fix her attitude, or I could—"

I raised an eyebrow to stop the judge's eager-to-please mouth vomit before others in the courtroom caught on to his obvious bias towards me.

Stella sucked in a breath of air, and I turned to look at her.

The anger in her eyes had melted into fear, with a delectable hint of loathing as she turned her glare on the judge.

"Well, Stella, do you need a few days in a cell?" I asked casually. "Or do you think we can straighten out your attitude problem on our own?"

Her hazel eyes flicked back to me.

Then her lips parted, as if she were going to say something.

Instead, her gaze fell to her shoes.

"Good girl," I rasped against her light brown hair before turning back to the judge. "No, your honor. I think it was just a momentary lapse in judgment. She is, after all, just a girl who lost both of her parents. I'm sure with some proper guidance, she'll *behave*."

Stella sucked in an indignant gasp as she attempted to wrench her arm from my grasp.

I held firm.

The judge nodded. "Very well."

With her arm still securely in my hand, I squeezed a little harder, as a warning.

Then I marched her through the wooden double doors of the courtroom and down the hall.

"Let me go," she growled under her breath as we passed several curious onlookers.

I pushed her over the threshold of the nearest conference room. "Careful. You are in no position to be making demands."

Then, I turned and locked the door.

CHAPTER 3

LUCIAN

These conference rooms were used for holding prisoners for final conversations with their attorneys before trial. Which meant the walls were thick, the locks secure, and there were no cameras.

If I wanted, I could flip that skimpy schoolgirl skirt she was wearing up to expose her ass and whip it with my belt, and there wasn't a thing she could do about it.

Rubbing her arm, she narrowed her gaze on me. "How dare you."

"You might want to watch your tone, little one. The only thing that should be coming out of your mouth is an apology."

"An apology? For what? You bribed the judge to... to..."

She didn't even know how to put into words the trap I had so easily set for her.

The bars of my gilded cage had closed so rapidly around her, she never stood a chance.

However, she was wrong about one detail. I did not bribe the judge.

God no. Bribes were too easily traced or turned into extortion. Their greedy hands were always out for more. Absolutely not. Bribing a judge was bad business.

Blackmailing a judge, on the other hand...

Crossing my arms, I leaned against the door, further blocking her only exit. "To what? Do as your father asked?"

"He would never," she said, her eyes wide.

The lie slipped easily from my lips. "Your father was a smart businessman. He wanted the best man possible to watch over his precious daughter."

"I don't believe you."

I raised an eyebrow. "Whether you believe it or not, is immaterial. It's now been affirmed by the courts."

"A corrupt court."

I smiled. "A court nonetheless."

"He hated you," she fired back. "He would have never trusted you with anything. He called you an unethical, evil bastard. There is no way my father gave a man like you control over *my* estate."

Heat traveled up my spine as I rotated my shoulders, letting the anger flow through me before I grabbed her by her frail neck and pressed her against the wall.

Usually I would react with almost disturbing calm to such an attack, but there was something about hearing those sweet, full lips disparage my character that had swiftly and alarmingly gotten under my skin.

Stella's fingers clawed at my hands, the gold bangles on her wrist clinking against the old masculine watch that was far too big for her.

I pressed my body against hers, pinning her to the wall, still holding her throat firmly in my grasp. She could breathe in raspy gasps, but that was more than she deserved.

"Listen closely to me, little one. It doesn't matter what lies your father told you. The facts are simple. You belong to me now. I will now control what you do, where you sleep, and who you associate with. You can't even buy a fucking cup of coffee without my permission."

"I am twenty-six, an adult. I should have access to my own money."

If this world were a fair place, then she would be right.

She would have access to her money, and it wouldn't have been so fucking easy for me to control her.

Too bad for her, life was anything but fair.

Fortunes and empires were built by men bold enough to claim what they wanted.

Men like me.

And at this particular moment, Stella was in my crosshairs.

I needed an obedient wife with connections and breeding. Her fortune certainly helped as well. She would bear the next brood of Manwarring sons. Maybe she would give me children that obeyed.

It would be a challenge at first. I would have preferred a more mature woman.

The young still harbored silly notions like love and happily-ever-after. They talked incessantly about nothing and had no real drive or experience. Spending time with people her age was tedious at best. To have someone young seemed like an unavoidable chore.

But then there was the lure of witnessing her come into her own, as the woman I suspected she was capable of becoming. It would be like watching something at the very moment of creation.

How fascinating that would be.

It helped that I would be the one molding her, training her.

Like the omniscient god so many amusingly suspected me of being.

The gold in her gorgeous eyes glowed with fiery indignation. "You paid the courts off."

I shrugged one shoulder as I focused on her mouth. "Semantics."

Tears filled her pretty eyes and spilled down her cheeks. "Why are you doing this to me?"

Leaning so close I could smell the sweet vanilla of her perfume, my lips skimmed her jaw as I whispered into her ear, "Because I have plans for you, pet. Plans that include making you my wife."

Her golden eyes widened with understanding, or maybe it was more fear. "I will never marry you. Hell will freeze over before I—"

I cut off her words, pressing my lips to hers.

She fought me for a second, squirming against my hold.

That only made me tighten my grip on her throat and press against her harder.

She needed to learn she could fight me—but she'd never win against me.

Her only option was to submit.

CHAPTER 4

STELLA

*D*ark, unholy fire ignited in my veins.

For weeks, I had been so cold, as if I were frozen from the inside out.

Sitting by the fire or drinking a steaming cup of tea brought no warmth.

Nothing broke through the chill.

Until his unwanted kiss.

It was wrong. So freaking wrong.

He was an unrepentant, arrogant bastard.

He was twenty years older than me.

He was the devil who'd just stolen everything from me.

But his touch was the only thing that had managed to crack the frigid layer around my core.

With his body pressed against mine, the icy cast covering my skin cracked and broke away.

And when his lips touched mine, it all melted.

I melted.

A chilling fog had crept over every corner of my life since the accident.

It didn't matter how many layers I wore or how high I turned the heat on. Even long baths with scalding water that left my skin raw and bright pink did nothing to warm me.

Until Lucian Manwarring had the audacity to touch me.

His kiss was dangerous.

I was holding a knife by the blade, heedless of the blood dripping over my fingers, focusing only on the warmth of the crimson drops.

I couldn't let this happen.

With as much strength as I had, I shoved him back.

He broke the kiss and grinned down at me like he'd just learned my darkest secret.

I had given up something… and he was going to use it against me.

My stomach soured.

This man, this tall barbarian in a suit, had stolen from me.

He had taken all of my inheritance. And worse than that, he was taking my freedom.

All of my plans for the future were fading like wisps of smoke.

As if I were no more than a petulant child, I wanted to stomp my foot and exclaim, 'no fair'.

I was an intelligent, fully capable, legal adult. Unlike half the heiresses I knew who seemed to think it was a stylish accessory to brag about their time in rehab, or getting kicked out of numerous universities, or needing their family to write a check to pay off an injured suitor.

I was a well-educated, even-tempered, mentally stable, responsible woman in her prime who had done what she'd been told her entire life. I hadn't even so much as had a boyfriend, let alone a pregnancy scare.

There was no legal reason any of this should have happened to me.

Other than that I had a shitty lawyer and a corrupt judge.

The way that judge had talked down to me, and the way my lawyer, a man who was supposed to advocate for me, had just given in, was infuriating.

Ice-cold anger surrounded my heart, strengthening my stomach, and finally, I was able to have an appropriate reaction.

I let my hand fly again, ready to strike Lucian across his handsome face, not caring how much hitting a jaw that firm stung my palm.

This time, I used my left. My right was still throbbing from the first hit.

Unfortunately, Manwarring was expecting it.

He grabbed my wrist mid-flight and pinned it to the wall next to my head.

"You already used your one shot," he growled, lowering his face to mine again. "If you try to strike me again, I'll take off my belt. Understood?"

Take off his belt?

As in *spank* me?

He wouldn't dare!

"Fuck you," I bit out, trying to pull my hand out of his grasp.

His cold, dark gaze lowered to my lips.

Without my own volition, my tongue flicked out to lick them.

He swept his thumb over my lower lip. "Such dirty words from such an innocent mouth."

He was taunting me, and I didn't appreciate it, or the way his vile words made my heart speed up with something far from disgust.

"Let go of me," I said, gritting my teeth.

He tightened his grip on my wrist while his other hand moved to my hip. The tips of his fingers pressed into my flesh as he squeezed. "No."

"I said, let go of me," I said again, trying so hard to keep the anger and hatred in my voice so he didn't see my truth.

I didn't want him to know that his touch felt good. It was so warm, it was almost painful, in the same way that sinking into a hot bath after being in the cold hurt for a moment until your body relaxed into the most delicious, soothing heat.

I mustn't give in to that warmth. It was flamed by the fires of hell, obeying its master here on earth.

A bit dramatic? Yes. Untrue? Absolutely not.

"Trust me, little one. You're trapped in a game you can't win."

"Trust you? I'd rather eat glass, you manipulative bastard."

"There's that dirty mouth again."

His lips slammed down on mine.

I tried to fight, to pull away from him, but was drawn to the painful heat of his embrace.

His fire was too tempting, daring me to submit.

Lucian's kiss was both tantalizing and dangerous, like sin.

The second I opened my lips to him, he took full advantage, sliding his tongue into my mouth, not just tasting me.

No, he was claiming me.

He let go of my wrist just to put that hand back at my throat.

He wasn't choking me, but he kept a tight enough grip to prove the threat.

More than just taking my money, he was taking everything.

In that terrible, unrestrained moment, I didn't care.

His hand was so warm, it fractured the constant cold around me. His other hand roamed my body, groping my breasts over my shirt.

Lucian's hard cock pressed against my lower stomach, holding me in place.

I wasn't very experienced with men.

I wasn't experienced with men at all, actually.

Until this man had stolen my first kiss, I had been untouched.

Even with my limited experience, he still seemed uncomfortably large.

He was not supposed to be for me. Just as I was not made for him.

But that didn't stop his lips from moving down my neck.

With a vicious twist, he tore my shirt open. The delicate pearl buttons snapped then pinged and clattered as they skittered across the floor.

The cool air caressed my sensitive flesh, but that did not last.

His gaze trailed over my body, quickly heating my skin.

I sank my fingernails into his shoulders. "This is wrong. You have to stop."

It did nothing to deter him as he pressed his cock harder against my stomach, making sure I felt every inch.

"You cannot win. Submit to me," he rasped against the sensitive skin just under my jaw.

His words brought the cold back.

This time in the form of a spike of frozen fear down my spine.

Submit?

What does he mean by that?

CHAPTER 5

STELLA

*D*id he mean sex?

Here? In this public conference room?

Over this scarred and used table?

Holding onto my virtue into my twenties had been a choice.

I knew my worth.

And despite what Lucian might think, I'd also taken my responsibility as an heiress seriously. No man was going to *one night and flight* me, ruining my chances of an advantageous marriage.

I had a plan for my life, and it included marrying well and being a respected, high society matron. As an alumnus of Brearley Academy, I intended to continue the commitment to charity and community service instilled in me at the distinguished Upper East Manhattan school.

I might have been young, but I knew how the world worked.

Money bought a person influence.

And influence gave a person power for change.

With my fortune and a good marriage, I could influence

legislation and policy as well as affect real change in people's lives through better education, supporting the arts, scholarships.

The sky was the limit.

My parents had never believed in my altruistic vision, especially my father.

While I grieved for their loss and would never have wished them harm, their deaths had freed me.

Finally I could realize my goals and have a real purpose in life beyond being the dutiful daughter.

And none of this included becoming the kept, trophy wife of Lucian Manwarring.

People jeered behind his back that his first wife had really died of hypothermia instead of in childbirth. While I thought that was an impossibly cruel thing to say about anyone, even him, I couldn't help thinking there was a reason why his name hadn't been attached to any woman since her death twenty years ago.

The man was nothing but a ruthless monster, intent on amassing power and an even impossibly larger fortune to lord over everyone.

With renewed determination, I resisted him.

"Get off of me!" I cried out as I struggled within his embrace.

With both of my hands on his muscular shoulders, I pushed as hard as I could.

He didn't move an inch. "Make me."

"Please," I begged again as his mouth then moved down, pulling one of my nipples out of my bra and sucking the tip, nibbling just enough to give it a slight twinge of pain with the pleasure.

My core tightened, and I bit into my bottom lip to stop myself from moaning.

My pussy pulsed with need.

His mouth felt so good. The illicit pressure built in my core as a flush of heat moved from my head down to my toes and back again.

"Tell me what I want to hear, and I will reward you," he said before sucking on my other nipple while pinching the first.

His other hand moved down my side. Grasping the hem of my skirt, he wrenched it high over my hip before sliding his hand under my ass. The tips of his fingers played with the elastic edge of my panties.

"I don't know what you want to hear." I was practically panting, but I didn't want him to know I was on the verge of coming apart at the seams.

My brain was screaming no, but my body was begging for more.

"Tell me you'll be a good girl for me. That you'll do as you're told."

My first instinct was to tell him what he wanted to hear.

To tell him that I needed him to touch me more. That I would be a good girl for him.

Then I opened my eyes, seeing past his shoulder and the room around us. It was a stark reminder of where we were, who I was with, and why.

With a strength I didn't know I had, I pushed aside the hormones, the need, and the craving for his heat. "Go *back* to hell, Lucian Manwarring."

CHAPTER 6

LUCIAN

"*D*o you want a chance to rethink those words, little one?"

It had never been my intention to fuck her in the courthouse, but if she continued to defy me, I wouldn't be responsible for my actions.

The idea of bending her over that nearby conference table and pounding my cock into her from behind until she screamed for mercy had a strong appeal.

This lack of control was not characteristic of me, but there was something about her.

I had to resist the urge to squeeze her throat tighter until I controlled the very breath that entered her lungs. I wanted her on her knees, begging me for her very life.

I wanted her grateful for the slightest kindness I deemed to show her.

I wanted her.

Pure and simple.

Wanted her in a way I hadn't wanted another woman... in well... a very long time.

It didn't make sense, but then again, I wasn't exactly thinking with my brain.

Logic had no place in this.

"You may be able to force a puppet judge to take my fortune, but even you couldn't force me to marry you."

My thumb brushed over her lower lip. "So naive."

Poor little thing didn't realize just how much power I wielded in this city.

If I wanted her for my wife, she could protest all the way to the altar, and it wouldn't make a difference.

She would be my wife.

Morally wrong? Probably. Not that I gave a damn. "Keep fighting me, and there will be consequences."

I backed up just enough to let her body slide down mine before stepping away from her.

Stella's gaze darted around the room while she gripped both sides of her shirt, trying to cover her full breasts with her hard nipples peeking through the delicate pink lace of her bra.

"Consequences?" She barked out a laugh. "What more could you do? You've already taken everything from me."

"I haven't begun to take from you."

"Is that a threat?"

"It's a promise. I have decided you will be useful for my future plans. And I won't allow your childish temper tantrums to stand in the way of what will be a lucrative and beneficial merger of assets between us."

"A merger! Do you hear yourself? It's a marriage, not a business deal."

I shrugged one shoulder. "Same difference as far as I'm concerned."

She crossed her arms. "Well, you can just *merge your assets* with some other woman, because I'm not interested."

My fingertips rubbed the center of my forehead. Fuck, I

hated tedious complications. "Once again, you are assuming you have a choice. I'm not sure how I can make myself clearer. This is happening."

She bared her teeth. "Over my dead body."

I chuckled as I shrugged out of my suit jacket. Twisting off first the left, then the right diamond cufflink, I said, "That could be arranged. After the honeymoon, of course."

Stella lurched backward as if she'd been struck. "I'll go to the media."

"I control the media."

"The police then."

"Them too."

She slid along the wall farther away from me. "You can't get away with this."

The heavy cufflinks clattered against the conference table surface as I tossed them aside before reaching for the buckle of my belt. "I already have."

Her eyes widened. "Stay away from me."

"No." I unbuckled my belt and slowly pulled it from the loops.

I bent the belt in half, then tested it against my thigh. The leather did give a satisfying snap, and the sting was intense. Perfect for what I needed it for.

"What are you going to do with that belt?" Her voice was shaking as she pressed her body against the wall.

"Whatever the fuck I want," I growled, reaching out and wrapping my hand in her hair before pulling her away from the wall and bending her over the large conference table in the middle of the room.

I held her down by the hair with one hand, then lifted her skirt and pulled down her white satin panties with the other.

Her ass was a perfect, unblemished porcelain white.

It was probably why she was such a brat. She had never been punished.

That changed now.

Her entire body tensed as the belt made a whispered slice through the air before it cracked against her delicate flesh, leaving a bright red streak diagonally across both cheeks.

She squirmed under my grip, but I pressed her down harder, not letting her move as she cried out.

I let the belt fly again, crossing the first mark with another. Then again and again as her screams and yelps morphed into sobs.

"Someone help me!"

"No one can hear your screams," I leaned down to whisper in her ear while my hand ran over the red-hot skin of her ass.

"I'll be a good girl, I promise. Please. It hurts." She sounded so sweet begging, but that didn't stop my hand from moving down her punished ass to in-between her thighs.

Nothing could have prepared me for what I felt. Her pussy was swollen, aching for me, and practically dripping wet. Had she been this wet when I sucked on her sweet little nipples, or was it my kiss? Or perhaps she got off on being spanked?

Interesting.

My fingers explored between her soaked lips to find her impossibly tight little channel. "I haven't begun to hurt you. You're about to learn the painful cost of crossing me."

I slid two fingers in deep, pressing against her G spot as I watched her squirm and cry for me. My thumb moved down to her clit and worked in quick little circles.

Her tight cunt pulsed around my fingers, showing me how good she would feel impaled on my cock.

"Oh, God. Please, don't!" she begged again as she rose on her toes.

Her pleas sounded so sweet on her lips.

"Are you beginning to understand, little pet? I own you. And no one would dare try and save you from me."

CHAPTER 7

LUCIAN

I thrust my fingers in deeper, meeting a resistance I hadn't felt in years.

It was hard to believe she was untouched. How a woman in this day and age made it to twenty-six without getting fucked, I would never know.

A rush of possessive pride roared through my veins. It was similar to the rush I got when I crushed an enemy in the board-room, but so much more satisfying.

Like being the first to own a priceless gold artifact or painting.

There was treasure, and then there was untainted, unspoiled, pure treasure.

I stared down at her skin as if it gleamed like polished gold— the only fingerprints on it, my own.

I yanked her hair back, so I could see her face as I moved my fingers deeper inside her, pressing against that G-spot that I now knew no one had ever touched before. There was a sinking suspicion in my gut that told me she hadn't even found this plea-sure spot herself.

My gut was always right.

Stella's cheeks were bright red and tearstained. And if it wasn't for the way her lips were parted in awe and her eyes closed, I would have thought that she was actually in pain.

I knew she wasn't.

I knew she liked this.

Her body was begging me for more.

Her wet heat gripped my fingers, pulling them in and urging me to keep going.

With two fingers, I press down on her G-spot while I rubbed tighter circles with my thumb on her clit, giving her just a little more pressure.

The cutest little sighs and moans escaped her lips as her body tensed under me, and her thighs shook.

The lure of knowing I would be the first man, the only man, to ever fill her, drove me to near primal force. Yet I resisted the urge to claim her tight sheath. I would not breed the future Mrs. Manwarring on a fucking table for criminals.

That wouldn't stop me from punishing her, though.

"Have you learned your lesson yet, pet?" I teased her.

"Yes," she said with a gasp.

"Good girl. Now, don't come yet," I growled, pushing into her harder. "That's an order."

"I don't know how to stop it," she cried out.

"If you come before I give you permission, I'm going to make it impossible for you to sit down without thinking about me for days," I warned.

She muffled another cry between her clenched jaw, her hands tightening into fists on each side of her head, and despite herself, her hips pressed down, with her ass tilted up, giving me an even better angle.

I knew she hadn't intended on doing that either.

But that just made it all the sweeter.

Stella may not have wanted me, but her body sure as fuck did.

I kept up the pressure even as I pushed her higher and higher, her pussy pulsing against my fingers. Her hands rolled into fists so tight, her knuckles whitened, and cries of pleasure and pain escaped her lips.

"Do you want to come for me?" I asked, knowing every time I spoke, it racked her up a little tighter.

"No," she whimpered petulantly.

I chuckled. Taunting her was too much fun to pass up. "What was that, little one? Did you just ask me to tan your pretty ass with my leather belt again?"

She shook her head. "No, please! Don't."

"Then you better come up with a more pleasing answer to my question. Now."

She sniffed as she balled her fist against her lips, muffling her words. "I want to come for you."

"Say it louder. I want to hear you beg for it."

"Please, make me come. I want to feel… to feel… your hands."

"But, bad girls don't get to come. Bad girls get spanked hard and are left with wet aching pussies and no satisfaction." I growled the words, and she whined, her hips wiggling as she tried to get more friction. "So, are you going to be my good girl now?"

"Yes," she moaned.

"Then be a good girl and show me how you come."

No sooner had I said the words than her back arched painfully as her pussy clamped down hard on my fingers and wetness gushed onto my hand.

I kept working her through her orgasm as her body shook. I kept up the pressure, letting her ride out every single wave of pleasure.

It would be such a shame to let this perfect, aching pussy go to waste.

It would be so easy to press my cock into her right now while she was so willing, so desperate for it. But only a real bastard would take a woman's virginity while she was bent over a conference table.

I toyed with the idea for a few more moments, fingers still buried deep inside her as her breathing evened out as she came down from the endorphins.

Over the years, there had been several things that made me a bastard, a son of a bitch and even a mother fucker.

Fuck it. One more sin wasn't going to take me even further into hell.

I unzipped my pants and put the head of my aching cock at her entrance, ready to push in as she went completely still.

"Beg," I demanded.

She opened her lips, but was interrupted by a knock on the door.

"Dammit," I swore under my breath as I remembered where I was and tucked my hard cock back into my pants.

Another knock, this one more demanding, sounded at the door.

Tossing my suit jacket over her prone form, I commanded. "Stay there."

I opened the door to the bailiff, standing there looking awkward as hell. He couldn't even meet my gaze.

"What?" I demanded.

"It's… uh… sir… we wanted to make sure everything is in order. This room is booked in twenty minutes."

Before I could tear into him, Stella with her skirt down and her blouse hastily put back together under my jacket, pushed her way out of the door and ran down the hallway.

She could run all she liked, but there would be no hiding from me… or my intentions.

CHAPTER 8

STELLA

"*I* just don't understand." I fumed, slamming my teacup down into the porcelain saucer, instantly silencing the entire room.

I looked around the lovely room with its creme walls with splashes of natural green all lit by a massive glass skylight. The tearoom in The Wharton was a more refined and less garish version of the tearoom at the Ritz-Carlton in London. It was light, airy, and welcoming.

Now all the ladies were staring at me, looking down their noses with expressions that ranged from mild irritation to annoyance. A few were downright furious I had interrupted the vibe of the service.

I gave the room an apologetic and abashed look, communicating my sincerest apologies before turning back to my table.

My mind had been racing since leaving the courthouse.

I didn't know what to do.

How was I supposed to deal with any of this?

The only thing I could think to do was get help from a few friends.

In life, we all knew it wasn't what you knew, but who you knew.

Connections in high society were everything.

Maybe one of my friends had a father or a brother who was a brilliant enough lawyer to help me through this.

Hopefully, another one was a psychiatrist, because after what I had let happen in that conference room, I was clearly in need of psychiatric intervention.

Of course, that would only happen after everything else was settled.

Otherwise, it would be used against me.

If a man saw a professional for help, he was being smart.

If a woman did it, she was weak.

After I left the courthouse, I sent out several SOS text messages, and my friends rallied around me.

Within twenty minutes, I was sitting in my favorite chair, at the head of my favorite table at The Wharton, with a calming chamomile steaming in the pot in front of me and women glaring at me.

I'd kill for something stronger than tea in this moment.

Unfortunately, with a woman of my stature, it didn't matter what I did as much as what it looked like I was doing. A single glass of wine at the bar might be perfectly fine, but a well-timed photo of that single glass of wine could write a false, inflammatory story that most would believe over the simple truth.

After all, a socialite falling to the dangers of drugs and alcohol made a much better story than a rich girl having a bad day. No one cared about the truth. They cared about the story.

They didn't even need to try too hard with the story.

A talented photographer could take fifteen to twenty pictures of me in a single night, take it home, and change the background of the bar, the dress I was wearing, and the levels of wine in my glass to make it look habitual. I couldn't risk it.

No wonder some of the older women snuck whisky into their tea.

It was technically against the rules, but we all knew they did it.

"So what does that mean?" one of the girls asked, pulling me back into the conversation.

"It means that I have somehow entered a time loop, and I'm now stuck in the fifties. Where a woman isn't allowed to have her own fortune. It means that despite being an adult, I now have an overbearing gorilla in a suit in control of my finances."

I left out the part about the "gorilla" being incredibly handsome and domineering, with a primal sexual energy that could make a woman lose all sense of propriety and place. Or that that same "gorilla" wanted to freaking marry me.

No point in boring my friends with the rougher details.

Thoughts of the rougher details brought back memories of his fingers inside me as he pulled a dark forbidden pleasure from my body. I'd never felt anything like that before. The mix of pain and pleasure had been exotic as well as erotic.

It was so incredibly wrong, and yet so deliciously right at the same time.

I pushed those thoughts away and took another long pull of my tea.

When I set my glass back down, Olivia, Amelia, and Charlotte were all looking at each other very uncomfortably.

Oh, damn. The man was their father! I should be more careful with what I said.

"Shoot, girls. I am so sorry. I know that he's your father and your father-in-law, but..."

"Oh no," Charlotte stopped me. "We understand. My father can be difficult—and complicated."

"What she means to say," Olivia interrupted her, "is that he's an arrogant, control-freak, who treats his family like he treats his company board, and does whatever he wants without any thought to anybody else, ever."

Amelia didn't add anything, but just took another sip of her tea, probably using that to silence her own thoughts on the subject. It was one thing to say something about a man as his daughter. But it was something else entirely to say it as his daughter-in-law.

"I'm still confused," Amelia said after a moment, putting down her cup. "Your lawyer didn't do anything?"

"No, he didn't argue it. He didn't fight for me. He didn't even give me a heads up on what was going to happen. It was like he, Lucian, and the judge had already decided everything, and this was just a formality."

"That can't be legal," Amelia said, careful not to talk about her father-in-law directly. "You are entitled to effective counsel."

"How do I go about filing something to overturn all of this?" I asked, resting my head in my hands for a moment.

"I have no idea," Amelia said. "Maybe I could ask Harrison? But he has been so busy lately with some cases. Even Luc is helping him with parts of it."

"Is that why they called Reid?" Charlotte asked. She was so smitten with her new husband, it was cute.

"I have no idea," Amelia said. "Oh, I know who you should ask. My new sister-in-law, Eddie. She is going to law school, and she is a brilliant paralegal. She'd have to be to impress Harrison. Maybe she could help?"

"Really?" I asked, sitting up, feeling a glimmer of hope.

Surely another woman wouldn't let me get steam rolled by the boys' club.

"Maybe. Between law school and helping my brother, she is really busy. She never has time to come to tea with Rose and me or go shopping. Maybe she doesn't like us, or we make her uncomfortable."

"You could never make anyone uncomfortable," Olivia said.

"Thank you. She is probably just really swamped with work. I think she is just as much of a workaholic as Harrison."

"Then it's a match made in heaven," I said with a smile that I hoped reached my eyes.

I tried to stay focused on the conversation at hand, but my mind kept going back to Manwarring Sr. and how his hands had felt on my body.

And how his cruel smile made my heart race.

What a twisted thing to think, let alone feel. That man had me all kinds of confused and mixed up.

The conversation around me continued as I tried to push thoughts of my encounter with Lucian out of my head. What he had done was unconscionable.

I could never let that happen again.

It *wouldn't* happen again.

I wondered how long I'd have to repeat that in my head before I believed it.

The truth was that I hadn't wanted it at first. But somewhere in there, while he was groping my body, stealing my kisses, and heating my core, everything had changed. My brain stopped protesting the violation and instead celebrated the unfamiliar domination of it all.

My desires turned dark, seductive, and erotic.

Ladies like me were not supposed to behave that way, especially about a man so much older than myself. It was unbecoming for a lady to act on something so primal.

Was it his anger, his hot temper, or was it something else that made his body burn like that?

I had always known that Lucian had a lust for life and for conquest. Not that I had seen it before personally, but I had heard my father's rantings and the rumors about what a vile man he was. The rumors covered everything from business deals done in bad faith to dealings with questionable enterprises.

It always made me wonder if he had ties to the criminal world.

He would hardly be the first man of his class to deal in the gray. But for most people, that meant insider trading, not brutish thugs, threats of violence, and mafia ties.

Of course, then there were the rumors about his lineage, those who said the Manwarrings did not belong in high society —education and net worth be damned.

He was not Old English money as he claimed to be, but instead came from impoverished Irish stock. They said that the Manwarrings made a fortune during prohibition with counterfeit whiskey. Those same people gossiped that it was to be expected that Lucian operated the way he did.

What else would you expect from a man whose fortune was built off of lies and deceit?

I had heard all of the rumors floating about them, but I never looked down on them for it.

I found the Manwarring clan to be interesting.

Every other family in our circle had been handed everything.

Many of the men never earned their titles or their wealth. They merely made back room deals on the golf course or in steam rooms and had other people manage everything.

So to see a family who took what they wanted instead of waiting for someone to give it to them, was intriguing.

My father, in particular, had hated Lucian Manwarring. I never knew why exactly, just that my father said he was a brute and did not operate by the rules of polite society.

The rules of polite society were built to keep those born with privilege on top and those not under their heel.

While Luc Manwarring was absolutely born into the same

privilege, I wondered if he felt the newness of his money, only a few generations from poverty.

If my grandfather had been the one to build the Deiderich name and fill its coffers, would my father have been the same?

Was it the generations of wealth that bred the primal savagery out of the other men in my class?

Was that what made Lucian Manwarring Sr.'s blood run so much hotter than anyone else's?

Was that why he could break through the ice still on my skin when nothing else could?

My mind drifted back to the things he had done to me, the way he'd touched me, and how even as he'd spanked me with that belt, it hurt, but the sting of each strike faded into a warm, soothing heat.

And then the way he made me react to him, that explosion of heat and pleasure he drew from my body as my own wetness trailed down my thighs.

Just thinking about it lit a small fire in my gut that melted the ice again. I had to push the feeling down.

Extinguish that flame with shame and regret.

Ladies like me were not supposed to feel like that.

It was the way he'd almost put his cock inside my core that filled me with the most shame.

Not only that he was about to push inside of me and take my virginity, but that I'd wanted him to. I was seconds away from pushing back into him myself when that knock sounded at the door and brought me back to reality.

Had I done so, I would have destroyed all of my plans for the future.

How could a man have made me feel so completely out of control that I would have discarded everything I believed in, for more of his touch?

The very idea of someone having that much control over me was terrifying.

"I just don't know what to do!" I said again, stopping the conversation at my table that I had completely lost track of. Again.

My mother would have been ashamed of me for that outburst, and I knew it was rude, but I just couldn't hold it in.

"Do you need to do anything?" Charlotte asked. "You still live in your own home. You still have access to some money. You just need to hold out for three years."

I didn't want to tell Charlotte that I was pretty certain her father intended to marry me himself well before those three years were up.

I also didn't want to point out that I was in this position because of her. It was her wedding we had been leaving when the accident had happened.

It was her father who had taken my money because she ruined his plans.

She disobeyed her father, and now she was living happily ever after with her husband, and I was paying the price.

I chided myself. Such thoughts were immature and churlish and completely unfair to sweet, kind Charlotte.

"I can't just do nothing. There is no telling what he will do in three years."

"Let me reach out to Harrison and his wife. This isn't the kind of thing they handle, but I am sure they know someone." Amelia reached across the table and put her hand on mine.

I clasped her hand and gave her a grateful smile.

Maybe I could get out of this before Lucian made too big of a dent in my lifestyle or my father's money.

"Okay, please allow me to pay for tea. It's only fair since I occupied the conversation." Just like that, I was back in a good mood and remembered the social graces I was raised into.

"Thank you," the others said as I handed my black Amex to the white-gloved waiter.

Feeling a little stronger and ignoring thoughts of Lucian touching me and the wetness between my thighs that those thoughts brought, I was able to refocus on the conversation at hand.

Charlotte was shopping for a new home for her and her husband, and there were so many choices: the Upper West Side, trendy areas like SoHo, or maybe even some grand estate just outside the city.

We laughed at the notion of living outside the city until we saw the dreaminess in Charlotte's eyes when she mentioned having a cozy place with a big kitchen to indulge her new cooking hobby.

Charlotte looked so smitten. I couldn't even begrudge her happiness, even when it cost me my family and freedom.

"Ma'am." The waiter had come back, standing next to the table awkwardly looking at the floor, a blush staining his cheeks.

"Yes?" I asked.

"I'm terribly sorry, but your card was declined." He took out a large pair of gleaming silver sheers and cut my black Amex in half.

The entire dining room gasped as they unabashedly watched my embarrassment.

I could feel the beady little eyes of every woman taking in each detail so they could tell the stories to their friends and destroy my reputation for sport.

"There has to be some mistake," I fumed as I gathered the pieces of black plastic off the pristine white tablecloth.

"No, ma'am," the waiter said. "If you cannot provide a valid form of payment, we will have no choice but to call the police."

CHAPTER 9

LUCIAN

"The credit cards are cancelled. The bank accounts have been placed in your name as trustee of the estate. The remaining assets will be under the umbrella of the trust within the next thirty days," my financial manager said over the phone.

I leaned back in my leather home office chair, enjoying the satisfaction of a plan coming together.

Stella would have to beg me for everything from this point forward. The only question now was how long it would take for her to realize it.

I checked my watch.

Perhaps I would have her on her knees by evening.

An intriguing thought.

Having her on her knees—begging.

There was something about her needing me that made my cock swell with interest.

Usually the idea of anyone needing me made my skin crawl. Men like me did not claw their way to the top and hold on to their empires with an iron fist by putting other people's needs above their own.

I pushed the images of Stella on her knees, with her big eyes filled with tears and her lips stretched around my shaft, out of my head.

There was more work to be done.

The house and other assets were going to take a bit of time, but with her liquid assets transferred, I now had control over her spending.

I told her she was going to have to ask permission even to buy a cup of coffee, and I meant it.

My office door slammed open.

Expectation hardened my cock.

Stella.

I was not accustomed to being denied something I wanted. Although it would have been brutish and borderline unforgivable to have fucked her in that courthouse, a gnawing need tightened inside my chest.

I hadn't felt such a keen, almost desperate need to possess a woman for a very long time.

There was just something about the innocent fire and smolder of intelligence behind those golden eyes that challenged me.

It had also been quite some time since I'd been challenged by something or someone.

"What do you think you're doing?" Olivia shouted as she and Charlotte burst into my office. "How could you be so cruel?"

Fuck.

Usually I would stand to greet them, but in my current state, that would not be possible. "What is the meaning of this?"

"You know what the meaning of this is. Stella is our friend. She just lost her family, and you are hurting her."

Olivia had always been the stronger of my two daughters.

Maybe that was my fault. Maybe I had given her too much freedom as a child. Maybe I'd hired the wrong nanny. Whatever it was, Olivia would have made a much better son than a daughter.

Charlotte had been much more amiable and obedient, until I let Luc hire that Texan cowboy to protect her. I might as well have hired a dog to guard a bone.

Now they were both married to wealthy men, but their marriages were wasted opportunities. There were no contracts, no deals that had been struck, no understandings. There wasn't even a single subsidy merger in either of their marriages.

I hated wasted opportunities for profits.

It was like burning money.

Luc was just as bad.

No, Luc's marriage was worse.

Unlike the girls, he knew better.

And just because my children destroyed their opportunities for a lucrative marriage, that did not mean I was going to let them do the same for me.

My hand flipped the leather portfolio on my desk closed as they approached. The last thing I needed was for Olivia to realize there was a prenuptial agreement already being drawn up.

Charlotte may not have recognized the contract, but Olivia would.

She was a shrewd businesswoman, and although part of me wanted to be proud of her for it, she was still shortsighted and didn't understand that the family business, my business, needed to come first. Always.

I twirled my heavy, black Mont Blanc pen between my fingers. "I don't appreciate either of you barging into my office unannounced with your shrewish complaints. Not that it is any of your concern, I am acting well within my responsibility as trustee of Stella's estate."

"Is that why you canceled her credit card, embarrassing her in front of her friends and her peers?" Charlotte asked.

I pressed the heel of my palm against the top of my thigh as I tried not to shift in my chair. My disappointment in seeing my daughters and not Stella added a heated edge to my tone as my erection cooled.

"Again. Neither of your concerns. The trust bank accounts and investments are being moved under my control. Had she bothered to talk to me like a responsible young woman instead of throwing a temper tantrum in the courtroom, she would have learned that and been given her new bank card."

Olivia's eyes narrowed as she crossed her arms over her chest. "How did you get new cards issued before the judge ruled?"

"Because the judge issuing the order was a formality. Her father's will stated I was to be the one handling her finances if she was unmarried when he died."

Charlotte huffed as she waved her arm at me. "But you hated each other. Why would he give you control over Stella's estate?"

She said estate, but all I heard was *control over Stella.*

Control over her body.

Control over her heated response.

Control over her pleasure.

Dammit.

I needed to get my meddling daughters the hell out of my office and go find Stella. Being denied earlier was fucking with my head.

"We were not on the best of terms when he died, but we had been close once upon a time. I suppose he never updated his will. Why is any of this your concern?"

Olivia's mouth thinned as she paced in front of my desk as if she were inside a boardroom. "Why is this so important to you?"

Apparently my daughter had missed her calling. She should have been an attorney. Soon she would ferret out the truth about my intentions toward Stella.

I couldn't let that happen.

Knowing she hated it when I took a shot at her business, I fired back, "Shouldn't you be buying another handbag or some other frivolous thing while you run your little magazine?"

It was a dick move, but effective.

Olivia's cheeks heated. "My business is just fine, Father."

"Is it? Have you seen your quarterly earnings? They looked a little anemic. Maybe you should talk to your brother or ask your husband for a little help improving profits."

Her profits looked fine. Actually, she was ahead of what I had estimated by about 8%, and she'd outperformed every single one of my expectations—but telling her that would make her even more suspicious.

"That's not... I... We aren't here—" Olivia stammered.

Mission accomplished.

"Instead of wasting my time and yours, why don't you two go and do something productive? If Stella wants her new cards, she will need to come to me for them."

Come to me. Come *for* me. *Semantics.*

Olivia glared at me, hatred in her eyes, as the blood drained from Charlotte's face.

Dammit. I may have overshot the mark. All I really wanted was them out of my office before they asked too many questions about my intentions toward Stella—not to start a whole new family feud.

Regret. An emotion I had little use for, crept into my consciousness.

With no intention of making an excuse for my behavior, or

hiding behind the fact that I was a young widower who'd suddenly and traumatically lost his wife, I knew I'd been a shit father. There was no point in insulting my children by trying to make amends now.

The past was the past.

The best I could do now was have us all stay out of each other's way.

"She is twenty-six," Charlotte said. Her voice was stronger, but her eyes were back to studying the carpet, an evasive stress reflex she'd done since childhood. "She is an adult, not a child. She deserves to have everything that is rightly hers in her possession. If she can't manage it or is frivolous, then that is on her. But it's her money and her choice. You have no right—"

"The court says I have every right."

Charlotte's eyes widened. "You're not going to marry her to Ziegler, are you?"

"The family's title has been stripped. They have nothing and are worth nothing. That is not the match I am considering for Stella."

There was no point in mentioning that I was the one who had petitioned to the crown and used my extensive influence to have the ancient title stripped in revenge for harming Charlotte.

She wouldn't trust such sentimentality from me, and even if she did, I wouldn't have deserved it.

And there was also no reason to mention that I had an entirely different groom in mind for their friend. Me.

Charlotte's shoulders relaxed, and the line that had formed between her brows disappeared.

"Is there anything else, or do I need to have a word with your husbands and tell them that you two both have far too much time on your hands?"

Both of my daughters swallowed the insult and then stormed out of my office just as quickly as they had stormed in.

They were angry of course, but no more than usual.

Charlotte would be pacified knowing I wasn't going to marry Stella off to that spineless worm.

The phone on my desk rang. I picked it up without saying a word.

"Sir, she is staying at the Aman here in New York."

"In one of the suites?"

"No, sir. She rented one of the long-stay homes. Her stay doesn't have an end date."

"Good. How is she paying for it?"

"Her family has a line of credit. It's the hotel her father used when guests or family would stay. The bill is sent to the family's financial manager and is paid monthly."

"Perfect." I slammed the phone down and relaxed back into my chair.

She was making this so damn easy.

CHAPTER 10

STELLA

*T*he nightmare always began as a dream.

I was in a gorgeous dark red gown, as far from white as I could get without wearing black.

It was for a wedding, after all.

I was genuinely happy, laughing and gossiping with my mother as we walked down the stone stairs of the performance art center.

We talked about the unusual wedding and the handsome man who stood by the groom in a big, black cowboy hat.

My father was all smiles, making jokes about the New York weather being bad for horses, and asking what happened when the brim of a ten-gallon hat was filled with snow?

Did the sides collapse, or did the cowboy notice how heavy it was and tip his head back and dump the snow on the poor frozen horse?

We laughed harder than the joke deserved, my joy aided by the several glasses of champagne and the few shots of whisky I had taken with the groom's brother.

It was silly, but we were all happy, almost giddy with the energy from the wedding, the drinks, and the snow swirling in the air, making it seem magical.

We'd watched Charlotte Manwarring marry the love of her life, a man who had saved her over and over, and then stolen her from the titled coward her father almost forced her to marry.

Before the wedding, my father even made a few off-handed comments about anyone being better than the Zieglers. He refused to expand further.

The entire wedding, I was enthralled, gushing to my mother about how Charlotte, a dear friend of mine, had gotten her happily ever after.

She'd married her strong, noble guard, who turned out to be a prince in disguise. I'm sure it was dramatic and full of issues, especially with her recent injuries. I didn't envy the dangerous path she had to take to get to where she was. But I envied her ending.

It was seeing her so happy that made my own heart ache.

I wondered if I would be so lucky as to feel that desire and love one day. I hoped that I could look at my husband the way Charlotte looked at hers.

"When will I find my husband?" I had asked my mother.

"As if there was any man in the world good enough for my baby girl," my father said, wrapping his arms around my bare shoulders.

"I don't know if I want a man who's good enough for me," I said, slurring my words just a little. "I want a man who's strong enough for me. I don't want a noble night like Charlotte has."

"Oh?" My mother laughed. "Do you want a prince?"

"You mean like Amelia and Olivia have?" I thought about it for a second, like it was a serious question.

They both had amazing husbands who were kind, doating, and loved their wives more than anything.

They even supported their dreams and ambitions.

Olivia with her magazine and Amelia with her school.

Each man was also set to inherit a fortune and would continue to grow their families' empire.

That didn't sound appealing either. "No, I want a king. I want a man who rules over a vast kingdom with an iron fist. The kind of man who takes what he wants and doesn't suffer fools."

"Sounds like you want a hard man," my father said, rolling his eyes when my mother and I both dissolved into another fit of giggles.

"It sounds like you want a cruel man," my father clarified. "There's nothing wrong with the cruel man as long as you are what he wants. The second he turns his gaze from you or decides that you are in the way of whatever his final goal is, you will regret that choice."

"No, that's not a king. That's a president." I wasn't even sure what I was saying anymore. But the math was mathing in my champagne-soaked mind. "I don't want a man who was just handed money on a silver spoon. I want a man who owns his empire because he took it by right and might. I want a man whose temper and fire for life runs hot. I want heat and passion and..."

"And," my mother interrupted, swaying on her Jimmy Choo heels, "a man who looks like Henry Cavill."

"That would suffice as well." I nodded sagely.

"I don't know who that is," my father groused, before he slipped on the stairs, barely catching himself and doing a little dance to make it look like it was intentional, a trick to amuse us.

My mother and I erupted into more giggles as we made our way down the stairs.

Our earlier conversation was forgotten in an instant as my father made grand proclamations about the need to dance, to enjoy life to the fullest, and he sung something else that was so slurred my mother and I just laughed.

Until I also slipped on the ice…

Straight into the arms of warm marble.

That was the thought which first penetrated my champagne-fogged mind. That I had just collided with heated stone. As if I were pressing my cheek against the warm marble of a carved fireplace mantle.

Then I looked up into the narrowed dark gaze of Lucian Manwarring, Sr. "I'm sorry, I—oh, it's you!"

Well over six feet tall, with a chiseled jaw and thick, bright silver and black hair, any girl would be forgiven for thinking the man a complete DILF.

Daddy-I'd-Like-to-Fuck.

I mean, holy hell.

He was like Christian Grey, the later years.

There was just something about an experienced man with money and power that was intoxicating, even better than champagne.

Who wanted to mess with an immature twenty-nothing who was filled with selfish misplaced arrogance and ego when you could have a man who commanded the attention of world leaders and business titans?

But none of that mattered.

Because Lucian Manwarring was the devil in an Armani suit.

A corporate raider with the morals of a marauding barbarian hoard.

My father both hated and feared him.

My attempt to break free was stopped by his strong grip on my upper arms.

His lips thinned as he wrapped the soft, heavy cashmere of his coat around me, pulling me against the warmth of his body, "Where is your coat, little one?"

The deep, rumbling tone of his voice sent a shock of awareness straight to my core.

Then, the dream shifted.

CHAPTER 11

STELLA

*T*he warmth from my skin faded as I watched from outside of my body.

I watched as we made our way, carefree and so full of life, down the stone steps. The dreamy, lovesick, and drunk, glassy-eyed look was clear on my face, with my bright pink cheeks and bright smile, as was the admiration on my father's face as he whispered something to my mother, who just giggled and blushed like a schoolgirl talking to her first crush.

We were the picture of the perfect, elite New York family out at an event with not a single care in the entire world.

We looked like nothing could touch us.

We felt like nothing bad could ever happen to us.

Except now, I knew what was coming.

I had relived this moment so many times.

I screamed at them *no, don't, it's not worth it. Stay a little longer. Get a hotel room down the street. Don't drive in this weather.*

I screamed with everything I had, but I didn't make a sound, and the figures paid me no mind as they made their way to the waiting limo idling at the curb.

It was completely futile, but I still screamed as the cold grip of what was to come clawed at my skin.

It didn't matter.

I had to try.

I followed them down the stairs, down to the limo, and even banged on the window, begging them not to go.

"Oh, it is so cold out tonight," my mom said, pulling her shawl around me.

I pushed it away. "I don't feel cold. In fact, the wind feels so good."

My body was still warm from the heat of Lucian Manwarring's arms. It was as if I could still feel the press of his fingers on my upper arms as the scent of his cologne still clung to me from where my body had connected with his.

"You'll catch your death," she said.

"Leave her alone. The car will warm in a moment, and we will be home before you know it. I called ahead and had the maids prep the fireplaces in the bedrooms."

"Oh, that sounds lovely. So sweet and romantic—"

"Please stop talking." I covered my ears with my hands. "I don't want siblings, and I *really* don't need to hear any of this."

I was teasing them, and both my parents laughed as they leaned over me to give each other a cute little peck that I pretended to be grossed out by.

Most of my friends' parents had an arranged marriage.

It was the norm in our society, but not my parents.

My parents had a love story that rivaled Charlotte's.

They had fallen madly in love and stayed that way. They never argued or fought, and if they had ever had a falling out, I didn't know about it. Even from the inside of this family, our lives were wonderful.

I had no reason to ever doubt that mine would stay warm, loving, and perfect.

"You guys are gross," I said, not really meaning it.

"Well, if you find that king you want so badly, you will be just as gross," my mother teased right back.

"When I find my king, we will be much worse, but in the privacy of our own home. Bleh."

Both my parents tipped their heads back, laughing hard.

My mother's bright smile and green eyes were the last things I saw before the world faded to black around me while my own cries echoed in my ears.

Next, I was back in my body.

Everything was so cold, and I couldn't move.

I opened my eyes to see my mother's face, now broken and mangled, her green eyes lifeless and dim, staring at me as a moan or rattle emanated from her open lips.

"Mom," I cried out and tried to move my hand towards her, but a dull, crushing pain shot through my entire body.

I choked on the scream that tore from my lips. Something was on top of me, making it impossible to move.

I got one hand free and reached out for my mother, not seeing the shard of twisted metal that was lodged in her throat until it was too late.

There was so much blood leaking from her red lips, soaking into her dress, which was a dark blue and now looked like an inky wet black.

"Mom, no, please," I called again.

My voice was hoarse, and I was so cold.

I needed help.

I needed to find help.

Where was my father? Surely, the police had to be on their way. Someone had to be around to help me. This was New York City, millions of people crowded into one tiny island.

Someone had to be close.

With as much strength as I could muster, I pushed the plastic divider off of my upper body.

It was hard.

The second I moved it, I was much colder, but it was easier to breathe. I tried to move my legs, but they were pinned down by something heavy and cold.

Something large and black. It wasn't a piece of the car.

It was fabric, not leather or metal. It took me a few moments to realize it was my father's body over mine. He was so heavy, I couldn't move him.

I cried out again. I was answered only by the howling wind blowing through the car.

"Please help." The words came out of my mouth, barely above a whisper. I was trying to shout, but it hurt.

Snow drifted in through the broken glass and torn metal.

I looked out of the window closest to me, and it was just a solid white wall.

But if there was snow floating in, it had to be coming from somewhere. My mind was still fuzzy, and it took me a moment to realize I wasn't on the seats.

I was on the roof of the car.

We had somehow flipped over.

My mother was dead, and I hadn't seen his face yet, but I just knew my father was gone too.

"Help!" I cried out again, ignoring the screams of pain from my ribs as I tried to project my voice.

The window on the other side of my father was shattered, but I could only see out a few inches that weren't blocked by a wall of snow. Those inches were covered with jagged pieces of glass. Even if I could get out that way, I would gut myself in the process.

There had to be a way out the front.

Maybe the driver had been able to get out and go for help. It took several agonizing minutes before I was able to actually get on my hands and knees. The shards of broken glass cut into my palms as I slowly made my way to the front of the car.

The driver was still buckled into his seat, hanging lifeless upside down with his blood dripping down into a puddle on the roof of the car. The way his head had been bashed in by the steering wheel was going to haunt my dreams forever.

Next to the ever-growing puddle of blood was a silver flask. It had to have been the driver's. Had he been drunk? Had he killed my parents? My heart was cold, and I couldn't even muster the energy to hate him, not yet.

My stomach rolled as I squeezed my eyes closed and looked away, trying to regain enough composure to figure out how to get out of the car.

The windshield was shattered, but it was also blocked in by snow, and the passenger-side window had the same problem. The only way out was through the open window on the driver's other side, and I couldn't get past the driver.

"Help!" I screamed.

I kept screaming it over and over, my voice getting stronger with each pass until my throat felt like it was on fire while the rest of my body was freezing. I kept screaming as long as I could, but eventually I didn't have the strength.

My eyes slid closed as I collapsed on top of more pieces of broken glass, and the world went dark again.

There was no way to tell how long I was out. It wasn't until I heard a faint voice calling that I was able to open my eyes again.

"This is the New York City Police Department. Is there anyone still in there?"

"Yes," I tried calling out, but my throat was too dry, too raw, and my lungs hurt too much to take a deep breath.

"I don't think there is anyone in there, cap," the voice said.

I tried to call out again, but it was useless.

I had to make some noise. They couldn't leave. I had to tell them I was here. If they left, I would die, cold and alone.

All because of one stupid limo driver who thought he could get away with drinking on the job in the middle of a snowstorm.

I wrapped my fingers around the cold slippery flask, now covered in half-frozen, thick blood, and hit it on the roof of the car.

Nausea rolled in my stomach as I struggled to keep a grip on the frigid metal, but I struck it again and again.

"Wait, I think I hear something," one of the voices said, and I nearly cried in relief.

I hit harder, faster. I was so close to being saved, so close.

"I don't know," another voice said. "I don't hear anything."

With as much strength as I had, my entire body still and nearly frozen, I hit the flask on the roof harder and faster again.

I silently begged them to save me before I froze to death in this icy tomb with my parents.

And just as always, I found myself longing to return to the safety and warmth of the devil's arms.

CHAPTER 12

STELLA

*M*y heart raced as I tossed in my bed.

Despite the heat in the room, I was still so cold.

I had turned the furnace up before going to sleep, as well as the gas fireplace in the room.

For anyone else, this room was probably stifling, but I was still cold.

The banging of the flask still sounded in my ears.

My ribs ached where they had been broken, even though they were long healed now. The doctor called it psychological phantom pain.

I knew what it meant.

It meant my body had healed, but the scars on my mind could be permanent.

There was no way to know yet. I did know they hadn't even healed over.

The same nightmare played over and over in my head every single night. Half of it was memories from the accident. Half were gaps that my own brain filled in from a mix of horror and guilt. My throat was raw, and I didn't know if I had been yelling in my sleep again or not.

All I knew was that everything was so cold and aching every single time I woke up from that nightmare.

Part of me was scared that one night I would fall into a deep sleep, that same nightmare replaying over and over in my head, and I would never wake up.

I was terrified that I would be trapped in that frozen hell forever.

That I would never again feel anything but a cold, dull ache.

Then Lucian Manwarring had touched me.

And the memory of his warmth, his strength, his power, and my own strange longing to return to his arms, washed over me.

Even as the nightmare still tried to keep its hold with the insistent, terrible clang of that damn flask against the car metal.

My eyelids fluttered open.

The banging didn't stop.

It took me a moment to realize it wasn't still in my head.

It was coming from the front door of the suite. I grabbed the plush hotel terry cloth robe from the chair by the bed and wrapped it around me to answer the door.

It was barely eight in the morning. I had no idea who would be at my door.

No one even knew I was there.

I had told the staff that I was going on a vacation and that they would be paid to keep the house up. My friends all thought I was at my parents' estate.

I didn't want anyone to know that I was too weak to face my demons.

Or the devil, Lucian Manwarring. Not yet.

After the accident, I hated being at home.

I'd tried, but it was too painful.

Every moment, I expected to see my mother around the corner on her phone, laughing and gossiping to one of her friends, or my father barking orders to a business partner.

The home that was once filled with so many happy memories was just a painful reminder of what I didn't have anymore: a family.

The banging got more insistent until I ripped open the door, half expecting Lucian to be there with an incredulous look on his face.

Ready to tell me what other freedom of mine he was taking the liberty of stealing.

Perhaps he had commandeered my jewelry. Maybe he'd decided that the degree I'd pursued was not worth my efforts, so he went ahead and shredded it. Maybe he had taken it upon himself to decide that I had too many shoes, and he was going to sell them all.

Or maybe he just wanted to prove he had more power, so he was here to take my cell phone and ground me like a child for a month because he could. Because I came to my senses and ran before he had the chance to push me further than I was comfortable with, he was going to punish me.

My cheeks heated at the memory of his belt on my ass.

Most men of our class and his age sought company outside the marriage bed, and their preferences generally went to much younger women. Most men Manwarring's age would have had two or maybe even three girls my age or even younger on speed dial. That wasn't unusual. It was almost expected. God knows every wife looked the other way.

Lucian didn't even have a wife to answer to, let alone any other women.

He hadn't even broached the topic of marriage with any number of suitable women since Charlotte and Olivia's mother died when they were children. The gossip mill ran rampant with conspiracy theories on why he remained a bachelor even with three children to raise.

Everything from keeping a harem in the basement to preferring the company of men. Though that last one had been disproved several times.

He just didn't seem to want a wife.

That, of course, had not stopped every mother with an eligible daughter from practically throwing the girls at his feet every single year.

He never even noticed.

Didn't seem interested in marriage—until now—until me. Lucky me.

I swung the door violently open. "What?"

The hotel manager was there, dressed in his freshly pressed suit. Classic black and white. The staff here always dressed impeccably in suits that were tailored to perfection, but just mundane enough to be a uniform. I gave him a kind smile. He had always been one of my favorite people.

I ran a hand over my face, then through my hair. "I'm sorry. I mean, good morning, Augustus. What brings you by so early? I'm not due for my breakfast or a wake-up call for another hour."

Augustus had been the manager at this hotel for nearly a decade. Since my family had such a large account with the hotel, he had always handled our reservations and accommodations personally.

It was so weird to see him at my door.

Usually he was in the lobby, behind the desk, or tending to the guests. The way he guided the other staff to everything always reminded me of a conductor.

He signaled to the bell hops when to get luggage, directed the housekeeping to each room, and he oversaw everything with such incredible fluidity that it all seemed as if it was done by magic.

"I'm sorry, miss." He shifted on his feet back and forth for a moment and then looked at the door frame just to the right of my head. "I'm afraid we have a bit of a delicate problem."

Whatever it was, he did not want to be there. He wouldn't look me in the eye or use my name. Every other time he greeted me, it was always 'Hello, Miss Stella.' 'Good morning, Miss Stella.' 'I hope you have a wonderful day today, Miss Stella.' He had always greeted me with a bright, sincere smile and respectful eye contact.

I didn't know if he was embarrassed for me or just uncomfortable with whatever the delicate situation was.

"What seems to be the problem?"

"There is an issue with your bill, ma'am. Payment for your suite has been declined." He still wouldn't look me in the eye.

Immediately, the shame and horror of having my black Amex cut at the table returned.

My lungs burned, and tears gathered in the corner of my eyes. Suddenly him not looking me in the eye made sense.

He was sparing me the embarrassment of having him witness a particularly hard moment in my life.

Staff like Augustus, and those he trained, saw everything and nothing at the same time. A spill was made, a maid was there cleaning it before the person who had made the mess noticed. Luggage needed to be handled, a bell hop was there as you exited your doors. A man brought a hooker to his room, the staff were too busy to notice. The same man's wife came in, and they hadn't seen him.

In the hotel business, discretion was the better part of valor. I used to laugh when he said that to staff. I would joke with my mother about what they must know. I didn't understand what my mother meant when she said, 'they will never know anything, at least nothing anyone will ever hear.'

"I can get you another card," I said, regaining my composure.

"My family has been coming to this hotel for years. You know that I will pay. I am just having an issue with my credit card company. I will have the new card today."

"I'm afraid that will not be possible." Augustus raised his hand, cutting me off.

That was when I remembered.

I had never had a card on file for this room. The second I arrived here, fresh from the hospital, still heavily bruised with bandages holding my body together, so many orange bottles of pain pills and antibiotics rattling in my purse, my hospital ID bracelet still on my wrist, Augustus had greeted me with a look of horror.

He had practically fawned over me, without breaking that distinct, professional distance people in the service industry maintained at all times.

Everything from back then was fuzzy, at best, but I remembered him guiding me to a chair in the lobby and sitting me down so carefully. I had a cup of the most amazing chamomile tea brought to me while he called my family's money manager to arrange payment and had housekeeping arrange one of the long-stay suites.

He even had the house doctor go over the care instructions the hospital had given me. The doctor was so sweet, taking all my medications, verifying the doses, and having them delivered when it was time for them, with either water or food, depending on the medication.

The doctor had a counselor come in and hold grief counseling sessions in the comfort of my room so I didn't feel alone while I healed.

Augustus even had the kitchen prepare my favorite meals—meals that were designed to help me heal—a perfect blend of comfort foods and nutrition.

Now, I was being kicked to the curb with nowhere to go. That didn't make sense.

"My card was never on file," I said, narrowing my eyes at Augustus.

"No, ma'am."

"The bill had always been sent to my family estate and handled with a very generous gratuity."

"In the past, that was how it worked," he confirmed. "And your family's generosity has never gone unnoticed."

"What changed? The money manager is the same. You called yourself to ensure there would not be an issue with payment. Are you worried that I won't be as generous? Is that why you've come banging on my door before I even had my coffee?" My words and tone were far harsher than I had intended. But it was what it was.

I was cold, tired, and still reeling from yesterday's embarrassment, and today's indignation added more than I could handle.

"Ma'am." Augustus's eyes hardened as he looked at me directly. Apparently I had crossed some line, and I was no longer entitled to the faux feeling of privacy. "It is quite simple. I received a call this morning. The funds for this room are no longer available. You have ten minutes to pack your things, and then security will be up to escort you from the building. With or without your belongings."

"Who called you? They were lying." I stomped my foot like a petulant child and was immediately embarrassed.

My mother and I would have mocked someone who was behaving how I was.

She would be ashamed of me.

"The call was made by your trustee, Mr. Manwarring. He informed us none of your extravagant lifestyle will continue to be covered. He did ask that I relay a message."

"What's the message?" I bit out.

My blood pressure was rising, and my hands balled into fists as more cold tears built behind my eyes.

He cleared his throat. "You were a bad girl for not asking him for permission."

With that, Augustus looked down his nose at me in disgust, turned on his heel, and walked away.

CHAPTER 13

LUCIAN

"Mr. Manwarring, this is Augustus from—"

"Is it done?" I barked into the phone.

I needed to know how much longer I had to wait.

She was fast becoming an obsession. I was impatient to get my hands on her again, and maybe a few other body parts.

"Yes, sir," the man on the other end said, no doubt picking up on my limited patience. "She left ten minutes ago. Her room has been cleared, and the transfer came through just a moment ago. Her bill is paid in full."

"Good." I slammed the phone back into its cradle and turned my attention back to the spreadsheets in front of me.

Something was wrong.

Deiderich was wealthy.

Everyone knew that, but looking at his wealth, all clearly labeled in ordered cells showing money flowing in and out, he had more money than he should. Even with his little princess living full-time at one of the most expensive hotels in the world with round-the-clock medical care, spending nearly six figures a month, there was more money coming in than going out.

That wouldn't be unusual, except for his untimely death.

His assets should have been frozen. The lawyers and accountants were still dividing everything up.

Only a portion of the estate should have been available to his daughter, with his businesses bringing in less after his death, not more. The stocks in his own company should have plummeted after his death, especially with no heir apparent. Even if just temporarily, it would have been normal for there to be some flux.

There was nothing, no signs of anything slowing down or taking any kind of dive. His assets were as strong as ever, even growing, which was not possible.

Something very... unethical had to be fueling this.

Maybe Deiderich was more of a man than I thought.

I sat back in my chair and stared at the numbers, trying to figure out what the fuck Deiderich had gotten himself into.

Was he part of some shady underground dealings? Maybe running with the morally depraved rich and their sick little islands? Deiderich certainly had the money and influence, but he didn't seem like the type.

He didn't seem skeevy enough for underage girls and blow.

Maybe he ran his own outfit, using his legitimate businesses to traffic weapons or drugs.

That didn't fit either.

I couldn't see him interacting with the lower classes to sell such merchandise, but it was still a possibility. It wasn't like true drug kingpins dealt with the sellers and buyers of illicit goods.

God knows I never did.

But that still didn't feel right.

He was too white-collar for something like that, but that didn't make sense either. Most white-collar crimes that would bring in that kind of money would end with his death. He wouldn't still be making that kind of money with insider trading, corporate espionage, or stock manipulation.

He was dirty.

Looking at these numbers, there was no other explanation.

I just couldn't figure out how.

Luc would have been able to figure it out, but if it was something below board, I didn't want him to know.

Not until I figured out if it was something I could do instead.

Luc had already severed our ties with the Irish mob like it was nothing. His ties with the fucking Astrid DA were an extreme inconvenience.

It was such a shame, as Harrison could have been used to our benefit. Instead he seemed to be using Luc to his.

If I could take Deiderich's place in whatever shady business he had going on, I needed to do it without Luc's knowledge or involvement.

I raised my children to be strong. It had gone well until they bit the hand that fed them. I would not make that mistake again.

My exploration of the spreadsheets stopped when the doors of my office banged open with another unwanted interruption from a spoiled intruder.

She was not going to get off as easily as my daughters had.

Stella stood in my office in front of my desk with her fists on her hips.

She was dressed in another skirt that hit her mid-thigh, but now those sexy legs were covered in thick black stockings.

I wondered if that was to cover the marks I had left on her ass and thighs. My mouth watered just thinking about how wet she got when I spanked her sweet little ass.

"How dare you!" she screamed at me, drawing my attention from her shapely legs back to her tear-stained face.

"I'm afraid I'm going to need you to be more specific." I closed the laptop, not wanting her to see what I was looking at.

I wondered for a moment if Stella would have known what her father was into.

She might have the answers I was looking for.

I dismissed the thought just as quickly.

The last thing I needed was for her to figure out that I was digging into her family's finances and the estate that would have been hers had I not interceded.

Thankfully, the loose papers that were spread out when Olivia and Charlotte were there had been neatly gathered and moved into a locked drawer.

"You know what you did." She crossed her arms over her chest, trying to be defiant, but all she managed to do was to push her perky breasts up, giving me a particularly enjoyable view in her deep V-neck sweater.

I wasn't sure if I approved of her wearing something so revealing for anyone's eyes but mine.

Maybe next time I got her alone, I would have to mark up those pretty breasts along with her pretty little ass to make sure they were for my eyes only.

"I do a lot of things, though it seems like I am being far less productive as of late. The women in my life just don't seem to want to let me work."

"What gives you the right to cancel my accommodations? I'm homeless now because of you. I demand that you call the hotel back immediately and fix whatever it is that you broke."

Her voice didn't waver like it had at the courthouse. It didn't shake. She didn't look at her feet or above my head. She stood firm, her shoulders pushed back, her jaw clenched, and her eyes full of fire and hatred staring straight into mine.

Had she been a man approaching me like this, I might actually have been impressed with the direct and almost forceful way she spoke to me.

"Calm down," I warned. "I did not leave you homeless. You will be staying here with me."

"You had no right!" she screamed.

Just like that, all of the respect I almost had for her melted away.

"I have every right," I yelled back, getting to my feet and placing my hands flat on my desk.

I gave her the same menacing expression, the same wordless warning that I'd given every other asshole who dared enter into my office and make demands.

And just like every other person who stood before me, she shrank.

Her shoulders, which had been pushed back defiantly, were now rounded in front of her. The hands that had been crossed in some type of power pose were now gripping her sides, trying to protect herself.

And her eyes that had boldly met mine were now firmly on the floor.

"I—" Her voice cracked.

"No. You come into my office, barge in here without so much as knocking, like you own my fucking house or are in the least bit entitled to my time, and then yell at me? I don't think so. We are going to have a conversation right now that more clearly defines our roles so you better understand your place in the world, and what is and isn't appropriate behavior."

"I—" she tried speaking again, but I wasn't having any of it.

"Sit down now." I pointed to the chair in front of my desk and stared her down until she finally moved.

She sat in the chair, curling her arms around herself, trying to make her body as small as possible.

When she was seated, her eyes still on the floor, I took my seat.

"Apologize," I demanded.

"What?" She looked up at me, fresh tears gathering in her eyes, making them shiny and bright.

"You barged into my office, interrupting my workday. You did not knock, and you did not make an appointment. The days of you acting like a spoiled little bitch are over. Apologize, and we will go over the new arrangement."

"And if I don't?"

"Have the marks from our first lesson faded so quickly? Though I probably should tell you, next time will not end so pleasantly for you." I sat back in my chair to have a more civilized conversation. "As soon as you apologize, then we can go over the arrangements, and you can get your new cards."

She stared at the floor for another few moments, watching as she kicked her legs under the chair, her chest moving up and down with deep breaths. She was trying to work up the nerve, going over and over it in her head and trying to figure out how she'd gotten into this situation.

She could sit there and think about it all she wanted. It wasn't going to change a damn thing.

"I'm sorry." Her words were whispered, barely audible even in my silent office.

"You're going to need to speak louder."

She huffed out another breath, then sat up in her chair and tried to make eye contact again. "I'm sorry that I came into your office without knocking or an appointment, sir."

"Good girl. That wasn't so hard, was it?" Being intentionally condescending may have made me an asshole, but it didn't mean it wasn't fun.

Her cheeks turned a darker red, and her little hands rolled into tight fists. "No, sir," she said between clenched teeth.

"Good, so let's go over your new arrangements. I've spent the last several days going through your family's estate and seeing what has been coming in and out. I'm afraid your father was not as financially savvy as he let his investors believe. Really, he's barely a step above a Ponzi scheme at this point," I lied.

"No, that can't be—"

"I'm afraid living in hotel suites is just not financially responsible given your current situation. Thankfully for you, I have generously agreed to let you stay here rent-free. This will give me some time to rearrange the estate and put you back into a positive cash flow. In the meantime, I do understand that you are used to a certain level of lifestyle, although I'm afraid that will have to be reduced greatly. I will be putting you on a monthly allowance of two hundred dollars."

"You mean two hundred thousand?"

"No, I do not. I will also be selling your family's estate. I'm afraid that's the only way to pay off the debts that your family has left you."

"That can't be—"

"But it is. It's all here in black and white, if you want to look it over." I opened my drawer and pulled out a file folder with her father's name on it, handing her falsified documents showing exactly what I wanted her to see and nothing more.

"So, you're saying I'm—"

"I'm saying you're extremely lucky that I have decided to take you in. I will be going over everything with my financial planners and seeing if I can turn this situation around at least enough to find you a proper husband."

"I don't believe you. My father would have never left me in financial straits. Not to mention my mother's net worth was in the hundreds of millions, and my father never touched that money."

"That you know of."

"I do know this isn't right. You can't—"

"No, the court says I can do whatever I deem appropriate. I am the trustee of your estate, such as it is. I am the one that controls everything you own, and I have decided the appropriate thing to do with you is to keep you here under my roof and give you a generous allowance of two hundred a month."

"You won't get away with this," she said, getting to her feet.

"I already have," I said, standing as well. "As your trustee, I decide what's good for you. I decide what you deserve, and if you were smart, you would learn how to make the best of that."

"Fuck you," she spat at me.

"Your father really didn't teach you any fucking manners, did he?" I moved around the desk, as she backed away from me.

CHAPTER 14

LUCIAN

She pressed against one of the built-in bookcases that lined my office.

When her back hit the wooden bookcase, I wrapped my hands around her throat and squeezed.

Not hard enough to restrict her breathing but hard enough that she would know I could.

"This is your life now, and if you're going to be a little brat, I'll treat you like one."

"You wouldn't," she sneered.

I tightened my hand and ran the other one down her body to her plump little behind.

"There is no bailiff here who's going to knock on the door."

"I don't care." Anger burned behind her eyes, and I grabbed a handful of her ass, watching as her face crumpled in a wince of pain.

I knew my marks were still there.

"Are you going to be my good little girl?"

"Never," she said, and I raised my hand and spanked her, pressing her mouth into my shoulder to muffle her screams.

I spanked her over her clothes three or four more times, feeling the thick fabric of the skirt and the leggings no doubt padding my strikes. But that didn't matter. With the bruises I had left with the belt, she would feel every single one.

When I pulled her away from my shoulder, she was breathing heavily, tears leaked down her cheeks, and a flush of red went from her almost angelic face down her neck and disappeared under the low V-neck of her sweater.

I didn't know what about that made her so fucking appealing.

The next thing I knew, my lips were pressed to hers, my tongue pushing between her teeth, exploring her mouth.

She could say she hated me all she wanted, but that didn't change the fact that I could feel her body press into mine. Her hands rested on my shoulders while her fingers dug into my suit and held me closer.

Fuck, I had never been so hard so quickly in my life.

She pushed me back, and I let her. I wasn't done with this fight any more than she was.

"I won't be treated like this."

I kept my hand wrapped around her throat and moved my thumb to tilt her chin up, making her face me. "You will be treated exactly how I decide you will be treated."

"I don't want to live here. I don't want to be around you."

"Fine," I said, taking a step back and motioning towards the door. "Then leave. But you leave without a single cent. The only thing you will have are the clothes on your back."

"But, you can't—"

"If you choose not to stay here, then you are forfeiting every-thing. You can go live on the streets for all I care. I wonder what's going to happen to a pretty thing like you when you try to sleep on a park bench. I hear Central Park can be a little dangerous at night, especially for a little girl like you, all alone in the world."

"I can make my own way. I am not some helpless damsel in distress."

"Oh?" I mocked her. "What are you going to do for money?"

"I'm sure I can find a job with—"

"With what? All of your experience? Do you think someone's really going to hire some spoiled rich girl who lost her fortune? You weren't raised to work. You were raised to make a lucrative marriage match—to someone like me."

My body was still pressed to hers, pinning her against the bookshelf, and I leaned down, about to retake her sweet lips when she pushed up and kissed me.

I let her have control for a moment until she pushed me back again, and this time, she tried to slap me.

I caught her wrist mid-air and used it to flip her around, pressing her front against the bookcase and wedging my foot in between hers.

I kicked her legs out and then gripped both of her wrists in one hand.

"When will you learn that bad things happen to naughty girls that need to be punished?" I growled in her ear as I pressed my hard cock against her ass.

She tried to stop the shiver that ran down her spine, but it was easy to see. She was getting off on this as much as I was.

"Or maybe that's what you like being?" I said. "Is that it, Stella? Do you want to be my bad girl? Does getting punished make your pussy wet? I bet I could strip you down now, bend you over my desk, and fuck you hard enough to make you scream my name."

"You're disgusting." Her voice was shaking with need.

She probably lied to herself and assumed it was anger, belying how her ass pushed into my hips.

"Maybe, but you like it. What does that make you, I wonder? You can lie to me all you want, but your body tells me how much you want me. Maybe next time you misbehave, I won't just spank you. I'll put you on your knees and show you exactly how a good girl behaves. You'd probably like that too, wouldn't you? I bet your cunt is dripping wet thinking about my cock going deep into your throat. You'll look so pretty with your golden eyes staring up at me while you swallow my cock."

"You don't get to control my life."

I had to bite back laughter. She couldn't deny the dirty things I was whispering into her ear, so she tried to change the fucking subject.

"Watch me."

"No, you're not my father. You can't—"

"Oh, sweet little brat. I have no interest in becoming your father."

I whipped her around and picked her up, throwing her over my shoulder and caressing her ass before leaving another sharp swat that made her cry out. "I, however, will be your husband."

CHAPTER 15

STELLA

"**Y**ou can't do this!" I screeched, trying to break free from the hold he had over my legs.

His arm was like a bar holding my thighs to his chest as his shoulder dug into my stomach.

I was trying to claw at his back through the suit that he was wearing, or kick him, anything. It was pointless.

I didn't see a single maid or butler or anyone in the hallways. They must have heard the commotion and avoided facing it.

The fucking cowards wouldn't even stand up to their boss when he was doing something they knew was so wrong.

"You can't do this!" I yelled again, slamming my fist down on his back.

"Watch me," he said with a dark laugh before he slapped my ass again. The sharp sting sent a shock of pleasure up my spine, and I had to bite my lip to stop myself from groaning.

I hated how much I loved the way that made me feel.

"Why are you doing this to me?" I cried, trying to kick harder until he moved his arm from the back of my thigh down to my ankles, making it impossible for me to kick and also, at the same time, making me feel very unsteady on his shoulder.

I had to grab the sides of his suit jacket to keep from falling.

"Because you like it," he growled. "Isn't that right, baby girl?"

"No, let me go." I said the words that I knew I should say, even if it wasn't the way I felt.

Disgust, revulsion, and hatred should have been burning their way through my veins. Instead, it was something much different giving me this incredible warmth. I didn't want to name it.

If I named what I was feeling, then there was no way I could lie to myself about it.

It may have been denial, but I was going to hold on to it with everything I had.

"You want me to let you go? Fine." He pulled me from his shoulder and threw me on a large bed with a firm mattress and the most incredibly thick goose-down comforter I have ever been on.

Before I could get up, he grabbed my ankles, pulled me across the black duvet towards him, and pulled off my shoes, tossing them to the other side of the room.

"You can't do this," I said again. I felt stupid repeating the same things over and over, like somehow it was going to change something. I knew it wouldn't.

Deep down, I didn't want it to change anything.

This was going to happen.

I knew this was going to happen.

I wanted this to happen.

I just didn't want to want it to happen.

"I'll make you a deal, baby girl. If I pull down your tights and your little pussy isn't dripping wet for me, begging for my cock, then I'll let you go. I'll set you up in one of the spare rooms, and I'll let you stay there unbothered."

"What?" There was no way he meant that. He couldn't have meant that.

"No? You don't want to take our wager? Is that because you're as wet as I think you are?"

"Let me go," I said again.

"Sure, if your pussy is dry, and your body isn't begging for release, then absolutely."

He didn't wait any longer.

He reached under my skirt, grabbed the top of my tights, and ripped them off.

"Please," I said. "Don't." I couldn't remember why I was fighting him.

The way his hands ran from my ankle up my thighs, leaving the most delicious trail of heat, I didn't want him to stop.

I wanted him to make all of me burn, to chase away the cold, and banish it. I wanted to feel warm and alive again. His touch made me feel that.

"All in due time, baby girl." He grabbed the center of my favorite pair of La Perla panties and ripped them off, tossing the expensive black silk on the growing pile of my clothes.

My new monthly allowance couldn't even replace those!

"Last chance, tell me you want it. I'll be gentle and teach you how to ride my cock like a good little girl. Or lie to me, and I'll fuck you like a bad girl. Which will it be?"

That same heat that had risen from my ankles to my thighs when he touched me burned all the way up my body to my cheeks.

I wanted him. I knew it, he knew it. There was no denying it. But I couldn't say it out loud. Shame kept my lips sealed shut.

"Time's up." His hand went between my legs, two fingers plunging straight into my pussy, stretching me.

I couldn't stop the moan that escaped my lips as my back

arched in complete submission. Even if he couldn't feel it on his hands, he could see how much I wanted it.

"I'm sorry, what was that, baby girl?" he said, pumping his fingers in and out of me while he pulled apart the buttons on my shirt to expose my breasts.

He pumped his fingers in and out harder, making it hurt just a little as he brought me so much pleasure, and his hot lips wrapped around my nipple.

This was so wrong, but how could something that was this depraved and this humiliating feel so good?

There was no use trying to fight it anymore, so I let my legs fall open, giving him full, complete access to me while my fingers slipped into his hair and held his mouth to my breast.

If this was going to happen, I might as well take advantage of it.

"Are you going to keep lying to me?"

"I don't want you," I said as I arched my back, pushing my breast back in between his lips.

"Such a bad liar," he growled, standing up and hovering above me.

"I'm not lying," I lied.

He smirked down at me, and I could only imagine how I looked, lying on his bed on top of his black duvet, my shirt opened and showing off my chest.

One cup of my bra pulled under my breast, pushing it up, the hardened nipple wet with his saliva. My legs were wide open while my skirt was up around my waist.

My pussy was dripping wet.

It had been wet before he fingered me. But now it was so much worse. I could feel the need pulsing between my legs.

I watched as his eyes took in every single inch of me, and I liked the way it made me feel.

It was wrong. I knew it was wrong, and I should have felt shame, humiliation, and just dirty. But I didn't.

I felt warm, hot even.

He made me feel seen in a way that I had never experienced before. The way his eyes hungrily ran over my body made me miss the feel of his hands.

"Bad girls get punished," he said.

That was the only warning I had before he reached down and spanked my pussy, sending a sharp shock of pain and heat licking up my spine. And he did it again before grabbing my ankles and using them to flip me over and push my skirt up.

"You're going to take your punishment for lying to me. I'm going to spank this perfect ass, and you're going to count and say thank you after every single swat."

I tried to squirm away from him. I tried to move, but he put his knee on the small of my back, pinning me to the bed.

"When I'm done punishing you, I'm going to make this pussy mine. And if you're a good girl, I'll let you come."

"And if I refuse to be your good girl?"

"If you're a bad girl, and you don't take your punishment… well then, it's not your pussy I'm going to fuck." He placed his thumb against my asshole and rubbed tight circles over it.

It felt different, depraved even.

I had already felt how big his cock was in the courthouse. I didn't think he'd fit in my pussy, so he definitely wouldn't fit there.

"Are you ready, baby girl?"

I bit my lip and buried my head in the comforter not wanting to say it. Not wanting to be so complacent, even if I did want it.

"Answer me," he said, pushing his thumb into my ass.

"Yes, I'm ready," I cried out.

CHAPTER 16

STELLA

"*G*ood, girl."

The first spank wasn't hard.

He wasn't trying to hurt me.

Just warming me up.

And that was exactly what it did.

His softer spanks heated the skin of my behind. It was almost relaxing.

"One. Thank you," I said obediently, noticing how every time I submitted, a pulse of need ran through my stomach to my core.

He swatted me again, this time a little harder. The sharp smack made my skin tingle with anticipation for more.

"Two. Thank you."

He kept each hit gentle, going over my ass and my thighs until I got to eight. Apparently, eight was the magic number where I was warmed up and ready to be punished.

His first real punishment spank caught the delicate flesh where my behind met my thigh.

I bit back a scream as tears filled my eyes, but that wasn't the only thing that happened.

The sting from that spank seemed to ignite something else deep inside me, a yearning that I didn't know how to understand. I could suddenly feel my pulse in my clit, and I needed friction. I needed him to touch me and give me satisfaction.

"I don't hear you," he said, the threat clear.

"Nine. Thank you."

The next slap was on the exact same place on the other side. This time I was expecting it, and my hips angled up to give him more access as the pain and pleasure hummed through my veins.

"Ten... Thank you..." My words were sobs instead of spoken.

Hot tears ran down my face, but they didn't feel like tears of sadness or even anger. They felt like cleansing tears of release.

The next one landed across both of my ass cheeks, and I jumped, letting out a yelp of pain.

"Eleven. Thank you."

My hips angled up even further, giving him more access to my ass and my thighs, and my legs spread just enough so he could see how wet I was for him.

A bead of arousal ran down my lips to the duvet cover.

I knew he could see it.

His fingers slid between my lips, circling my clit before running back, spreading my own wetness from my clit all the way up and around my asshole.

My body stiffened, but I didn't move. I didn't argue. I didn't fight. I was giving in to him.

Suddenly, his hand was gone, and then just as quickly, it was back again. His palm slammed against the center of my cheeks, his fingers slapping down over my most sensitive skin.

This time, I screamed, and fresh cathartic tears rolled down my face.

"Say it, baby girl," he threatened as he rubbed more moisture over my behind. "Let me hear you."

"Twelve. Thank you."

"Have you learned your lesson?" He moved his knee off of my back and pulled me to the end of the bed. Letting my legs hang over the edge.

"Yes, sir," I said, not moving.

"Shame, your ass looks just as tempting as your fresh little cunt. The next time you misbehave, I won't just spank you. Do you understand me?" His thumb pushed into my ass again, going in further than before, making it burn.

"I understand, sir."

"Too bad you didn't understand sooner. This could have been a lot gentler if you'd just behaved," he growled, sending shivers up my spine as I twisted my fingers into the soft duvet cover, bracing myself for what was going to come next.

I expected him to just push in and take me from behind.

Instead, he grabbed my ankles and used them to flip me over.

He ripped at my shirt and my bra, making sure every single inch of me was exposed to him.

My skirt was still flipped up around my waist, tears still streaming down my face.

"I want you to look at me as I take you. I want you to know that no other man is ever going to fuck you like this."

"Yes, sir," I said, my core clenching at the thought.

"Stay right there. If you move, I won't let you come."

I froze, not wanting to make him madder than he already was.

He stepped back and stripped off his suit, first exposing his chest.

I knew he was fit. I could feel that through his suit.

What I didn't expect were biceps that looked like they were carved from marble and an eight-pack that I wanted to run my tongue down.

He looked better than the pop stars I'd posted on my wall when I was younger. He wasn't as thin as those men. He didn't have the super-toned body of male models and actors who spent hours in the gym to have the measurements of a Dorito.

No, his body was thick.

A larger frame packed with layers of muscle and power. This was a man who'd earned his abs through hard work, not paying a trainer. I wondered how he'd gotten like that. He had to do more than just sit behind a desk all day.

"Like what you see, baby girl?" He smirked as he noticed me staring.

I looked away, and he came over and grabbed my chin, pointing my face back towards him. "Answer me. Do you like what you see, baby girl?"

"Yes." My cheeks burned with embarrassment again, but I couldn't look away from him.

"Look all you want." Then he gave me another searing kiss that left me aching for him. Then he stepped back again, and I could see the outline of his hard cock in his dress pants.

My mouth watered, and I had this urge to get down on my knees in front of him, but he had told me to stay put. So I held on to the duvet as if that could somehow hold me in place.

He undid his pants, and as they fell to the ground, I could see just the tip of his cock peeking out of the elastic waistband of his tight black boxer briefs.

My mouth watered even more as he gripped his cock over his boxer briefs giving it a few sharp tugs, which I was pretty sure was for my benefit, before sliding his boxers down.

When he stood again, fully naked, his cock stood upright and proud, heavily bobbing with every step he took towards me.

I couldn't rip my eyes away from it if I wanted to. The head was dark red, almost purple, with a single clear bead of liquid at the tip.

I licked my lips again and swallowed, wondering what it tasted like, wondering what he would feel like in my mouth.

"Not this time, baby girl. I need to feel that tight pussy squeezing me. But don't worry. You'll have plenty of time to get those sweet little lips on me later."

The sound of his voice brought me back to reality, and I remembered what he was going to do.

Where he was going to put that massive thing.

I might not have been experienced, but I could do basic math, and I knew that the math was not going to math.

His huge hard cock was not going to fit inside of me. There was no way my body was made to take something that big.

He took a step closer, and I scooted back on the bed, still staring at his cock.

"Where the fuck do you think you're going, baby girl?"

I shook my head, not able to say anything, not knowing what to say as I moved back even faster.

I got to the edge of the bed and tried to make a break for the door.

Lucian let me get maybe three steps before he was on me, one hand around my waist, the other on my throat.

"What happened to being a good girl?" he growled.

"Please," I whined.

"No, you said you were going to be a good girl." He pushed me away from him just enough to rip my shirt and my bra from my body, leaving my top half completely exposed.

The only thing I had left was my skirt.

"What happened to you doing as you're told? Was one punishment really not enough? Did you need me to spank you harder or just tie you to the bed?"

"No, I can't. It won't fit." I clawed at his hands. "Please, there's no way."

He laughed at me, pulling my body against his.

As soon as his bare skin brushed against mine, instant

warmth overtook my body, banishing the cold that had crept inside of me again and making part of me relax a little.

I still fought him, but not nearly as hard as I wanted to.

"It will fit. I'll make it fit." With his hand still around my throat, he pushed me against the wall, holding me there like he had in the courtroom.

His hand went down my body, stopping just to cup my breasts for a moment and pinch my nipples before traveling down to my waist, grabbing me with both of his hands and lifting me up against the wall.

He pressed his body to mine, holding me up with his entire body, and my legs immediately went around his waist.

My ankles locked behind him.

His entire body was pressed to mine, and it felt so good.

His skin was so hot, and his body surrounded mine, making me feel safe.

It was kind of funny. The one thing that I really needed protection from was the only thing that had made me feel safe in months.

"Please," I said. "It's going to hurt."

"Yes," he said. "It is. But you're going to do it anyway."

He leaned back just enough that my body slid down his, and I could feel his cock at my entrance. He lined us up, pinning me against the wall so I couldn't move.

"Please."

"So strange. Your eyes are begging me not to, but your pussy is practically screaming at me to fuck you. I can feel your juices dripping down my cock. That's how wet you are." He leaned down to whisper in my ear, sending shivers over my bare skin. "That's how much your body is begging me to claim you."

He didn't wait for me to plead again or anything.

He thrust up, pushing all of himself inside of me in one fluid, agonizing push.

I could feel the second he pushed past my maidenhead, the searing pain making me cry out. It burned as if I had been stabbed.

Lucian held me there for a moment, letting me feel every single inch of agony.

Then he pulled out and did it again.

Over and over, but every single time, it hurt less. As the pain dissipated, it was replaced by something else, something addictive.

"That's it, baby girl, take it. Love it. Does it still hurt?"

I nodded.

"Does it feel good too?"

Again, I nodded as he angled his hips to brush against my front wall, and fireworks exploded behind my eyelids.

A deep, satisfying moan pulled itself from my throat, and he laughed.

"Yeah, that's it, baby, take every inch of it and get addicted to my cock. This is the only dick that will ever be inside this tight little cunt. I own you, now."

"Yes, sir."

He grabbed my upper thighs, digging his fingers into the fresh marks that he had left during my spanking, sending another shock of delicious pain through my body as he pushed into me harder, faster.

The more he pushed into me, the better it felt, and soon, I couldn't control my cries of pleasure. I didn't want to.

I could feel the pressure building at my core, and I knew that he was right.

I was going to be addicted to this cock.

There had to be a way out of this before he ruined me forever.

CHAPTER 17

LUCIAN

Three times.

I took her three more times until we both passed out in my bed, with her cuddling into my arms, her body pressed against mine so she didn't sleep in the wet patch she had left.

It had been some time since I had been with a woman who was so greedy for pleasure that I was able to push her to the point of soaking through sheets.

There was something supremely satisfying about that.

I had not intended to miss an entire day of work the day before.

But, if my plans were to go the way I needed them to go, I had to make sure Stella had no other options.

Taking her virginity, as well as her money, left her pretty much in my hands.

There was no other bargaining chip a girl like her had.

It was 4:00 a.m. when I woke up. The alarm clock on the side of my bed told me that I still had another hour of sleep if I wanted it.

I didn't. What I wanted was still fast asleep in my arms.

So I took her.

I shifted her body until she was lying on her stomach.

I could see the bruises I had left on her thighs and ass in the soft, ambient pre-dawn light that was coming from outside.

Just having this girl in my arms was enough to make my cock harder than it had been when I was in my twenties. I could outperform every man my age, but with her, I could outperform any man in the city.

I pulled her hips up, and even in her sleep, she was so desperate for me that she pulled her knees up and responded as I pushed them apart.

I pressed my cock inside her more gently than I would have preferred, but I knew she would be sore. I used that to my advantage, glorifying in the delicious groan of pain and pleasure coming from her lips.

Her pussy was still soaking, although I wasn't sure if it was more from my come or if she was still greedily wanting more.

Stella Deiderich was a cock-hungry little thing, and she was all mine.

I hadn't counted on that.

It was actually going to make my plans easier and much more enjoyable.

She woke as I pushed fully in, her back arching and her hips adjusting, giving me better access.

I thrust in again, and she moaned, pushing her hips up further, begging for more.

There wasn't time for marathon sex this morning. So I reached down under her and tweaked her sensitive, swollen little clit as I fucked her slow but hard.

Her walls instantly fluttered around me, sending waves of pleasure up my spine. I gritted my teeth and held on, wanting to make it last just a little longer.

"Come, Stella," I demanded with a quick sharp slap to her ass, and her body obeyed.

God, that level of control felt amazing.

She collapsed under me as I kept going, fucking her like I owned her. Because that was exactly what this was.

I owned her body and soul, and as soon as she accepted that, her life was going to be easier.

When she came again, I let go and filled her tight little cunt to the brim for the fifth time. I made a mental note to have a staff get her the morning-after pill.

Her belly swelling with my child so soon would raise the attention of people I didn't want to deal with quite yet.

"Where are you going?" she asked, her voice still slurring with sleep.

"Shower. You stay right there. Do not move. Or else."

She sleepily nodded as I went to the ensuite and took a scalding shower, rinsing the sex sweat and everything else from my body. I did what I did every morning in the shower and planned my day.

There was a lot that needed to get done and not a lot of time to do it. Not to mention adding the mystery of whatever the fuck her father had been up to. There was so much work to be done, transactions to unravel, and meetings that I could not put off.

I was barely holding the O'Murphy family back from trying to murder my son and the DA, as it was.

I really should not have spent all day fucking, but a day between her thighs was hard to pass up.

It was tempting to do it again, but some plans needed to be made, and I needed to make sure she understood exactly where she stood in this situation.

It was going to be far easier for me if she behaved.

And I just didn't have the time to deal with a spoiled little girl throwing temper tantrums.

I got out of the shower with the towel wrapped low around my waist and went back to my room to dress for the day.

Stella was sitting up now, the blankets pulled tight over her body like they could somehow erase the intimate knowledge I already possessed.

"What happens now?" she asked, her voice low and timid.

"When we are in this room alone, you will refer to me as sir."

I hadn't planned on making that a rule, but something about the way she moaned it while I was balls-deep inside of her or the way she said it as I was spanking her was just so unbelievably hot. I wanted to hear the words from her lips constantly. There was no way I was going to let that go.

"Why?"

I looked at her, raising my eyebrow, the only warning she was going to get. There wasn't time to properly spank her again this morning, but she didn't need to know that.

"Why, sir?" she repeated, a tint of red coloring the tops of her cheeks.

I think she liked it too.

"Because it pleases me. That's all you really need to know."

"Okay, sir." She took a moment while I went to the closet to get my suit for the day.

I grabbed a suit that was a particular favorite. It was one of many that I had made on Saville Row. All my suits were custom-made and from the finest materials, in the English style. But this one with the wool blend in the dark grey check was always my favorite when dealing with the Irish mob.

The single-breasted jacket was unmistakably English. Even the subtle grey check pattern spoke of refined British taste. It always irked the Irish, even if they didn't know why. It never failed to knock them off their game and give me the upper hand.

"What happens now?" Stella finally worked up the nerve to ask.

"Whatever I want to happen, baby girl. But as far as my plans with you, I'm going to sort through the financial mess your father left you in, and you're going to spend every night in this room grateful for the opportunity. In public, you're going to act like the most gracious and thankful little ward anyone has ever seen. If anyone asks you, you are to tell them that your father trusted me to ensure your future, and that's exactly what I'm doing."

"Yes, sir," she answered obediently, making my cock stir.

"In private, you're going to be my perfect little submissive baby girl. You are going to do as you're told at all times, without complaint. You are going to sleep in this bed every single night and let me take you however I please, and you are going to be grateful for it. Or I'm going to continue punishing you until you're grateful for it anyway."

"Yes, sir," she said, her voice cracking as tears filled her eyes.

"After a respectable amount of time, we will announce our engagement."

"But—"

I crossed the room and snatched her chin, tilting her head back. "Was that an objection?"

She bit her lip then shook her head.

"Good. And you are going to follow the rules. At all times. Is that clear?"

"What rules?"

"The rules I am making just for you."

I hadn't thought of any rules, but it was a good idea.

A woman like her needed rules to follow.

She craved to be a good girl, to be rewarded just as much as she was punished. It was only fair to give her clear-cut rules to follow.

"You are to behave at all times. I don't even want you talking to another man who might get the idea of spending some time with what belongs to me. Do you understand?"

"Yes, sir." She said the words, but her eyes went down again.

"It's not all bad. If you're a good girl, prove to me that you can be trusted, then I'll give you an allowance that will be more to your liking. But if you disappoint me, if you fail me, I will strip you of everything you own and toss you out in the cold. Do you understand?"

"Yes, sir. Please not the cold."

Her tears were falling down her face now, and she seemed more worried about being cold than homeless. Whatever worked to keep her in line.

"Good. Now, what do you say to your sir?"

"Thank you, sir."

"Good girl." I stood back up and went to get dressed, standing next to the bed, and letting her watch me. I liked the feeling of her eyes on me. I liked knowing that a woman who was around half my age was still so enthralled with my body.

"What happens after?" she asked.

"After what?"

"After you figure out what went wrong with my father's finances. Do I just get everything back when I'm twenty-nine, like the judge said?"

There was a hopeful lilt to her words that was actually adorable.

She was hopelessly naive if she thought she was ever going to see a fucking dime of her estate. Her father really did leave her too sheltered.

"No, we will be married by then."

"What? You said after a respectable amount of time. I thought that would be a few years."

There was no fucking way I was waiting years to make this

treasure truly mine. Another man would snatch her from me before then.

"In six months," I repeated more firmly, "we will announce the engagement, and you will start planning our wedding. You will be married to me by the end of the year."

"Why would you want to marry me? You said I don't have any money. There was nothing of value..."

"Because I have plenty of money. I have power, and I have influence, and it is well past time for me to take another wife. You are destitute, but beautiful and well-bred. So if you can prove that you can be a good, obedient ward, then I will turn you into my perfect submissive trophy wife."

"I still don't understand."

"There's nothing to understand. I want you to be mine, so you will be mine. You will behave, you will follow the rules, and you will spend every night showing me how grateful you are in this bed. In return, you will have access to whatever you need. Whatever you want, I will have new black Amex cards made with an allowance that I deem appropriate. Currently, you're at two hundred a month. Prove to me in the next week that you're a good girl, and I'll increase it by one hundred percent. Keep behaving, and you'll get more money."

"So you're paying me to sleep with you?"

"No, I don't pay for sex. I'm incentivizing you to follow the rules. I'm being far more gracious than I have to be. The fact of the matter is that you are going to marry me because that's what I want. And I always get what I want." I tucked my shirt into my pants and grabbed the belt, folding it in half and cracking the leather.

She jumped as the loud, sharp snap cut through the early morning air.

"If you misbehave, not only will your cards be taken away,

but I will show you what happens to bad girls. Or was one lesson not enough?"

"No, sir. I understand."

"Good," I said as I looped the gray and navy-blue silk tie around my neck and slid it under my collar.

"But, what if…" Stella's words trailed off, and I turned to face her as I tied my tie on with nothing more than muscle memory.

"What if what?"

"What if I'm not ready to get married?"

"You're twenty-six years old. You're plenty old enough."

"I know I'm old enough, but what if I'm just not ready? What if I want—"

"What you want is irrelevant when it contradicts what I want. Now get dressed and meet me downstairs for breakfast. You are to be fully dressed and at the breakfast table by 7:00 a.m. every morning, do you understand me?"

"Yes," she said with a bite to her tone.

"You want to try that again?" I asked, looking back in the mirror at my perfectly tied Windsor knot.

"Yes, sir. But what am I supposed to wear?"

CHAPTER 18

STELLA

This had to all be some deranged fever dream.

Or maybe I had died in that car, and this was my hell.

Was this all punishment for making fun of Mitzy Buller's braces in the third grade? I had apologized for that.

I stared at Lucian's back as he walked out of the door, closing it behind him.

If looks could kill, I would have set his gray suit on fire with my eyes alone.

Not that he cared. Not that he asked what I wanted at any point. The only thing he cared about was that I called him sir. And didn't break his rules.

I didn't know which I hated more, the fact that he made me do it, and it felt so demeaning, so embarrassing, and just wrong, or the fact that every single time those words came from my mouth, there was a pulse of pleasure between my legs.

It was so messed up.

This man, this gorgeous, older man.

I was friends with his daughters and daughter-in-law, for

Christ's sake. He couldn't be serious. The rules he had given me were completely asinine, and I didn't believe what he said about my father's money for a second.

Lucian had told me to get dressed, but I had no clothes here.

I hadn't been allowed to take anything from the hotel suite. Everything was being held until I could figure out a way to pay my bill.

What was I supposed to do? Fashion a dress out of his bed linens? God knew after the way he was with me last night that they were not fit to wear. He had done things to my body that left large sticky white stains over the black satin.

Heat burned my cheeks again as I thought about last night.

About how good everything was. The pain, the pleasure, and how they swirled together in a way that was intoxicating, and so warm. Last night I had slept in his arms, and I wanted to feel like I should be sick about that. I wanted to feel like that was something horrible, but the only thing I felt was warm.

The truth was that it had been the best night of sleep I'd had since the accident.

It was the first time I had slept through the entire night without those dreams haunting me. The first morning I had woken up to the feeling of his cock sliding inside of me, my muscles aching from soreness, and it still felt exquisite. It was far better than waking up to the echoing, pounding sound of the flask hitting the roof of that limo, or having the image of my mother's lifeless eyes seared behind my eyelids when I first opened them.

I thought back to how he'd touched me, expecting the revulsion to hit any minute, but it still didn't. Instead of that, a slow creeping warmth glowed in my core again, and I couldn't help the way my fingers slid down my body, stopping to pinch my nipples like he had, thinking about the way his hot mouth pulled at them before my hand slid down further to my wet, aching, and very messy pussy.

My finger had only barely touched my clit when the doors slammed open, and a parade of staff came into the room. Grateful that I was still under the blankets, I held them to my body and demanded to know what the hell was going on.

"Mr. Manwarring is having us deliver your wardrobe. We are to put it into the spare closet in this room so that you may get dressed. Mr. Manwarring has insisted that while we prepare your closets, we are also to draw you a hot bath so that you may cleanse yourself," a man with slicked back hair and a tuxedo with a bow tie and tails said, while looking down his nose at me.

"Excuse me?"

"Suzette is already drawing your bath. You have fifteen minutes before breakfast is served."

He turned his back on me but didn't leave the room.

Instead, he continued, directing the never-ending parade of other maids and butlers and what looked like a like a few gardeners as they brought in garment bags, hat boxes, and even the Vintage Louis Vuitton steamer trunk that my grandmother had given me.

It was everything that I'd had not only in the hotel room, but also in my rooms in my parent's estate.

He'd sent people to my home. Invading my private space, my parent's private space, without permission.

Lucian really had moved my entire life without my consent.

Then again, my consent didn't really seem to factor in on his list of concerns.

It was clear the staff was not going to leave. By the way the butler lifted his wrist out and tapped on his watch, I knew I was on a countdown clock.

This was ridiculous.

Tightening the sheet around my body as much as I could,

careful to cover every inch that needed to be covered, and not give the help a free peep show, I made my way into the large ensuite bathroom.

Sure enough, there was a maid there in a traditional maid's uniform, with the ruffled hat clipped into her hair and everything, leaning over the bathtub and filling it with hot water and some of the most delicious smelling oils.

"What is that?" I asked her. "It smells amazing."

"Mr. Manwarring had it brought specially for you. It's a bath oil designed to sooth your muscles and accentuate the scent of the perfume he got for you."

"What perfume?"

"Carolina Herrera's *Good Girl*. It really is a very fetching scent."

Of course, it was Carolina Herrera's *Good Girl*.

I took a deep breath in slowly through my nose and out of my mouth, stopping myself from screaming at the poor maid.

This wasn't her fault, and I did not take things out on the help. I found it tacky and gauche and refused to be one of those overprivileged, entitled women. I mean, I was overprivileged and entitled, or at least I had been, but my situation had nothing to do with the maid.

"Is there anything else that you need help with, miss?" she asked.

"No, I can bathe myself." The words may have come out a little too harshly, so I immediately followed them with, "Thank you so much for your help."

"Of course, miss," she said and dropped into a short curtsy before leaving the room.

That was odd.

I'd had a maid my entire life, and none of the staff had ever curtsied to me. Then I thought back to the butler and realized he had an accent and was an actual legitimate English butler.

Even the suit Lucian put on I was pretty sure was English. There was something about the subtlety of the check pattern in the dark gray, and the cut not only hugged his body perfectly so that it looked tailored, but there was also something in the way it was cut closer to his body, and how the shoulders seemed larger and yet still tapered perfectly to his waist.

He was not a small man by any stretch of the imagination, but his suit still gave him a sleek silhouette.

I shook those thoughts out of my head.

If he was an anglophile, that was the least of my concerns. His other quirks like making me love the things that I should hate and making me feel warm when everything else left me frozen— those were the things I should be more concerned about.

He'd only left me a moment ago, and the cold was already starting to creep in.

As soon as Suzette left, closing the door behind her, I dropped the ruined sheet to the ground and went to step into the steaming water.

Just as I feared, I didn't feel the warmth.

The water was hot. I could see how it pinkened my pale skin, but I couldn't feel anything but that icy grip starting to enclose my body again.

As quickly as I could, I scrubbed my body clean of his touch, hoping that ridding myself of his fingerprints would somehow clear my mind of the fog of hormones and lust.

I leaned back in the water. Even if I couldn't enjoy the warmth, I could at least enjoy the luxurious scents of the oils. The notes of vanilla, tonka bean, and jasmine floated around me, and I tried to focus on those luxurious scents. I ignored the fact that he was the one who had picked them out for me.

"Ten more minutes, miss," the butler called from outside of the room, his accent more pronounced now that I was listening for it.

"I will be out when I am ready and not a moment before," I responded.

Suzette may not have earned my annoyance, but the butler could deal with it. He huffed something under his breath, but I sank beneath the water so I couldn't hear it. I needed to block him out, I needed to block everything out and think.

Lucian Manwarring wanted to marry me.

He hadn't asked, he'd informed me.

Just like he'd informed me that my father was broke, that I was broke, and that I had to live reliant only on his goodwill.

I couldn't believe it. I knew people with our status could easily lose fortunes. I knew people like my father could hide the loss of money for a certain amount of time, but I just couldn't believe it.

My father was shit at keeping secrets.

Whenever he had a surprise for me or my mother, we knew something was up. Granted, he didn't talk to us about business situations, but if he was broke, he would be worried about it, and we would know.

I didn't understand how I was in this situation.

Could it be my fault? Should I have started working?

Or could I have done something of value instead of waiting for my life to begin once I got my inheritance?

I was twenty-six, one of the only girls in my friend group who wasn't already married.

Maybe that was my big mistake.

Waiting around to inherit my trust. Assuming I had plenty of time to choose an influential husband who aligned with my vision of the future. One who could help me get the right charity board appointments. One with the right political connections to influence legislation. One who was willing to become a power couple for change.

When I was eighteen, I should have insisted that my father set up my own corporation. That my trust fund be transferred into my name so I had assets of my own that couldn't be touched by anyone else.

That was always the plan, but I thought I had time. I should have had time. That time was taken from me by that drunk limo driver, and I would hate him forever.

Hating him wasn't going to get me out of marrying a man who was literally my best friends' father.

It wasn't going to get me out of this situation where I was forced to sleep in his bed every night, facing the dirty things that turned my body on. That made me feel hot, euphoric, and then so dirty.

There had to be options for me.

I still had to do something, I couldn't just sit here and let this happen.

Getting out of the tub, I stretched, letting the water slide off my body before I stepped into the cobalt blue kimono silk robe waiting for me. I wrapped it tightly around me as if that could somehow stop the chill that I was pretty sure had to be coming from within my body and went out to the bedroom.

It was blissfully empty, the entire parade of staff having left, and it looked like they were never here.

The room was immaculate.

The bed had been stripped and remade to perfection. The closet that was opposite where Lucian had grabbed his suit had been left open.

The closet was at least 15x15 feet, with a large set of drawers acting as an island in the middle of the room. The shelves and bars were full of my clothes, hat boxes tucked neatly at the very top, and even the shoes laid out in the individual little cubbies, all perfectly displayed.

This was not the clothing of a girl whose father was on the verge of bankruptcy. This was the clothing of a girl whose trust fund could fund a small country for her lifetime without ever running dry.

No, I needed to know what was really happening.

I needed to know what my options were, what was realistic, and how I was going to be able to get free from all of this mess without a ring on my finger, or worse, a bastard growing in my belly.

My parents had spent hundreds upon hundreds of thousands of dollars on my education. I had excelled in courses that other girls struggled in. I was accepted to a top university and graduated top of my class.

It may have been general education in general business courses since I was going to need to play the part of a perfect wife, but that didn't mean that was the only thing my degrees could be used for.

My parents had raised a strong, educated woman, and I could do what I needed to do to survive without them.

I could be independent.

I just needed a little help.

There had to be some way to get me out from under Lucian Manwarring and his theft of my family's legacy.

Pushing my shoulders back, I grabbed my own pink power suit that completely channeled Elle Woods energy and paired it with the perfect pink crystal Jimmy Choos.

I was a badass, stylish woman who planned to take her future by the balls.

First, I needed to talk to my lawyer to figure out my next steps.

CHAPTER 19

LUCIAN

Stella, the punishment-craving brat, was making me wait.

If I had the time, I would have gone up to my room myself, reminded her how valuable my time was with a belt, and then forced her to sit still to eat breakfast with me.

Sadly, I didn't have the time for that this morning, and I sent Hamilton to deal with her for me.

He apparently didn't have to go very far.

I could hear them arguing just steps outside of the formal dining room.

"No," she said. "I have appointments that I have to see too."

What appointments could she possibly have? I didn't know, and truthfully, I didn't care. She needed to learn the rules of this house.

Rule one: if you lived in this house, you ate breakfast at this table every single morning.

I couldn't hear exactly what Hamilton said, but after a moment, he directed her into the dining room.

I stood as a gentleman should when a woman approached the table.

She was dressed all in pink, her arms crossed over her chest like a little angry Barbie.

With a quick wave, I signaled to Hamilton that I would take care of getting her seated and he could let the chef know that it was time to serve breakfast.

Even though now we were running four minutes late.

He quickly pivoted on his heel, turning to anticipate my needs. I have to say, Hamilton was my best investment. I'd picked him straight from the Prestigious Butler Academy, Bespoke Bureau in London.

Classically trained, British Butlers were a must in my line of work. Not only did they anticipate needs, but they were discreet and always distinctly aware of who signed their paychecks, and their loyalty was unflappable. There had been many times my son tried to bribe him to keep his mouth shut about sneaking out. Each time, Hamilton took the bribe and then immediately reported my son's whereabouts.

You could only buy that kind of loyalty.

He'd be discreet about what was going on between Stella and me. He also managed the rest of the staff with an iron fist, ensuring that they worked at the same level he did. At all times.

Stella could pout all she liked.

It wouldn't matter this time.

She would be learning her lesson soon enough.

I walked around the long, elegant table and pulled out her chair, motioning for her to sit.

Her lips twisted like she wanted to refuse, but I raised an eyebrow.

Thankfully, she was quick enough to learn that that expression was a threat, and one she should heed.

Sulking, she stomped over to the seat, and then her breeding took over, and she gingerly sat while I pushed in the chair. I didn't miss her slight wince once she was in the chair.

"Is this really necessary?" she said, crossing her arms.

"Yes," I said, moving back to my side of the table.

Less than thirty seconds after I sat down, Hamilton stepped into the dining room and held open the door for the kitchen staff. They placed the breakfast items on the table: pastries as well as omelets, coffee, tea and juices, fresh fruit, toast, and potatoes in three different ways. As well as a plethora of breakfast meats.

I stood again and selected for Stella.

In time, I would let the staff serve her, but this time, I would take care of it. She was far too thin. She needed to eat more. I piled her plate high with eggs, potatoes, bacon, and toast. Snatching a small crystal cup of cut fruit, I placed it all in front of her.

"I can't eat all this!"

"Try," I ordered as I turned to make us both a cup of coffee. Already knowing how she liked it from observing her at a cafe cart outside the courtroom, I added a sugar substitute and a little skim milk, then set the cup in front of her.

I loaded my plate up next with the proteins and carbs I was going to need to fuel my day, as well as a large cup of hot coffee.

"So what are your plans today?" I asked as I took my seat.

"Just a few errands to run," she bit out.

"Good, then let's make this quick. Let's go over the rules that you seem to have already forgotten."

"I haven't forgotten anything," she said, staring daggers at me.

"Really? I haven't forgotten anything what?"

Her face paled as she looked at a maid and the footman, who stood by the door, waiting to see if we needed anything, and Hamilton, who stood beside him.

"In this house, the staff sign ironclad NDAs. When it is just us and the staff, we are in private."

"I haven't forgotten anything, sir," she said between clenched teeth, and I barely heard it.

It was good enough for now. I understood that she was embarrassed by the way her cheeks glowed, and even the maid had a blush on her face as she stared down at her toes.

Hamilton had no expression at all.

Still, I wasn't going to fault her for being embarrassed.

"Let's go over all of the rules again and give you more details, shall we?"

"Yes, sir," she said as she picked up her fork and stabbed a piece of cantaloupe.

"Good. Breakfast is served at 7:00 a.m. in this dining room, and if you are in this house, you will be here at 7:00 a.m., fully dressed and ready to enjoy your first meal. This is the meal where we will go over our itineraries, and I will let you know if there is anything pressing that I need you to do that day."

"Is there?"

"Is there what?"

"Is there anything pressing that you need me to do today, sir?"

"As a matter of fact, there is. You need to be here and ready to leave with me at noon."

"Where are we going?" she asked.

"If I had wanted you to know where we were going, I would have told you."

"Yes, sir," she said, staring back down at the plate.

I took a sip of my coffee. It really was the best blend. I had the beans flown in from Marrakesh. Batcha coffee was the only coffee I drank, and I could tell by the way her eyes lit up when she took a sip of it herself, Stella liked it too. And that told me a very valuable truth. She could not afford to be poor.

Her tastes were already too delicately honed to a life of excessive pleasures to ever survive the working class.

"I'm not going to go through an entire list of do's and don'ts, but there are certain things that I will be expecting of you."

She didn't say anything. She just set her coffee cup back on the table, folded her hands in her lap, and waited.

"You are to accompany me to events, to be on my arm presented as my ward. You know how these events are. You know how to behave, and I expect you to behave as such. If you have any questions about what is and isn't inappropriate at any given event, look for one of my daughters. They will tell you exactly what I expect."

"Yes, sir."

"You are also to stay out of my business. That means you don't pry into conversations that you do not belong in. If I am having a conversation with a business associate while you are on my arm, you should be talking to their wife or their daughters, or looking around and not listening. Those conversations are not for your ears, is that understood?"

"Yes, sir."

"In return, you get a roof over your head. You are able to buy whatever you want, and then as I mentioned earlier, in six months we will announce our engagement. Then you will have another five months to plan the wedding. I believe your new card was given to you?"

"Yes, sir."

"Good. The event we're going to later is not formal. It will be outside, more of a garden party. Buy what you need. Do what you need to do to be presentable by noon."

"Yes, sir."

She was trying to go for malicious compliance. Saying only what I told her she could say. She could do that all day long. Every time the word *sir* came from her lips, my cock twitched.

"Good girl," I said before I drained my coffee and stood to head to work.

I had a meeting in twenty minutes, and I had to get into my office at the financial district. There was some business I preferred not to handle in my home.

Hamilton was already waiting by the door with the travel mug of my coffee as well as my copies of the paper which I would skim over in the car.

I stopped when I reached Stella and watched.

She sat there, her arms neatly folded and her breakfast barely touched.

"Do not leave this table until your plate is empty."

"Yes, sir," she bit out through clenched teeth.

With a chuckle, I rewarded her reluctant obedience with a kiss on her forehead, confident in her complete submission to my demands.

CHAPTER 20

STELLA

The very last thing I was going to do was buy a fucking garden party dress today.

That breakfast was humiliating.

To make it worse, the majordomo of the house wouldn't let me get up until I finished my plate. He watched me eat like he was scoring my posture and fork positions.

Judging by the scowl on his face, he disapproved of my table manners, which was ridiculous.

I had been brought up in the best prep schools. I had been taught proper etiquette and manners since I was a child. Lucian could have brought the King of England for dinner, and I would know the proper etiquette.

When I was finally allowed to leave the table, I stormed up to my room, or rather our room, and sat on the bed, trying to figure out what to do. I had two hours before my lawyer would be in for the day.

After the judge ruled against me, I'd tried to reach my lawyer, and again, several times over the next few days. His secretary had been blocking me. It seemed the only way I would be getting ahold of him was to march into his office and demand his attention.

That was my plan, but I had some time to kill first.

I activated my new card and researched conservatorships in the state of New York.

There was so much information, it was starting to make my head spin.

I dug some of the documents out of my purse, needing to reread them. I still couldn't understand how he'd gotten away with this. Scanning through the paragraphs of indecipherable legalese, I looked for something that almost made sense.

Then I found it, right in front of me, in black and white.

IT IS the court's opinion that the sudden death of Ms. Stella Jane Deiderich's family has left her grief-stricken and in a position where she cannot be trusted to maintain her family's estates. All assets that would have been bequeathed to her by her parents are to be placed in a trust with Mr. Lucian Manwarring, Sr. In addition to managing her finances, Mr. Manwarring will also be appointed her power of attorney as well as her health care proxy. The list of duties appointed to Mr. Manwarring is as follows...

THE LIST AFTERWARD WAS IMPRESSIVE. It systematically notated that the court had taken away every right I had.

Sure enough, in the middle of that list, it stated that Mr. Manwarring got to decide where I lived, if I went back to school, everything.

He had the right to void any contracts I signed without his approval, including but not limited to leases, employment contracts, and marriage licenses.

I'd give him this much: his lawyers and that judge may have been corrupt, vile men, but they were thorough.

I wasn't allowed to do anything, at least not until I got back to my lawyer and made him face me and tell me how to fight this.

If Lucian Manwarring expected a docile little ward he could intimidate, threaten, and play with, a little mouse he could turn into a submissive and an obedient housewife, he had another thing coming.

I was still a Deiderich, and I would fight this.

As soon as my phone said it was 8:30 a.m., I had to go.

My lawyer began his day at 9:00, and I needed to be the first person he saw.

Getting out of the mansion was a little trickier than I had anticipated.

The English butler, whom I now referred to as Jeeves, at least in my head, seemed to be everywhere. I wasn't sure if he was going to stop me from leaving again. Since his boss wasn't here, maybe I was free to do as I wanted. No one had told me I wasn't allowed to leave.

However, I knew that if he saw me go, he would immediately tell Lucian.

There shouldn't have been a way he could track me, but on the off chance he had put something in my bag or had some other invasive way to track me, I didn't want him to know ahead of time where I was going.

It took a fair bit of sneaking and going down a long hallway with my back pressed against the wall.

I even had to double back twice to avoid Jeeves or another maid who reported to him.

Finally, I got to the front door. Just as I gripped the handle, a nasally English voice came from behind me.

"Mr. Manwarring asked that I remind you there is an outing to attend at noon."

Busted, but that didn't mean I had to let him know he had won.

"I understand."

"May I inquire as to where you are off to this morning?"

I turned and looked him in the eye as I pushed my shoulders back, a position of strength my father had taught me. "No."

"Be back on time. Otherwise, the master of this house will be displeased." He looked down his nose at me. "Maybe then he will take my suggestion and put you to work with the rest of the entry-level staff instead of giving you a free ride you do not deserve."

"You don't know what I do and do not deserve."

"I know enough," he said, turning on his overly polished heel and walking away.

A cold fire burned in my belly, fueled by rage and embarrassment. It didn't slip my notice that even my anger was now cold.

Even when I tried to slam the door behind me, it simply glided shut with a very unsatisfying click.

This house was the worst.

I called an Uber, put in my new card info, and went straight to my lawyer's office.

The ride wasn't too bad, and I had even managed to calm myself down a bit. I had every intention of walking into that office and tearing him a new one, but I was at least calm enough that I could act like a well-mannered lady while doing it.

Logically, I knew a hysterical woman never got what she needed, only ridicule, and I needed the lawyer's help. And for him not to send me a bill until whatever we were going to do was done.

When I stepped out of my car, I got an alert from my banking app informing me I had $163.00 left on my card. All of the poise and composure I had managed to find instantly evaporated.

"You have to get rid of him," I said when I stormed into my

lawyer's office, his secretary trailing after me, telling me I couldn't go in there.

My incompetent attorney was just taking a sip of his coffee when I came in, spilling it down his cheap, ill-fitting suit.

I hoped it burned.

It was a cruel-spirited thought, and I immediately regretted it.

Then he shot me a look of annoyance like I was a child who was running wild and interrupting his work instead of a paying client who needed his help.

Suddenly, I didn't feel so bad.

This man was supposed to be on my side. He was the only help I had, and he saw me as a nuisance.

I didn't understand it. My father had used this firm exclusively for nearly twenty years, so they stuck me with what I was hoping was a first-year associate nepotism baby.

I didn't give a fuck who his uncle was. After the amount of business I gave this firm, how was I not treated better?

"Ms. Deiderich, did we have an appointment?"

"No, your secretary is refusing to schedule anything. Apparently, you are all booked, so I thought I would come down here and see if you could fit me in between meetings." I made a show of looking around the empty room. "What do you know? It looks like you have time now."

"Ms. Deiderich, please, this is not how things—"

I held up my hand, cutting him off as I took a seat on the other side of his desk. "What he is doing cannot be legal. He is ruining my life."

"There is nothing I can do," he said, grabbing napkins from a drawer and dabbing at his shirt like it would do anything.

He gave up and hit the button on his phone, asking his secretary to get him a new shirt. The snotty bitch asked if he would also like her to get security.

"Do it, and I'll bring my complaints to your boss's boss, and then I will take out an ad in the Washington Post about this firm intentionally tanking cases. I will ruin this firm and your career. My father may be gone, but my name still carries weight."

"No, security will not be needed," he said before sitting back in his chair. "What are you expecting me to do here?"

"Your job?" I sounded bitchy, but it needed to be said. "You sat there and watched. You said nothing as they stole my money and treated me like a child."

"What would you have me do?" he asked, standing. "No, really, what would you have me do? Manwarring owns half the judges in the city. His son married the DA's sister. There is nothing this man can't touch. If we drag it in front of another judge, the same thing is going to happen, but maybe this time, he will call you incompetent. Maybe this time, he says you need round-the-clock inpatient psychiatric help because you are unstable. He can have the court claim you are a risk to yourself. Do you really think he can't buy a doctor as easily as he bought the judge? He will lock you up and throw away the key."

"That isn't fair."

He scoffed. "Fair? Jesus, you are a child. Life isn't fair. Boo-hoo, you have someone holding on to your assets for a few years. He can't really do much with them. They are still yours. He just manages them for the next three years. So you have a trustee, so what?"

"So what?" I practically screeched. "So he had me kicked out of my hotel. He had my cards canceled, and he made me move into his home."

"When you say he canceled your cards, do you mean he has taken all funds from you?" the lawyer asked, his eyebrow raised as if I had piqued his interest.

"Yes, well, kind of."

"What do you mean, kind of?"

"He gave me a new card, but it has a limit. That is unacceptable."

"The room he has you staying in? Does it have a solid roof?"

"Yes, but what does—"

The lawyer raised his hand, cutting me off. "Does it have heat and a bed? Do you have access to running water?"

"Yes, of course, but that doesn't mean—"

"It means you have it better than most people in this city. No judge is going to take you out of Manwarring's care because you have an allowance." The way he rolled his eyes as he said 'allowance' made me grind my teeth.

"I understand that I am still very fortunate, but—"

"But nothing. There is nothing I, or any other lawyer, can do for you."

"There has to be a way out of this."

The lawyer stared at his now empty coffee cup longingly for a moment, then focused on me. "Your best option is to just wait. You have only three years, or until you get married."

Three years was too long. Lucian Manwarring was going to force me to marry him in less than one.

"I understand you believe that is my best option. I am asking what my other options are."

"You have none unless Manwarring is somehow unfit—"

"How do I prove he is unfit?"

The lawyer didn't even bother hiding his disrespectful eye roll. He wouldn't have done that to my father, and I was getting really tired of men not taking me seriously.

The lawyer held up his hand, spread his fingers, and counted off the ways.

"Mismanagement of funds, which, even if he did that, you don't have the ability to prove. Failure to file the required tax documents, which, let's be honest, is never going to happen, and even if it did, he could explain it away as an accounting error. No judge would fault him for that. The man doesn't file his own taxes."

"What else?" I demanded, ignoring the way the walls were slowly creeping across the floor, closing in on me and making it harder to breathe.

I focused on controlling my breath as subtly as possible while staring the lousy lawyer down. The last thing I needed to do was have a panic attack in this office. He would absolutely call 911 and have me rushed to the hospital just to get me out of his office.

"Or breach of fiduciary duty or conflict of interest. None of which would apply here."

"What else?" I asked again, knowing there had to be something. The system was not set up to protect women, but there was always some loophole, some grey area, some loose string. I just had to be clever enough to find it, and brave enough to pull it off.

"There is nothing else unless he was physically abusing you, which clearly is not the case, or neglect, but you already admitted you were fed and housed. Unless he was somehow incapacitated or you got married…"

"Wait, if I got married, then I would get my money and property back?" Immediately, the plots of a thousand Lifetime movies scrolled through my head.

I had no interest in a husband or falling in love, but maybe I could pay a man to marry me, and then pay him to leave me alone, then divorce me when I was of age.

Maybe some handsome artist who needed time free from a job to create his art? Or maybe a Parisian baker with a sexy accent who wanted to intern in the amazing New York bakeries and just needed a green card.

"Yes, but to get married, you will need your trustee's written permission."

Well, there went those dreams.

It was probably for the best. No self-respecting Frenchman would come to the United States to learn how to bake. It just wouldn't happen.

"Ok, you mentioned incapacitated. What does that mean exactly?"

"If he is in some way physically unable to do his duty as a trustee. If he were in some kind of accident or a medical issue arose, left him incapacitated. Though I should tell you. Manwarring did a full physical to prove that he was more than capable. The man is in perfect health. That avenue isn't going to give you the options that you're hoping."

Incapacitated. Something about that struck a nerve.

The lawyers didn't say he had to be sick or in an accident. He just had to be unable to perform his duties as a trustee.

Of course, the most common way that would happen would be if there was an illness or injury, but I didn't think those were the only ways. I remembered reading something in the contract about being incapacitated, but I couldn't remember what it was. It was just on the tip of my tongue.

"What other ways could he be incapacitated?" I asked.

"Look, there's not a loophole here for you, and I don't have time for this. Nothing short of prison is going to get you free of him."

Prison, that was it.

My father did not speak about business in front of me or my mother often, but I had heard him say things.

He hated Lucian Manwarring, and my father did not hate without cause. He had said once in passing to someone at a party that it was a miracle that Lucian wasn't in prison.

He had a reputation for making questionable deals and bending the law.

Amelia had mentioned once that Harrison wasn't a fan of her

father-in-law or really most of their class. He also had a reputation for wanting more and wanting to prove he wasn't just another rich man playing at ruling the world.

Maybe he would see taking Lucian Manwarring down as a way to do that.

"So, just to be clear," I said, standing and tucking my Kelly bag under my arm. "You are saying if he is in prison, then I get my life back."

The lawyer eyed me warily. "Yes, but I don't like where your train of thought is going."

"Where my mind is, is no longer any of your concern. I will schedule an appointment with your secretary if I need anything further. Have a nice day."

I practically ran from his office.

Lucian would be home soon, which meant I only had a few hours to find something and get it to the DA.

CHAPTER 21

LUCIAN

"**M**r. Manwarring. Your late morning appointment is already in your office," my secretary said as I stepped off the elevator after an off-site inspection of several of my dock warehouses during the first half of the morning.

"Why did you let him into my office?"

"I didn't. I couldn't stop him."

I shook my head. Her primary responsibility was to keep people the fuck out of my office. That included my son, and it damn well included Ronin O'Murphy.

How hard could it be for a woman alone to stand up to one of the biggest Irish mob bosses in the city?

The only reason I wasn't firing her on the spot was because Ronan was not at my desk snooping through shit. He was sitting at the side table setting up the chess board, which was how we preferred to do business.

If a man was cunning enough to talk strategy while playing chess, it could tell you more about the person on the opposite end of the table than doing just one or the other. I knew that if a man's strategy changed in the game while we were speaking, then his strategy had changed in the conversation as well.

If a man who was usually indecisive with moves had a sudden rush of confidence, that meant he was hiding something.

If a man who was usually decisive paused too often and took too much time making simple moves, then he didn't have all the information. There was some other influence at play.

Ronin was the first man I'd never been able to get a solid read on while playing chess. He was also one of the few who could give me a run for my money.

Most men I could beat in under twenty moves. A few took a little longer, and Ronin and I ended in stalemates more often than we finished the game. As far as we were both concerned, a tie was just as bad as a loss.

"Ronin," I said, stepping into my office. "Did my secretary offer you coffee?"

"She did, but I know she doesn't brew the good shit until you're in the office."

I laughed like it was some kind of joke, but it was the truth, and he knew it. I signaled to my secretary to make a pot.

I took the seat opposite Ronin, setting my briefcase off to the side. Truth be told, I really didn't need it. Ronan was the only reason I had to come into this office today. Everything else was better done where there were fewer snooping eyes.

It was Ronin's turn to play white. So he moved his pawn to E4. Classic opening. I immediately balanced it, moving my pawn to E5.

His next move was a knight to F3. Aggressive. Something was pissing him off.

"How's business, Ronin?" I asked as I moved my knight to C6, mirroring his moves on my side.

"Work is being made more and more difficult by your son and his brother-in-law." He moved the bishop to C4. He was in a mood. "I thought Luc married that Astrid bitch so he could control her brother, not join his side."

"You know my son is his own man, and I can't control him. I didn't raise weak children, though with how stubborn they are sometimes, I wish I did," I said, moving my bishop to C5.

He stared at the board, nodding, thinking. He wasn't thinking about the move. He was too good of a player to have to stop and think this early into a game.

He was trying to figure out the strategy for dealing with me and whatever the fuck was on his mind.

He moved a pawn up one to C3 before leaning back in his chair. "I don't think you understand how serious this situation is. Your son is friends with the DA and is giving him privileged information. Information that implicates a lot of people in the family. And we know the District Attorney has his eyes set on a higher office. It looks like he's trying to use us to get him there. It doesn't help that his mother has decided that my men are at her disposal."

"Jesus fuck, what is Mary Quinn doing now?"

Her involvement in my daughter's shooting by Zeigler could not be proven, but I had my suspicions. The entire sordid mess had her dirty paw prints all over it.

I moved my knight to F6. It wasn't the best move. I could have slid my bishop over, taken a pawn, and moved into a position to check. But I didn't want to antagonize Ronin before he got to whatever his point was.

The look he gave me told me he knew exactly what I was doing and didn't appreciate it.

"Mary Quinn is doing what that stuck-up, stick figure of a bitch does best. Sticking her fake nose where it doesn't belong." He curled his lip in disgust as he moved a pawn to D4, blocking my bishop to take a different pawn and block the position to take his queen.

"Is she really the biggest problem you're having right now?" I asked, moving my bishop down one and putting him in check.

Ronin was off-kilter this morning. Something was going on with the Irish families that he wasn't ready to tell me, but he needed me involved.

He blocked my check by moving his bishop to D2, and I saw him fray a little bit.

Something big was about to go down.

"Talk to me, Ronin. What's happening? How can I help?"

"You can help by getting Mary Quinn the fuck under control and getting her son out of our business. I also want your son to get the fuck out of our business. When he cut us out of Manwarring Enterprises, and all of the distilleries, we lost our primary way of cleaning money."

"I understand that."

"No, I don't think you do. If the DA starts bringing us in, and we go down, then we are taking you down with us. Not just your business. We're not going to let you pull some bullshit with a fall guy in accounting. No, we are personally taking you down. You and I will share a fucking prison cell."

"That's not going to happen," I tried to interrupt him to calm him down. He was having none of it.

"If we are not made whole, then we are coming after you and those you love."

Ronin did not make idle threats. That didn't mean I was willing to be threatened in my own fucking office.

"Who exactly do you think you're talking to? I have had this deal running with your family before you were born. You will not come into my office and threaten me, boy. You do not threaten my family. I threaten yours. Just because I sit in this glass tower, don't think I don't remember where the fuck I came from. Or how I got here."

"That doesn't change the fact that we need to—"

"You need to shut the fuck up and let me handle it. I heard you. You need another way to clean money and replace the income you lost. I have a plan that is in the works and may prove to be far more profitable than I intended."

"What plan?"

"It's too early to give details. I have been working with your family for years. I value this relationship and understand how delicate it is, even if my son does not. Let me handle it."

"You know what happens if you don't," Ronin said.

I knocked over my king, even though it was never in any danger. Not as a sign of defeat, but a symbol of bending a knee.

It made my stomach twist in anger, but I held it in.

Life was a game of chess, and just like in chess, sometimes you needed to sacrifice a pawn or even a king to win in the end.

I was playing the long game.

CHAPTER 22

STELLA

*M*y heart raced as I pressed myself against the wall, listening for the footsteps coming down the hallway.

Doing this was stupid, but I had to try.

The footsteps got closer, and I just knew they belonged to the evil butler. He was going to rat me out if he caught me, and then there was no telling what Lucian would do to me.

The lawyer's words played over and over in my head, as well as the image of the healthcare proxy listed on the court documents.

If he caught me here, he really could toss me in a mental institution and throw away the key. Just because doctors no longer diagnosed women with hysteria didn't mean they didn't treat it.

My eyes stayed closed tight as I listened to his footsteps get closer and closer.

Maybe I did deserve to have a trustee.

Maybe I wasn't an adult.

I couldn't even sneak down a hallway and get into an office without being caught by the butler.

Then, in a moment of pure luck, the footsteps turned a corner and walked away from me. I hadn't been caught, not yet, anyway.

I counted to ten silently in my head, making sure the coast was completely clear before I continued creeping down the long hallway to Manwarring's office.

The large wooden door was thankfully unlocked, and it was easy for me to slide into the room, barely opening the door and closing it behind me. Again, I stopped and listened, making sure no one had followed me, no alarms were going to go off, and I was safe.

With an almost compulsive need, I slowly counted to ten in my head, waiting for something to happen, someone to pop out of a closet or the butler to walk in and drag me out after being alerted to my trespassing by some silent alarm. When nothing happened, I let out a breath of relief that made my lungs ache.

I had made it successfully into his office. Now, all I had to do was find something that I could take to Harrison Astrid.

His computer was the most obvious place I would find anything truly damning.

If I could find something there and take screenshots, maybe email them to myself, delete everything from his computer, or even just take photos with my phone that would give Harrison enough for some type of search warrant, then I could be free.

It did occur to me that I may not even have to go that far. Just having the information might be enough for me to blackmail my way to freedom. I just didn't know if I was strong enough to go through with that. But from what Amelia had told me about her brother, Harrison absolutely was.

Whether or not I decided to go the legal route or the blackmail route really didn't matter unless I could find something incriminating.

I sat in the large leather chair that was behind the massive, imposing wooden desk. There was no computer on top of the desk, so I opened drawers, trying to find something.

Thankfully, Lucian kept a tidy desk, and it only took me a moment to find the sleek silver laptop. Of course, it was Samsung and the newest model. As carefully as I could without smudging anything, I lifted the top to see the battery was full, but the screen was locked.

There wasn't even a place to type in the passcode. It required a fingerprint ID.

Fuck.

I did not have the technical skills required to try to break into a laptop, even if it had a password as simple as one, two, three, four. There was no way I was going to be able to get into a computer that had biosecurity.

I set the laptop on the desk and dug through the drawers—but found nothing in the front middle drawer other than a few pens and pads of paper.

Carefully, I put the laptop back in that drawer and closed it. The ones on the side held more office supplies as well as a bottle of lubricant and a few condoms. I didn't want to think about what he had done on this desk before.

Putting all of that back, I went to the other side. The smaller top drawer opened, and it looked like there were a few leather portfolios. I pulled them out, set them on top of the desk, and went through them.

He had a background check on my notes about doctor visits from over the years, including notes from my psychiatrist when I was sixteen. But these notes had been changed.

When I was fifteen, I had been riding a horse that stepped into a gopher hole and broke his leg. The fall shattered my arm, and I'd watched as a new ranch hand fresh from Wyoming or somewhere came over to my prize-winning horse and shot him in the head.

The ranch immediately fired him, against my wishes, because of the way he'd handled it. According to my father, I shouldn't have had to witness it, but I was glad I did.

Butterscotch was my horse, and it was my job to calm her and assure her as she passed.

After that incident, I was given painkillers for my arm, and my parents insisted that I get checked out by a psychiatrist to make sure there were no lasting effects from the trauma of seeing my pony die.

I was sad, but I understood what happened. I understood that killing the pony was doing it a service because his leg would never heal right. The horse would have spent the rest of his life in excruciating pain.

It was a hard lesson to learn, but I'd learned it with the grace and poise that was expected of me.

The notes I read in front of me were something completely different. They insinuated that I had not taken the incident well and that I had coped by abusing my pain medication.

It was ridiculous, but it didn't matter.

The doctor's signature was at the bottom of the page, right under where it diagnosed me as having an addictive personality and a problem with impulse control. The forms were fake, but they looked real.

If the wrong judge saw this, and if this was what Lucian used, then there was no way I was going to get out of this situation.

This information was dangerous for a woman like me.

Women nowadays joked about hysteria and being medicated, lobotomized, or any number of other gruesome things that men used to do to get rid of women.

Most women didn't realize that for the elite class, the class that had old money that came over on the Mayflower with a fortune already intact, these practices were still very much alive.

No, they no longer manually stimulated a woman in a doctor's office to reach orgasm and cure her of impure thoughts, at least not at any of my appointments.

However, there were repeated keywords that doctors used. Hysteria had now become manic episodes, or depression, having a nervous disposition, unbearable fatigue, hormonal imbalance, anger issues, the list went on and on.

I'd thought it was a thing of the past, too, until my mother's friend Dorothy Howard's husband had decided to leave her, trading her in for his secretary.

He'd wanted a divorce. She'd said okay. He forgot that the vast majority of his wealth came from her. When he saw how much of the estate she would get to keep, the house in the Hamptons, the jet, and even the vacation home in the Bahamas that his mistress loved so much, instead of divorcing her, he had her committed.

My mother and I visited her a few times. The grounds were beautiful, the staff was pleasant and attentive, but she was gone. They had her on so many medications the bright, funny woman I had called Aunt Dorothy had disappeared.

Lost somewhere in a haze of drugs and red Jell-O.

She died within the year.

The official diagnosis was suicide. They said that she had been storing her medications and then took them all at once, overdosing.

That was an interesting side effect they never told you about taking antidepressants. If you weren't depressed, or if they gave you the wrong dosage or the wrong medication, it could make you depressed.

My mother cried for a week when she died, and my father had been by her side comforting her.

I promised myself that I would never forget what happened to Dorothy, but clearly, I had if I had let myself get into this situation.

I kept flipping through the pages, stopping only when I saw another name I recognized. Doctor Sylvia Roth, OB-GYN.

Lucian actually had the results from my last pap smear and vaginal exam. Not only that, but there were extra notes, things I did not ask her to look at. There were notes talking about my fertility. Saying that I was at the perfect age and in the perfect health to carry strong healthy fetuses. There were even notes saying how symmetrical my ovaries were.

Why would he have this information? Why would anyone have this information other than my doctor herself? For how long had this man been planning on taking me?

I tore out the pages from my OB-GYN, as well as the records from my psychiatrist. No one needed these. Ever.

I slid the leather portfolio back into the drawer.

I made sure it was in exactly the same place and that the drawer looked undisturbed before I moved it back in. I was about to reach for the next drawer when I heard more footsteps just outside the door.

Immediately, I dropped to my knees, crawled under the desk, and prayed it was just the butler dropping something off, or maybe he was walking past the office on his way to somewhere else.

I hid in the cramped footwell, my heart beating against my chest and a cold sweat breaking out on my brow.

Of course, it was cold.

Everything was cold.

Even the Persian rug's thick fibers dug into my legs, scratching my delicate skin, and felt cold, but I did not move.

Not until I heard the footsteps make their way back down the marble hallway.

I hadn't heard the door open, and I was pretty sure I was still alone, but I still gently peeked my head out and looked around the office.

It was still completely empty, completely silent.

I stared at the bookshelf, the one that he had pressed me against the other day, kissing me, touching me, and igniting a fire inside me. I looked away and ignored the bloom of warmth in my core.

Apparently, all I needed to do was think about him, and that fought off the ever-present chill.

I reached for the last drawer on his desk, the deepest one that in my experience usually held hanging file folders. I pulled and the drawer did not budge an inch. Just under the handle, I could feel the brass keyhole.

Of course the documents that I would need would be under lock and key. Unfortunately for Lucian, I really was a bad girl when I was a child.

My father had a very similar desk, and that drawer was where he'd hidden his stash of candy. I was fairly certain my father knew I snuck into his office when he wasn't home to steal candy, so he'd locked the drawer. Then he pretended that he didn't know when I picked it and stole candy anyway.

Older desks were larger than their modern counterparts. They were heavier and statelier. They were also not nearly as secure.

I slid the top drawer all the way out then, laying it on the floor next to me. Then I reached in and flipped the lock on the bottom drawer.

It pulled open easily, and I was able to slide the top drawer back in place. It was heavy and awkward, but I got it in and no one would ever be the wiser.

I was right. The bottom drawer did have hanging file folders, all labeled with initials and dates. I grabbed the first one, and it was nothing but a list of first names in one column, dates in the next, and then what looked like probably bank account numbers and amounts.

The next was more of the same, but the amounts were getting bigger. I kept thumbing through files, looking for something that screamed evidence.

It would have been so much more helpful if Lucian had just labeled a file folder *Evidence That Would Get Me Thrown In Jail.*

Sadly, I wasn't that lucky.

I thumbed through pages, wondering how as a college-educated woman, I didn't understand a damn thing on here. Maybe I should have gone to business school instead of finishing school.

Pages and pages of numbers and dates and just first names. That couldn't be normal. Surely the accounts would have to have last names attached to them. But nothing gave me any indication if these were deposits or withdrawals, money transfers, or receipts of payments for purchases.

"Well, well, well," Lucian said.

I peeked over the desk to see him standing at the door, leaning in the door frame with his arms crossed. He didn't look mad. It was so much worse. He looked amused.

"What exactly do you think you are doing?" he said, taking a step inside and kicking the door closed behind him.

I reached back and clicked the lock as quickly as I could. I put the papers back into the bottom drawer, keeping just a few out, tucked under my knees.

"I was just looking for a pad and paper," I said in the sweetest voice I could manage. "Your butler wasn't any help. So I had to go find it myself."

I stood, picking up the pages with one hand, hiding them behind my back, pretending to straighten my suit as I slipped them under my jacket and tucked them into the waist of my skirt. They wouldn't hold forever, but it might be long enough to get them to my room.

"I don't believe you. Hamilton would have never let you into my office."

"I didn't say he let me into your office," I said, assuming Hamilton was the butler. "I said he wasn't helpful when I asked for a pad and paper."

"What did he say then?"

"He said that little orphans should work in the kitchens, not sleep in the master of the house's bed."

Lucian tipped his head back and laughed, and I used the momentary distraction to make sure the pages were secure at my back.

"What were your rules, Stella?"

"I am to behave, at all times, call you sir in private, and accompany you to events where I will continue to behave as a grateful ward until you announce our engagement in six months." I repeated the asinine rules he'd given me while staring at the ground.

Caving to him like this made my stomach flip in a way that wasn't entirely unpleasant, and I didn't want to think about it.

"And what else?" he asked, taking a threatening step towards me.

"I'm to stay out of your business," I said.

"And are you?"

"Yes, sir." I hated how my core warmed when I said those words. They shouldn't have turned me on the way they did. He should not be the only source of warmth I had.

"Then why did you try to get into my computer?" he asked, reaching over the desk to slide open the drawer.

"I didn't, sir. I promise."

"Oh, baby girl. That was exactly what I was hoping you were going to say."

He opened the laptop, hit a few keys, and turned it around to show me a photo of my face taken when I opened it.

"I…" I had no idea how I was going to cover this up. "I'm sorry, sir. I just wanted a bigger allowance," I lied.

"You lied to me, little girl." He reached down and undid his belt buckle.

CHAPTER 23

LUCIAN

"I'm sorry, sir."

"That was a very bad thing to do." I pulled my belt free from my pants in one fluid motion. "You know what happens to bad girls."

The way her bottom lip quivered as I took off my belt made my cock swell, and her eyes filled with tears as she looked around, trying to find her escape.

There was no escape for her.

There would never be an escape for her, but I liked that she still had hope.

"No, please," she said as I laid the belt across the desk.

"Bad girls get punished. Spanking clearly doesn't work, so let's find out what will."

With one swift movement, I lunged across the desk and grabbed Stella by the throat, holding her still, not letting my baby girl run.

"No, I'll be good," she whined as she tried to pry my fingers from her throat.

Careful not to squeeze too tightly, I moved around the desk, holding her in place.

"Oh, I have no doubt you will be very good. Get on your knees," I said when I stood in front of her, releasing her throat.

"What?" She looked at me, eyes wide as I threw my belt down on the desk, letting her know I wasn't going to use it on her but keeping it close in case that plan changed.

"You want to be behind my desk, fine." I unbuttoned my pants and pulled down my fly. "I'm going to show you what you should be doing when you're in here. Down. On. Your. Knees."

Her eyes held this incredible combination of hatred and just a little bit of desire with a touch of fear. Her eyes were so expressive.

I always knew what she was thinking and what she was feeling.

Stella sank her teeth into her bottom lip as she stared at the floor before lowering herself down.

This girl was going to be the end of me. She sank down to her knees, and I took my already hard cock out.

"Show me how good of a girl you can be," I said, placing the head of my cock on her full lips. "Open," I demanded.

Her soft, pink, glossy lips slowly opened while her brilliant eyes flicked up, staring up at me. Her cute little pink tongue quickly darted out and licked the tip of my cock.

I didn't think she'd even meant to do it. Instinct was taking over.

She may be fighting her desire for me, stuck with the images of what she thought she wanted, but her body was already so in tune with my needs.

Stella could fight it all she wanted.

I even enjoyed the challenge, but soon, she would figure out it was too late.

She was mine—her money, her property, her body, and her

soul. Everything she thought was hers was mine, and I had no intention of giving up my claim.

Her lips stayed parted just slightly, and her warm, damp breath felt amazing, but I wasn't here to let her tease me.

I was here to punish her.

I slid my hands through her silky hair, tilting her head up just slightly before I gripped her hair by the roots and forced my cock to the back of her throat.

"Take it, take it all," I told her as she struggled. "Just relax and take it."

Tears pooled in the corner of her eyes, one escaping and making a trail down her heart-shaped face.

When it looked like she was struggling to control her gag reflex, I pulled her off my cock, and let her catch her breath while running my hand through her silky locks, soothing her.

She choked, coughing and gagging, and I gave her a moment to regain her composure.

Without letting go of her hair, I sat down in my leather office chair, and as soon as she had gathered herself enough, I guided her head back to my cock.

"Suck it like a good girl, and I won't have to choke you with it. But if you misbehave, I will fuck your pretty mouth until your lips are bruised, and your throat is sore. Is that understood?"

"Yes, sir," she said before leaning down and taking my cock between her lips.

She sucked me so sweetly at first, only taking the head in her mouth. Her movements were hesitant and delicate at best, but I gave her a moment to get used to the new feeling. I usually was not a patient man, but as she was tasting my cock, her sweet little cunt was getting wet for me.

It was much harder to deny how much she wanted me when her mouth was stuffed with my cock, and her cunt dripped for me. Still, this was supposed to be a punishment.

I grabbed her hair again and pushed her down, forcing my shaft to the back of her throat. I held her there for a long moment before pulling her back up to the head.

Again, I pushed her back down, and she, like the natural little submissive slut she was, took to cock sucking like a pro.

She kept her lips sealed tightly with the perfect suction. Her mouth almost felt as good as her cunt, so tight, hot, wet, and willing.

If I wasn't careful, this wasn't going to be a punishment at all. If she wanted to get on her knees and suck my cock like a good girl, then she could earn it.

Tightening my grip in her hair, I pulled her off of me and to her feet. She stared at my hard cock sticking out proudly from my pants as I ripped open her shirt and groped her perfectly firm and perky breasts.

Jesus, most women had to pay for tits this exquisitely shaped, but even the most talented surgeon couldn't make silicon feel like this—the perfect balance of fitness and give.

Her eyes were still on my cock, making it stand taller, prouder.

"Take off your panties, then lie on the desk. With your head hanging over the edge."

"What?" she asked, her eyes getting big, and she almost looked scared.

"You're enjoying the taste of my cock too much. This is a punishment. I'll let you take your time licking my cock like candy when you have earned it. For now, I am going to fuck your pretty face while I spank your naughty little cunt until you learn your fucking place."

"I'll be good, please." Tears filled her eyes, but she also pressed her thighs together.

The dirty girl wanted it.

I just knew she was wet and aching. She was going to stay

that way, constantly on edge and desperate for my cock until I decided to let her have it.

By the end of the year, I would have Stella's body trained to be wet and aching for me every time she saw me.

Every single one of my conquests, every single success, would be celebrated with her mouth around my cock, before she rode me like the thoroughbred she was. The frustration of every setback would be taken out on her pussy, with me fucking my anger out on her perfect body.

Hell, every dull, pointless meeting that should have been a fucking e-mail my assistant read would be tolerated by having her under my desk, her mouth keeping my cock warm until I had the time to fuck her.

All I had to do was break her first.

"Desk now, or I use the belt." It was an idle threat, but she didn't need to know that.

Stella hung her head low and nodded before reaching under her skirt and sliding down her pink lace panties, and I made a mental note to give her a separate allowance for lingerie.

Maybe I would just open an account at a store and let her go wild, spending as much money as she could on things I could rip from her body.

Once her panties were in a small pile on my floor, the middle clearly a little damp, she hopped up on the desk and got into the position I'd asked for, her head hanging off the table at the perfect height.

I pulled her bra down so it pushed her tits up like they were being offered to me, then flipped her skirt up, exposing her bare and already glistening pussy lips.

I had no idea how I was ever going to work at this desk again without a raging hard-on. This view was worth the distraction.

I lined my cock up with her mouth and pushed my cock to the back of her throat. I held myself there for a moment, trying to clear my mind and not fill her mouth too early. The key to making any punishment effective was making sure it lasted.

Pulling out of her throat was almost painful, so I slammed back in, followed by a few more hard, slow thrusts, getting her used to the sensation of my cock down her throat and my sack smacking into her face.

Stella was being an exceptionally good girl.

Her hands stayed flat on the desk even as I made my thrusts a little less deep and picked up the speed. I made sure to take my cock out of her mouth every few thrusts to let her greedily gulp down some air before thrusting back in.

Stella wasn't just lying there taking her punishment.

She was actively sucking at my cock, using her tongue to create more pressure, more friction. Just when I was starting to wonder if maybe she liked this, her thighs pressed together.

She was getting off on this, on being punished, or maybe it was being used.

I wasn't sure which, but I fully intended to take advantage of it.

"Part your thighs," I bit out.

Her knees bent up, but her thighs didn't part like I'd demanded. I thrust my cock to the very back of her throat, making her swallow it all, and when she struggled, needing to breathe, I backed off, taking my cock from her lips, watching a single, silver strand of spit go from the tip of my cock to her tongue.

"I said part your thighs." I kept my words low and slow, almost growling them out in a threat.

Her knees were still bent, her feet planted next to each other on my desk, and she slowly opened her knees, exposing the shame she felt.

It wasn't just that she was exposing the most intimate parts of her body. No, she was exposing her dirty secret.

She was showing me the evidence that confirmed my suspicions.

Stella Deiderich liked it when I fucked her throat.

Her pussy was soaking wet, showing me exactly how much she had craved me. I hadn't even touched her other than groping her breasts a little. This amount of moisture wasn't from a little rough tit play. No, this was from the taste of my cock and the feeling of me bending her body to my will.

Breaking her was going to be so much easier than I had anticipated. She pretended to be a 'good girl,' she acted like it, even kept her innocence until I took that too. But she really was a slut, desperate to be owned.

I slid my dick back between her lips, and she eagerly sucked me down again just before I landed a sharp little slap to her upper thighs. Her body jolted with each hit, and I liked watching her jump.

Then I slid my fingers between her pussy lips, spreading her juices around. She moaned deep in her throat, sending the most delicious vibrations through my cock to my spine.

I pushed a little deeper into her throat as I slicked her clit and felt the gentle hum around my entire cock this time.

Fuck, this woman really was going to be the death of me. If I let her. I didn't lose to anyone, especially not some brat lying on my desk swallowing my cock.

I petted her again, and her throat constricted, gripping my cock as more moans traveled from her through to my cock. It became a game in my head, a challenge. I needed to prove that I owned her pleasure and her pain.

Stella was not going to make me come in her tight little throat before I was ready. There was also no way in hell that I was going to come down her throat without making sure she came first.

There was nothing wrong with me taking pleasure from a

woman and not returning the favor. If I just had her under my desk, sucking my cock, then that was fine, but the second I touched her dripping wet pussy, the second I gave her pleasure, I became determined to see it to the end.

Most men didn't care if they left a woman hanging. I, however, refused to start a project and then not see it through.

With one hand pinching her nipples and the other stroking her clit, I kept thrusting into Stella's mouth. She was sucking me down, and every single flick of my fingers over her tight little bud sent another moan vibrating through my body. It was almost more than I could take.

My balls ached with the need to release, and I had to clench my abs and count in my head. Anything to stop myself from spilling too soon. It wasn't going to be enough.

She kept moaning, kept humming with her lips so tightly wrapped around me. I was in danger of losing the game.

Then I remembered that I was the one who made the rules. I pulled my cock from her lips as I leaned down and sealed my mouth over her pulsing clit.

I expected her to moan or say something, but instead, her lips wrapped around my balls. She gently sucked and licked, still moaning, sending those damned good vibrations through me.

Fuck, I had never even thought that she would take it upon herself to take care of my balls so sweetly. The way her lips pulled as her tongue teased was too much.

I had to get her back on my cock.

It took me a second to get the angle right again so I could push down her throat far enough that she couldn't control anything and still lick and suck at her clit.

She wasn't able to move her lips over my cock, though she tried. I held her there, her neck bent back as I teased and tormented her pussy, my fingers digging into her thighs as her legs squirmed and shook, her moans and cries being absorbed by my cock, sending so much pleasure through my body.

Wild colors danced in front of my closed eyes.

I was so close to coming.

The way she tried to grind her cunt against my face and the way her legs were shaking, I could feel the tremble in her bones as I brought her closer and closer to her orgasm as I tried desperately to hold back my own pleasure.

Sweat broke out over my skin as my abs cramped with how tightly I was holding them. It didn't matter.

I never minded a little pain on my way to victory.

And with the way the trembling in her thighs increased and the pressure in her throat became almost unbearable, I knew she was close.

I focused my attention on her clit, licking and sucking the little bud until her back arched off the table hard enough that I was forced to let her thighs go as fresh moisture gushed from her.

Seeing her come like that, knowing that she came so quickly and so easily because she was already so turned on from serving me, was the single most gratifying win I had ever had.

I pulled out of her mouth and let her catch her breath for just a moment before guiding her back to her knees on the floor. I didn't even have to guide her lips towards me.

She leaned forward on her own, her hands on my hips, and swallowed down my cock, taking me as deep as she could.

I tipped my head back and closed my eyes, enjoying the feeling of success and triumph again as she gave me my reward, and then I gave her hers by coming down her throat in an almost violent explosion.

She swallowed as much as she could, and when I finally stopped coming, she sat back on her heels and looked up at me.

Stella was beautiful like this, her lips swollen, her eyes glassy, and a look of awe on her face.

I wasn't sure if that look was just from the powerful orgasm she'd had, understanding how much she loved making me come, or if she felt the same rush of power that I had when I controlled her orgasm.

Most men in my position didn't go down on their women. They saw it as an act of service, as something they did for them, and they got nothing out of it.

Those men were fucking stupid and probably terrible lovers.

They didn't understand the power of holding someone on the precipice, knowing that a single move would send their entire body rocketing into complete bliss. For that moment, you were a god. You held their pleasure, their life, their heart, everything in the balance.

Someone once said that everything is about sex, except for sex.

Sex is about power.

Being able to control your lover's entire body with just a simple flick of your tongue was power.

You controlled their brain waves, their heart, their ability to breathe, to think, to function, and even their hormones.

Their entire being was in your hands.

Stella had this incredible look of awe and bliss on her face, and I had to wonder if she felt that power too.

I shook the thought from my head. This had not gone to plan. I had caught her in my study, and I had meant to punish her, not teach her how much she would love getting on her knees for me. This should have been painful for her.

She should have been punished severely. Instead, I showed her a new way to control me, and I gave her an orgasm for her trouble.

Fuck.

"Get up, go upstairs, and get changed. We leave in an hour."

"Changed for what?"

"Excuse me," I bit out. "Do as you are told." I reached for my belt again, and she flinched.

The lust in the air fizzled out in a second as she got to her feet and grabbed her underwear. Whatever spell she was under disappeared, and she was back to her bratty self.

"I need to know where we're going so I know how to dress."

"We're going to a polo match."

"I don't want to go to a polo match," she said, covering her chest with her arms.

"Then it's a damn good thing I wasn't asking. Isn't it? Go get changed now, or you will go naked."

CHAPTER 24

STELLA

I didn't understand what had just happened.

Lucian Manwarring caught me in his office.

He had proof I was trying to get into his computer, and there was no way that he believed the lies that I had made up on the fly. My excuses had sounded lame to my own ears.

The look he had given me told me he knew I was lying.

It wasn't the first time I had lied to him.

It wasn't the first time I had disobeyed him, and every single time that I had done that, he had punished me in ways that left me aching and confused. This time, I wasn't aching, and confusion wasn't the only thing that I was feeling.

I wasn't sure what I was feeling. Satisfied for one, but somehow not. My body was still aching for something else. I just didn't know what, or I didn't want to tell myself what I still needed.

Of course, I knew what some men liked their women to do.

The notion of a blow job was not foreign to me, although I had never done it. I had heard the maids giggling about one of them doing it to somebody and how it was scandalous. I, of course, knew that men expected oral sex from their partners.

It was one of the easiest ways to keep them happy. Even the girls at boarding school had talked endlessly about different tips and tricks they'd learned from reading salacious magazines.

It always seemed like an unfortunate, disgusting chore that women were occasionally forced to do. Maybe not wives, unless it was their husband's birthday or they had bought a particularly lovely piece of jewelry, but girlfriends, mistresses, and not too long ago, probably secretaries.

What I didn't understand was that no one ever mentioned how good it felt, how it messed with your head and made the giver's body sensitive and filled with this addictive, buzzing sensation.

Those magazines also never said how getting on your knees for a man looked subservient and should have been submissive, but there was a strange kind of control with the act itself.

Even when he'd grabbed my hair and thrust into my throat, I'd still controlled how deep he could go. I still controlled how much pleasure he got from his actions.

I controlled how tight or loose I held my lips, how wet and how firmly I rubbed my tongue along his shaft. There was nothing he could do to force any of that. That was on me.

What I really hadn't understood was when he put his mouth on me. The women had never talked about that. I hadn't thought men did that type of thing.

That alone was a completely new sensation that my brain didn't have time to understand fully before I was overwhelmed with pleasure and massive explosions going on behind my eyes. The lack of oxygen from my only occasional breaths made me light-headed and seemed to intensify the entire experience.

Lucian had licked me and tasted my skin in the most private, personal places, and I wanted him to do it again.

I gave myself until I got back into my room to let my mind try to understand and absorb what had happened. There were so many feelings rushing through my body and so many hormones flooding my brain that I was having a really hard time making sense of it all.

It wasn't until I got back into the room and into the ensuite bathroom that I remembered the papers that were still against my back, held in place by the waistband of my skirt.

If he had removed a single piece of clothing completely, I would have been caught. But he hadn't, so I took them out and tried to look them over, sure that I might have something of value.

Lucian knowing how to confuse my mind and play my body like an instrument, didn't make him less dangerous.

It made it so much worse. Nothing had changed, and I still needed to get out. Having him in prison was still the easiest way to do that.

I looked over the papers I'd stolen, trying to understand what they were, and I realized they were completely useless.

There was nothing but numbers on the page. There was no key, no column headings, and nothing that told me what I was looking at or gave any context to the data. This could show money being bounced between hundreds of foreign accounts for tax evasion, payouts to organized crime, or the earnings report from McDonald's last quarter.

There was absolutely no way for me or anyone to know.

Maybe I could go back, look in the same place I'd found this, and find the first pages that would hopefully give some context to what I was seeing.

In the meantime, I stuck the pages between the mattress and the box spring, pushing them as far back as I could so the maids wouldn't accidentally brush them when changing the bottom sheet.

I heard a noise outside the door, and I wasn't sure if it was Lucian coming up to change or his evil butler coming to check on me. Either way, standing in the middle of the room smelling like sex and looking disheveled was not how either of them was going to find me.

As quickly as I could, I scampered into the ensuite bathroom and turned the shower on as hot as possible.

There may not have been a way for me to go back in time and erase what happened and how it made me feel, but maybe I could singe the memory from my skin.

The water was scalding, and it felt amazing.

With each pass of the loofah, I tried to forget what he had done to me, how he made me feel, and how much I wanted him to do it again.

Instead, I tried to replace the feeling of his mouth on me with that of my fingers. Maybe if I could bring myself to orgasm, I could erase the memory of the way his mouth had sucked at me, the way his tongue felt on my delicate folds, and how unbelievably and sensually intense the entire experience was—from feeling his weight pressing down on top of me, light-headed because his cock was blocking my airway, to even the slightly salty masculine flavor that had filled my senses.

I needed to erase all of it.

It didn't work, and I ended up coming apart in the shower with his name silently painted on my lips.

Getting out of the shower, I dried myself off as quickly as I could and made myself presentable.

I'd never been to a polo game, but I assumed it was the same for any outdoor posh sporting event.

A floral printed sundress in a pretty baby blue that would hug my curves just right. I used to love dresses like this. They were always so pretty and feminine. They looked modest, with their longer skirts hitting just below my knees and higher sweetheart necklines, but the thin fabric floated over my curves, and when the light hit it just right, you could see my silhouette through the material. They were what I called innocent and sexy.

Dresses like these used to be my favorite part of spring, but now they just left me freezing. But my comfort was hardly a concern for Lucian.

I put on the dress and paired it with strappy heels, a fabulous hat my mother bought me last year, vintage Chanel, so it would never be out of style, and then grabbed a matching cardigan to provide a pale attempt at fending off the cold that had come over me.

I stepped out of the large walk-in closet just in time to see Lucian coming out of his closet.

It was the first time I had seen him when he wasn't wearing head to toe black. Instead, he was wearing a blue blazer over a crisp white button-down shirt and cream linen slacks.

He looked like a man half his age and yet still just as powerful.

My admiration for his attire was cut short when he dropped a large duffel bag just in front of his penny loafers. I didn't know what was in the bag, but I did know it couldn't be anything good. He wouldn't have anything good in a duffel bag. It just wasn't who he was.

Men like him carried briefcases. Expensive leather and brass used to carry essential documents, files, and laptops. Duffle bags were for something different altogether.

"You look acceptable," he said, looking me up and down. Even his eyes left a trail of warmth over my chilled skin.

"Acceptance was exactly what I was going for."

The corner of his mouth twitched up just a little.

I would have missed it if I hadn't been looking so closely.

I had no idea why I was looking so closely. I pushed that aside as he motioned for me to follow him.

I expected to go out the front door, but instead, he took me to a back hallway that I hadn't been to before and pressed a button for an elevator. I said nothing as I stepped in, my hands folded in front of me, clenching the leather handles of my powder blue Kelly bag.

When the doors opened, we were on the roof, and a helicopter was waiting for us. Its blades were already spinning, sending gusts of wind to tousle my hair.

"Come on," Lucian said, grabbing my arm. I used my other hand to hold my hat to my head, and we both ducked down under the blades to get in. "Have you ever been in a helicopter before?"

I shook my head, knowing that if I said anything, there was no way he was going to hear me.

He nodded and put a large headset over my head, holding my hat in place as we took off.

The pilot checked in with us once before lifting off and taking us over to New York City.

I had seen videos of other people in helicopters.

I'd even seen clips from YouTube of New York City from drones. They didn't compare to actually being above the city flying over it.

Yes, I had traveled all over the world, but New York City was my world, and to see it in all of its gleaming glittering glory from a thousand feet in the air was spectacular.

However, that still didn't take my mind off of whatever could be in that duffel bag. I thought back to every movie I had ever seen and every book that had mentioned duffle bags.

Nothing good was ever in them.

I had seen everything from guns, to heads, to piles of money.

Soon, the gleaming steel towers and crowded roads gave way to lush green fields, and we touched down in front of a sign that said NY Polo Club.

"Where are we?" I asked.

"Patterson, New York. Driving here would take over an hour, and frankly, I don't have the time," he said, grabbing the duffel bag and dragging me through the open grass fields to several large white tents.

"Stella, you're here," a high-pitched feminine voice called.

I turned just in time to see Charlotte before she threw her arms around me and pulled me into a hug. She smelled of sweet floral perfume and mint.

"I'm here," I said, still not 100% sure what the hell I was doing there.

"Did you bring the equipment?" Luc said to his father, his arm firmly around Amelia.

Lucian gave his son the bag, and immediately Luc dropped it to the ground and opened it up.

I held my breath.

Inside were several different helmets, knee pads, and what looked like a few polo sticks. Or were they called mallets? I had no idea, but I was extremely relieved there wasn't a single stack of bound cash, firearms, or a severed head in the bag. At least not that I could see.

I released the tense breath I had been holding.

"Stella," Lucian snapped harshly, making me think he may have said my name a few times.

"I'm sorry, what?"

"Stay here with Charlotte and Amelia."

"Of course," I said, giving him a pleasant smile. I didn't mean it, but it was what was expected of me.

Luc and Lucian walked off, and I couldn't help but realize how similar they looked. Both were tall with broad shoulders, and they were both incredibly handsome. Lucian looked more like Luc's older brother than his father.

"Have you ever been to a polo match before?" Amelia asked.

"No, I haven't."

The three of us walked arm in arm back to the white tents where Charlotte's husband was sitting, looking extremely uncomfortable. He looked quite dashing in his suit, but although it was tailored perfectly to his body, it did not fit him at all.

"Well," Charlotte said, "let me introduce you to the best part of watching Luc and his father battle it out with other men on horseback."

"What's that?"

"The bottomless cocktails," they both said with bright smiles, and I noticed for the first time that Charlotte's eyes were not as focused as they should have been.

We took a seat at one of the benches, and almost immediately, a waiter wearing a white tux came over to our table with what looked like fresh mint juleps for Amelia and Charlotte.

"She'll have the same," Amelia said. Then she leaned towards me. "Trust us, they're the signature cocktail here. I don't know what they put in them, but I'm pretty sure it's illegal."

"If not, it should be," Charlotte agreed.

"They use your family's bourbon," Reid said, rolling his eyes and sitting back, his arm slung casually over his wife's shoulder. It was adorable, but he still looked so uncomfortable.

"That explains why they are just so good."

"So, does your father like to coach the team or something?" I asked, trying to figure out exactly what was going on.

"No," Charlotte answered. "Well, he's the captain of the team. Luc is chomping at the bit to take over, but I don't think Father is going to let that happen for several more years."

"It annoys Luc to no end that your father can still outplay men half his age," Amelia said, laughing before taking another long sip from her drink. "But Lucian is the captain of the team and the owner."

"He owns the team so he can be captain. That seems a little heavy-handed."

"No," Charlotte said, scrunching her nose as her eyes drifted up. "Father earned his place as captain years before he bought the team. The previous owner was talking about buying cheaper horses, like Kentucky Derby rejects or something, and said they would be just as good with some steroids or something, and Father wouldn't hear of it. He said he wouldn't destroy the sanctity of the game like that. So he bought the team and makes sure everyone has the best equipment and mounts money can buy."

"Really?" So he didn't mind playing by the rules when it was a game, but with my life, he would bribe judges and break as many laws as he needed to.

"Yep, the next step is to get this one out there." She patted Reid's arm.

"I don't play polo. I can rope a calf, but I refuse to get on a horse just to hit a little ball with a big hammer."

Amelia and Charlotte both teased him about life on the ranch and how now he was a big boy and could do big boy sports.

His response of football was met with more jeers and laughter.

I had to wonder, was this what my life would have been like if I'd had siblings?

The good-natured teasing and poking fun at each other while also knowing they would always have your back.

I envied Amelia and Charlotte. They had both grown up with older brothers who loved and protected them, and sisters who were like their best friends. Seeing them like this—so easily accepting of spouses into their circles and the relationship they had with their siblings extended to those spouses so easily, just to make their family larger—it almost hurt.

There was nothing quite like the joy and peace of others to make you realize exactly how alone you were in the world.

I was lost in my own thoughts, not really paying attention to what the others were saying, when I saw Lucian lead his team onto the field.

And it struck me again how unbelievably handsome he was.

He was sitting on top of his mount in polo attire, ready to do battle.

The look on his face was nothing short of fire and intensity.

This wasn't a game to him.

It was a war.

He sat on his horse in front of his men ready to lead them into battle like a true king.

CHAPTER 25

LUCIAN

She was a distraction.

My head should have been in the game.

I should have been focused, ready to take down the opposing team, but instead, I was watching her out of the corner of my eye.

Stella was sitting with my daughter-in-law, as well as my daughter and her husband.

Stella should have been safe.

And she would have been, despite the way the liquor flowed in the VIP tent, if she'd had enough sense to sit in the fucking middle.

Instead, she was sitting on the edge, leaving the married women in the center.

Every man at this club knew who Amelia was married to, and there was no way that a fucking security guard was going to let anyone near Charlotte.

Stella, however, didn't have that kind of protection from the vultures that liked to pick up women at polo matches for a quick nooner.

The fucking spineless bastards who liked to sit in the white tent, drinking the whisky I so graciously gave to the club at a heavy discount, and socialize like they didn't have a care in the world.

They weren't real men.

They were children who liked to pretend that they were refined enough to enjoy the art of polo, the mastery of the horses, and the thrill of the game, but without the balls or talent to actually play.

I couldn't count the number of times I've heard them laughing, joking about the number of women, usually someone's wife, they had lured into the forested area for a quickie.

Or how they'd sweet-talked so-and-so's daughter into blowing them in the stables.

I never thought too much of it, mostly because they knew who I was so they knew who my daughters were and that they were not to be fucked with.

But my status as trustee over Stella's estate was not common knowledge.

Her father was not a member here.

They would see her in that pretty blue dress and immediately assume she was fair game. Or worse, they would recognize her as a recently orphaned billionaire heiress and pounce on the opportunity.

The game began, so I poured my frustration into battle.

I rode harder than I needed to, stole the ball every chance I got, and definitely hit it with far more force than was needed to get it between the goalposts.

I also came very close to fouling several of the opposing team, even one of my own because they wouldn't get the fuck out of my way.

They should have known better.

It almost made me feel better, except every time I looked up, there was Stella, drinking a mint julep, laughing with Charlotte, Amelia, and some little fucker in a pink blazer and white pants who'd decided to take the seat next to her.

What kind of self-respecting man dressed like a pink lollipop?

The kind of man who wanted to be seen as non-threatening to innocent little girls like Stella.

Not that she was innocent anymore.

"Who did what?" Luc asked as he rode up next to me.

I just hit the ball between the goalposts again, and the crowd cheered as the rest of the team celebrated.

I wasn't satisfied. I wanted another, so I moved to be ready to reset.

"Stop for a second and talk to me. What crawled up your ass?"

"Excuse me?"

"You only play this aggressively if someone has fucked you over or tried to take what's yours. We all know the only thing you give a fuck about is the business. So if there's an issue at work, I need to know who did what."

"Nothing that concerns you." I hated how well he saw things.

He could prove to be a problem if he found out about my plan with Stella and got on his fucking high horse.

Luc moved in front of me, blocking my path. "Tell me."

Fuck. Why did I raise this boy to be strong and demanding?

"Somebody is trying to take something that is mine. But it has nothing to do with the business. It's personal, therefore none of your concern."

"You don't do personal." He narrowed his eyes at me.

"Well, I have four children, so obviously, I do. Just because I do not keep you apprised of my personal life, does not mean I don't have one."

With that, I led my horse around his and moved to the

starting position as the umpires were getting ready to throw the ball in the air again. I had no intention of letting these English fuckers score a single goal.

Just as the umpire threw the ball in the air, movement caught my attention in the VIP tent.

Stella had gotten to her feet, watching the match, but she was now a few feet away from my daughters.

And that little lollipop fucker was standing next to her, and he looked like he was about to whisper something in her ear or, God forbid, touch what was mine.

No one touched what was mine.

The umpire threw the ball, and I immediately went for it.

I ran it down the field as quickly as possible, lifting my arm back to hit it and angling it just right so I missed the goalpost completely but hit my true target.

The man talking to Stella crumpled to the ground as he was hit square in the balls. The man doubled over in the most satisfying way.

By the time I got to the side, he was coughing, gripping the grass, and several people were surrounding him.

"Sorry, it got away from me," I said, not even pretending to care.

He coughed out something I didn't give a shit about.

I turned to confront Stella, but she wasn't in the group crowding the man on the ground.

She didn't look like she cared about him at all.

Instead, those beautiful golden eyes were focused on me, her pupils blown wide and her lips slightly parted.

There was a hunger there I only saw when she was turned on past the point of no return.

I doubted she'd even known the other man had been there.

My girl only had eyes for me.

"Stella, are you okay?" I asked, looking down at her.

She nodded and traced her top lip with her tongue, making my cock stir.

I knew exactly how good those lips felt, and even though I had been in between them only a few hours ago, I wanted her again, and she clearly needed me.

"Behave, and you'll get a treat after the match," I growled out.

Someone handed me the ball, and I remembered we weren't alone.

There was only so much I could say to her right now, so I gave her another heated look and then took the ball back to the field to play, handing it to the empire to reset.

I tried to focus on the game, but my mind was still on her.

This time, when I glanced over, I saw her staring at me.

The asshole from earlier was nowhere near her, probably taking the hint that maybe his attention was best spent elsewhere or maybe going off to the emergency room for a testicle retrieval.

I really didn't care. What I did care about was that no other man dared go near her, and even if they did, I was pretty sure she wasn't even going to notice.

"Get your fucking head in the game," Luc came over and growled at me.

"The second you score as many goals as I have, then you can talk shit. Till then, sit your ass on your horse and do your goddamn job," I said before getting back to work.

The second chukka was finally over, and it was time for my team to take a quick break, get some water, and regroup while the spectators went out on the field for the divot stomp.

At the last minute, I turned around and went back towards the VIP section.

Luc could handle the pep talk. I may have been captain, but that didn't mean I did the whole warm-hearted speech or pep talk.

There were more important things to handle.

Stella looked so pretty in her blue sundress. Charlotte was on one side in a similar pink dress and Amelia a little further away in a green one.

Thankfully, Stella was just far enough away from them that I could talk to her without anyone overhearing. I hoped she had done that on purpose.

She kicked in a rather large divot and stomped it flat when I reached her.

"Are you having fun?" I asked, pulling up right beside her.

"I really am," she said, looking up at me, her eyes still wide. "I had no idea polo could be so..." Her voice trailed off, her cheeks reddened a little, and so did her chest.

"So...what?" I prompted.

"Forceful?" she asked, thinking about it. "I didn't know how violent it could be and how..." Her cheeks were a bright red as she grasped for the right words.

"Finish your sentence, baby girl."

"Hot," she said, her gaze on the ground in front of me.

I threw my head back with a laugh as I reached down for her.

Amelia, Luc, and Charlotte were all staring at me, but it didn't matter.

They were too far away to hear me, so they could think whatever the fuck they wanted.

"I know what you mean, and I'll tell you what." I reached down and ran my hand through her soft hair.

She pressed her cheek into my palm, looking up at me so sweetly.

Something about watching me had changed something in her.

I liked it.

"You keep watching me, thinking all of those filthy thoughts that I know are going through your mind right now, and when this is over, I'll show you how hot this can really make me."

I sat back on my saddle and watched her face turn bright red for a moment before I turned and trotted away.

I had so many plans for her as soon as this game was over, but there were two more chukkas to go, and I was going to send the Englishmen back across the pond with their tails firmly tucked between their legs.

The game flew by. I was suddenly in the zone.

I could still feel Stella's eyes on me, taking me in, probably objectifying me, but it somehow fueled me.

I wanted to win more than ever.

Not just for the sake of winning, though usually that was enough, but because I wanted to show off for her.

I wanted to show her exactly what I was capable of and that I had no problem going to war with men half my age and making them look like pathetic children playing a man's game.

I might have been older, but I was still in my prime, and she needed to know it.

By the time the game was over, my team had scored fifteen goals.

Ten of those were from me personally, and the other five were from Luc.

The English had scored none.

In most places, that would be unusual for a polo match, but between Luc and me, we owned this field. Nobody was scoring on my grass.

Now it was time for me to take my prize.

Usually, I'd be with my team, cleaning up in the locker rooms. Or if I had a bad game or didn't feel like talking to anyone, I'd go to my own private stable, clean up in my own suite, and be back in time for the award ceremony.

Today, I had a better idea.

I waved Luc off, signaling to him that I was going to go to my own stable.

Instead, I rode towards Stella and reached out my arm, offering it to her.

She looked up at me, her brows twisted in a question as she placed her delicate hand in mine.

In one swift pull, I hoisted her onto the saddle, her ass sitting solidly in front of me with both her legs on one side.

She gave the cutest little scream as she held on, her arms wrapping around my waist as she pressed her face into my neck.

Fuck the award ceremony.

I was taking my prize now.

"Hold on tight, baby girl. It's going to be a rough ride."

CHAPTER 26

STELLA

I had no idea where we were going.

I expected him to take me back to where the rest of the team was going or maybe give me a ride to the clubhouse while they were setting up for the award ceremony, but instead, he rode away from everybody else.

"Where are we going?" I asked.

"Somewhere no one can hear you scream."

I laughed nervously while trying to hold on to him, hoping that it was a joke.

He didn't smile.

My skin pricked with nervous tension, and I expected to feel that cold ball of fear in my gut, but I didn't.

I never felt cold when I was touching him.

He rode harder, and I held on to him as tightly as I could with my arms.

We rode to a small path towards the back of the property. It was surrounded by trees so densely packed that it reminded me of the forest that I would read about in fairy tales.

I had the sinking suspicion that these were the type of trees that hid secrets. They could hide witches, monsters, and women like me who would never be seen again.

"Please, tell me where we are going," I begged.

"I told you," he whispered into my ear, "we are going somewhere that no one can hear you scream. You were a bad girl today."

"I wasn't," I tried to argue. "I did what you told me to do. I stayed with your family. I stayed with Amelia and Charlotte. I didn't talk to anyone else. I didn't say anything that would embarrass you. I didn't talk about the situation that we are in. I was good."

"You talked to another man. You let another man encroach on what is mine."

"What? Who?"

My answer must have pleased him. There was a satisfied, almost smug grin on his face, but I still had no idea what he was talking about.

"You were drinking." He said it like an accusation.

"Of course, I was drinking. You never said I couldn't. And your daughter pushed a drink into my hand before I could say anything. I didn't get drunk."

"Did I say you could drink?"

"You didn't say I couldn't. You never said I couldn't drink. You're changing the rules on a whim, and it's not fair," I whined.

It was annoying even to my own ears, but I couldn't stop it.

Tears prickled in the corner of my eyes.

I held back my tears as he rode to a small stable nestled into the little wooded area, perched right in front of a picturesque lake.

It was so beautiful. The grass was a lush and vibrant green, and the lake was reflecting the gray sky. It was gorgeous, but something about it wasn't quite peaceful and joyful—it almost felt like a warning. Like there was danger just beneath the surface. There weren't even any sounds of wildlife.

No buzz of insects, chirping of birds, or even scurrying of squirrels.

Wasn't that a sign of an alpha predator nearby? I just knew the world wasn't holding its breath for a wolf or a bear.

They'd silenced themselves for Lucian.

I didn't say anything as we headed through to the stables or when he helped me off the horse before getting off himself.

"We are going to talk about what else you were doing during the match," he said, his back to me as he walked over to a wooden bench with brushes and other things to take care of the horses in this secluded stable.

"But I already told you I wasn't doing anything I wasn't supposed to. I'm sorry if you didn't want me drinking. I didn't know that."

"That's not what I'm talking about," he said, still not facing me. "I'm talking about how you were a distraction."

"What?" I had no idea what he meant. I was sitting quietly, talking with the people around me, mostly Charlotte. How was I a distraction?

"I could feel your eyes on me the entire match." He turned to face me, a metal tin in his hand. I couldn't see what it was before he tucked it into a pocket. "Do you know how it feels to have someone watching you so intently?"

"No, you're mistaken. I wasn't watching you."

Heat rose to my face at the lie. The truth was, I couldn't take my eyes off of him the entire match. The way he rode into battle. It was a game, but he didn't look like he was playing anything.

Lucian Manwarring didn't play.

He dominated.

The way he rode on that field was the same way he dominated me in the bedroom or his office. I would bet that it even applied to the way he did business.

He didn't play at being a CEO or a master of industry.

He didn't even play at legal proceedings.

Lucian Manwarring only knew how to wage war.

I never had a chance.

I couldn't take my eyes off of him the entire match.

I was captivated.

The words I told my parents the night they died about me not wanting a prince or a soldier but a ruthless king rang in my ears over and over.

He was a man who took what he wanted because he could.

Seeing him on that horse facing down other men with unbridled intimidation had been spectacular. No one would ever take anything from Lucian Manwarring. No one would ever talk over him, disrespect him, or even attempt to extort or blackmail him.

He was untouchable.

And I was watching him prove that him playing a simple game on horseback had made me weak.

I wanted him, but I didn't understand why.

I should hate him.

Every fiber of my being should be repulsed every time he touched me or looked at me, and instead, he set my blood on fire. Not with rage, not with hate, but with passion and need.

I didn't understand it, and I couldn't control it. No other man was ever going to make me feel like this again, and I had to decide what I was willing to do about it.

There was something else in his hand, something that he held at his side, just far enough back I couldn't see what it was. He took a step towards me, and I took one back. The way he was looking at me, I understood why the animals outside had stopped making noise.

Turning my head to look outside, to see if there was some

escape, some way I could run and get in public before he did anything, was a mistake. In that split second, he was on top of me, crowding me against the wall.

"I…" My voice trailed off.

What was I going to say?

I'm sorry I stared at you. I'm sorry I ignored everyone around me because I couldn't take my eyes off of you.

I couldn't say either of those things.

They were more than just an admittance of guilt.

They were an admission of want. That was a power I couldn't give him, not that that would stop him from taking it anyway.

He didn't say anything as he put his hand on my shoulder and spun me around to face the wall. His large, warm hand gripped my waist, before trailing down my side until he got to the hem of my dress.

Without a word, he flipped it up, exposing my practically bare ass. Sundresses required thongs.

There was nothing between my skin and his hand.

CHAPTER 27

STELLA

"*This* is your last chance, baby girl." His words were practically growled into my ear, sending shivers down my spine. "Admit you were watching me, or I will be forced to punish you."

"I wasn't..."

A sharp sting radiated from my behind and throughout my entire body.

He hadn't spanked me, not with his hand.

No, he had a riding crop.

The little bit of leather did not really leave any damage, but the sharp pain was still undeniable. I tried to stop my cry by pressing my lips together, but it didn't work.

He whipped me again, and with each impact, a yelp escaped my lips.

"Do not lie to me, little one. Tell me that you were watching me."

Tears streamed down my face as I said nothing. It wasn't out of defiance, not really. Each strike from the crop hurt, but then it left a hot, burning sensation on my skin. The sting faded quickly into something more, something better.

Tears streamed down my face, but they felt cathartic.

After a moment, he cropped me again, and this time, my cries of pain sounded more like moans of pleasure. Again and again, over and over, he struck me with the crop, no doubt leaving large red welts all over my behind and my upper thighs.

Then he placed the crop against the cotton of my panties, which had to be soaked by now. He pressed it against me, giving me the most delicious friction.

"Last chance, baby girl."

"I was watching you. I couldn't take my eyes off of you." The words flew from my lips. I didn't want to know how the crop would feel against my most sensitive flesh.

"Why? What did watching me do for you?"

"I didn't know what else to do."

He knew I was lying and gave me a quick but intense slap on my pussy with the crop. I cried out again. It was a million times more intense than the swats on my backside or even on the sensitive skin of my inner thighs. But with the increased pain came something else, too.

"Tell me the truth."

"I watched you because it turned me on. I watched you because I couldn't not watch you."

He threw the crop to the side and then pressed his body against mine, his hand slipping around my hip, under my skirt, and sliding into my soaking panties.

"All this time, I'm trying to punish you. But all I seem to do is turn you into a desperate, horny little cock slut."

His fingers stroked my clit, making me dizzy with desire, while his other hand moved to my throat. Not choking me, but holding me. "I bet I could put you on your knees right now, and you would hungrily swallow down my cock. Or I could bend you over and take you right here."

"Please." I didn't remember saying the word, but I could hear it coming from my lips.

"Oh, baby girl, I know this cunt is dripping for me. Desperate to be filled. But you are a bad girl, so you don't get what you want. I, however, am going to take the trophy I deserve. I've already fucked your throat raw and pounded your pussy until you screamed my name."

His fingers went from my clit, past my opening, into my asshole. He circled it with his thumb, spreading my own dampness around. "Now I'm going to take my trophy and claim your ass as well."

"Please. I was trying to be good."

I should have refused him.

I should have fought, but the way he touched me there, I hadn't even known that was something that would have been expected of me or that I'd want it.

He let go of my throat and reached into his pocket, pulling out the metal tin I had seen him slide in. He set it on a horizontal beam just above my head. I looked up to see the label. It was a balm made from honey and beeswax.

"This is going to hurt," he whispered in my ear. "But I think you like that."

He pulled me away from the wall and bent me over at my waist. Flipping my dress up and pushing my thong down to around my ankles.

I didn't say anything.

I let him move me.

My eyes slid closed as I tried to brace myself against the wooden walls.

His hand was either on my lower back, pressing me down

further, or on my thighs, spreading them before I heard him grab the tin and set it on my lower back.

My face burned with humiliation as I prayed no one came back here, but the rest of my body tingled with anticipation. There were so many things that he'd done to me that I didn't want to happen, but every single one ended up setting my body on fire. Every single one of them made me feel so unbelievably satisfied but also desperate for more.

The only thing I could do was hope that this was going to be just as intense, just as good. Even when he gave me pain, he gave me pleasure.

He was a king.

He was going to take what he wanted regardless of what I had to say about it. But when what he wanted had always given me such a dark pleasure, why should I fight it?

I jumped when he spread the balm over my backside, slowly working in one finger and then stretching me with two. The burn was instant and intense but faded after a moment. The more balm he used, the more comfortable it got, and the less my body tried to fight the intrusion.

But that was just a finger.

"I want to hear you say it again," he demanded as I heard his zipper go down, and a sound that could only be him spreading the balm on his cock.

"Say what?"

"You know what I want to hear," he demanded as he pressed the head of his cock to my ass.

"I was watching you," I said, as he slowly pressed into me.

I gasped.

It felt different than before. It hurt, but there was something else there, too.

He stopped only an inch inside of me, but it felt like so much more. "Why were you watching me?"

"Because I couldn't take my eyes off of you. I saw you riding that horse and..." I stuttered as he moved again.

"And?"

"And I wanted you. Seeing you in control like that made me wet, and I ached for you to dominate me the way you owned that field."

"What about the men who were talking to you?"

"What men?" I asked, overwhelmed. It was so hard to think while his cock was pushing inside of me so quickly, stretching me beyond my limits.

"Don't lie," he warned.

"I'm not. I don't remember any other men. My eyes and my thoughts were on you the entire match."

Finally, he was completely seated inside of me, and he held me there, not letting me move. Not that I would even if I could.

"Good girl," he whispered into my hair, leaning over my body.

I could feel the warmth of his chest and his arms through the thin fabric of my dress, and it made me ache to press against him. Instead, he stood straight, his hand holding my back at the angle he wanted as he moved.

Just like the first time he took my pussy, the first few full thrusts hurt, but with each pass, it hurt less, until suddenly, the pain was overtaken by pleasure. But this wasn't the same as before.

It felt different. Forbidden. It was a darker, more illicit pleasure that I didn't even know I could want.

"God, yes, just like that," he said behind me. "Keep taking it like such a good girl, and I'll reward you."

"Yes, sir," I breathed, keeping my hands flat on the wooden planks on the side of the stable.

"Fuck." He bit out the curse, grabbing my hips with both hands like he was trying to hang on.

I couldn't be sure, but I had the distinct feeling that Lucian Manwarring was starting to lose control.

He was losing control while taking pleasure in my body. There was something very satisfying about that, knowing the great king was going to lose his composure because of little ol' me.

I wanted more of that power, even if it was just a momentary illusion. I leaned down a little further, arching my back and pressing my hips up, giving him a deeper angle. It changed the way that not only my body gripped his but how he filled me, giving me a taste of more pleasure.

The fingers of one of his hands dug into my hip harder, but that didn't stop me, not even when his other hand came around me and stroked my clit.

I closed my eyes again, and I let the intoxication from the several drinks I had, as well as the light-headedness and over-whelming ecstasy, take control. The little voices in my head stopped telling me this was wrong.

They stopped telling me that he shouldn't be able to touch me like this, that I definitely shouldn't like it, let alone crave it. Those little voices finally shut up, and I gave in to the pleasure.

It wasn't long before my thighs shook, forcing me to put more weight on my hands to stop myself from collapsing. I held on for a few more minutes before the sweat ran down my brow and trailed down my back.

But I didn't want to come first. I didn't want to come before he did. I was afraid that if I allowed myself to go over the edge that what he was doing to me wouldn't feel as good. The little voices would come back and it would ruin the experience for me.

So I did what any good baby girl would do.

"Sir, am I allowed to come?"

"Oh, fuck," he said between clenched teeth. His cock felt like it was swelling even larger inside of me, and his words were spoken between gritted teeth.

"Please, sir?"

"Yes, come for me, baby girl."

Something told me that he was about to follow me over the edge, so I let go. Wave after wave of ecstasy flooded my body as I screamed out his name and came.

"Stella..." He came right after I did with a satisfying grunt and my name on his lips.

We both stayed there, not moving, just catching our breath for several minutes. Until he lifted my hand from the wall and saw the handprint I had left in blood.

"What did you do, baby girl?" he asked, still inside me.

"I don't know." My hand stung, but I hadn't noticed. The sensation had been lost among all the others.

He clicked his tongue in disappointment. "Splinter, come upstairs. We will take care of this now and get back to the crowd."

"Yes, sir."

He slid out of my body and tucked himself away before helping me straighten up.

Without warning, he swooped me into his arms and carried me up a set of wooden stairs at the back of the stable. I didn't have the strength to fight him. I laid my head against his chest and took the comfort where I could.

Upstairs, there was a loft with a large, jetted tub in the middle of the room overlooking the lake. The main room had a couple of chairs and a couch, but other than that, it was pretty bare.

He led me past the tub into the actual bathroom and started the shower. This bathroom, much like the rest of the apartment, was sparse but had what he needed.

After gingerly holding my hand and removing the splinter, he washed my body, spending extra time between my legs and making sure I was completely clean.

"Put your dress back on, but do not put on your underwear," he said from the shower. "Hurry. As soon as I'm done here, we're going to go back so they can present the trophies."

"You're getting a trophy?" I asked, not really thinking.

"I'm the captain of the team. We won the match. So, I get a piece of metal that will signify my victory. Though if I'm being honest, I already got the trophy I wanted."

He slapped my ass on the way past me to the closet where he kept spare clothes to change into.

That was enough to break the spell I was under.

He'd reminded me of exactly what I was to him.

To me, he was a king, a warrior, and a man who could show me all of the things that I didn't know my body could do.

To him, I was a trophy.

Something he could put on a shelf and show people what he won.

CHAPTER 28

STELLA

I didn't know why my body responded the way it did to Lucian.

I had no idea how to prove he was breaking the law.

There was no way for me to understand the numbers that I had found in that file.

If I didn't get out of Manwarring's house, out from under his thumb, and more importantly, out of his bed soon, then I never would.

Lucian Manwarring was not a stupid man, and worse, he was not an unobservant man.

Most men didn't pay attention to the world around them, especially the women around them. If it didn't directly involve them, they wouldn't care.

Lucian wasn't like most men.

If he thought something was off, if he had any inkling that I was planning something, then he would make a move to stop it.

He was a master at defense, so I needed to make sure he didn't think I was on the offensive.

So, I did the only thing I thought I could do. I was a good girl the rest of that night, with nothing but 'yes, sir' from my lips. When we were back around people, I was perfectly poised and behaved as a good ward should. Nobody would have any reason to expect that I was walking around the field without my underwear and my ass still aching from the riding crop and his cock.

I got up and dressed as I was expected to do, and I even had a pleasant breakfast before Lucian left for work.

He was even gracious enough to extend my allowance—it went from two hundred dollars a month to two thousand. It still wasn't enough, but I couldn't complain. I refused to complain. Instead, I smiled graciously and thanked him profusely. I didn't even shy away when he muttered something under his breath about thanking him the proper way after dinner.

After he left for work, I went up to my room and just waited.

Once what I thought was an appropriate amount of time went by, I went downstairs. I didn't stop to speak to the butler and pretended I didn't hear him when he called for me. Just because I didn't treat the staff like garbage, didn't mean I was willing to be talked down to by some uppity English butler.

The Uber I ordered was waiting at the curb, and I took it to the nearest library.

Signing up for my first New York City library card in my twenties seemed ridiculous.

But there I was.

I just needed to use the computers, and I had seen on some crime shows that the easiest way for people not to see your search history is to use a public computer. I thought about spending part of my allowance on a small laptop or tablet, but I wasn't sure if Lucian had some way to track my internet.

I knew his butler would rat me out if I asked for the WIFI password.

Three hours later, I was sitting at a coffee shop down the

road, sipping my caramel macchiato and looking over the stack of pages I had printed out.

I considered looking into my legal options while at the library, but what could I find with Internet Explorer in two hours that my lawyer, with his years of experience and law school, couldn't figure out? No, my energy was going to be better spent on finding a job so I could support myself.

Maybe if I got in front of a judge and proved that I was mentally stable, of sound mind and body, and financially responsible, then he would reverse the decision and give me my life back.

"Stella? Is that you?" a familiar and almost musical voice asked.

I looked up to see a woman I didn't recognize at first.

She was wearing a pantsuit from at least three seasons ago that didn't quite fit her right. She was gorgeous, her auburn hair pulled into a high ponytail, highlighting her light blue eyes, which had dark bags under them. She was a beautiful girl who looked like she was on the verge of a mental breakdown and holding her sanity together with duct tape. A sentiment I could very much relate to.

"I'm sorry, do I…"

"Oh, I'm so sorry. I think we've only met a few times. I'm Emma Zeigler. My brother is…"

"Of course. Your brother was going to marry Charlotte. We met at the engagement party."

I couldn't believe my eyes.

It was Emma, but she looked so different. At the engagement party, she had been dressed in a stunning gown, her face was perfection, and even her gorgeous hair was done in a complicated updo. She was absolutely radiant, and I remembered being so jealous.

This girl got to live the fairy tale fantasies that I'd had as a child. She was a wealthy, stunning woman with a fantastic accent, and she had a title.

"That's right," she said again, her now worn smile not reaching her tired eyes.

"Would you like to join me?" I asked, not forgetting all of my manners.

"Uh..." She looked around for a moment and looked like she was going to say no, then changed her mind at the last moment. "Well, maybe for a moment, if you don't mind."

"Not at all." I smiled and signaled for the waiter. "How have you been?"

"Well, I suppose you have heard the gossip about my situation and family?"

"No, actually, I hadn't. I'm sorry I've been kind of out of the loop lately."

"Oh, that's right. I am so sorry I heard about your parents. That must have been absolutely awful." She reached over and laid her hand on mine in a moment of true sympathy that felt genuine, and I appreciated the connection.

After the accident, when I woke up in the hospital, the room was full of flowers and condolences, but with the exception of Charlotte and Amelia, I hadn't heard from any of my friends. I guess it proved who my real friends were.

Emma looked down at the papers that I was holding and gave me a sad smile. "I suppose your circumstances have changed like mine have."

"What do you mean?"

"Your job hunt. That's actually what I'm doing here as well, applying for a waitress position."

"A waitress?"

"After Charlotte and my brother's engagement broke, a lot of information came out of the woodwork about my brother. It seems my family owed several creditors, and they were counting on Charlotte's money to pay them off. When that clearly wasn't going to happen, they called in the debts. My brother has run off somewhere to avoid prosecution, leaving me and my mother completely destitute. They even stripped our titles."

"So you're looking at waitressing?"

"I was an aristocrat. I was born and bred to be an aristocrat. The only career I was prepared for was being a wife to another aristocrat. I have no skills, no experience, and nothing but my willingness to learn. Unfortunately, five years of experience supervising event planners and choosing themes for parties does not constitute a successful resume. So I'm having to do... what do Americans call it? Pull myself up by my bootstraps?"

I couldn't help but giggle a bit. "That is what we call it, at least, I think. Have you found any good leads?" I asked, looking at my stack of papers, which so far had been full of jobs I wasn't qualified for, entry-level positions that required degrees that I didn't have, and positions doing exactly what Emma was trying to do—waiting tables.

I was delusional to think that that would cover rent anywhere in the city.

"Nothing," Emma said, leaning her head back. "I have had to sell the few possessions that Mother and I still had, all of them going to different consignment stores across the city. More than once, I was accused of stealing my own family heirlooms." She rolled her eyes. "But that has given me enough to put Mother and me up in a small apartment, but the money is running out quickly, so I need to get more coming in immediately."

I felt for her.

Worse than that, talking to Emma was making me realize exactly how much of an uphill battle I had before me.

I had no safety net anymore. If I tried to leave Lucian and stand on my own feet, I would crash and burn.

I had no real-world skills. I literally had no idea how to boil water, let alone hold down a job. My mother had always bragged about the "career" that I had when I was twenty, but that was just being a social media influencer.

Truth be told, I didn't even work at that. I didn't make a lot of money, and I had no real talent or even the business to monetize it properly. I just banked on the fact that I was pretty and rich.

I was no longer rich, so why would anybody want to listen to what I had to say?

How long until I had to sell my own clothes? Would I even be able to sell my own clothes, or would Lucian keep all of that, as well as the rest of my family's estate and inheritance?

There was always the option of using my beauty while I still had it to my advantage, but if that was what I was going to do, why not just stay with Lucian?

At least he was good in bed and knew how to make me come.

Emma looked like she was barely holding it together, and if she couldn't, what made me think I could?

"Have you gotten any interviews?" I asked, hopeful that Emma could shed some glimmer of hope on this dire situation.

"I've had a few interviews." She nodded. "But none that were acceptable."

"What do you mean acceptable? Like they didn't pay enough?"

Emma tipped back her head and laughed, a light musical laugh that I was sure was taught to her in the finest boarding schools in Europe—probably a finishing school that taught her how to laugh, when to laugh, and when to reach out and sympathetically touch someone's hand. My thoughts were racing, and I could feel my breath speeding up. The last thing I wanted to do was have a panic attack in the middle of this cafe.

"Unfortunately, dear, nothing pays enough. I don't even know what is enough anymore. I don't think I ever did. My childhood did not prepare me for the realities of life. I was brought up never to look at a price tag. I never thought about money. I don't even really understand how it works. All I know is that so far nothing has paid enough to cover basic living expenses for two people. I'm going to have to try to find three or four jobs but right now, I can't even find one that doesn't include some shady backroom deal with a manager who wants to grope me. God forbid Mother or I get sick. The health care here may be state of the art, but I don't know how normal people afford it."

"That sounds awful." I wished I could help her. "Are you just looking at waitressing jobs?"

"No, I've been looking for anything I can find, but I have no skills or training. I can have delightful conversations, but I never even learned how to type."

"Because it ruins your nails." I nodded.

In certain circles, that made complete sense, though now, looking at my life through a different lens, it felt ridiculous.

"Because it would ruin my nails." She nodded as if she felt as jilted by our class's restraints as I did.

"So if you're looking for work, I take it that your parents left you in the same type of situation that my brother left me in."

How did I tell this woman that no, my father had not left me destitute, but every penny I had or that he had was stolen by a man who wanted to keep me as a trophy wife?

That I had the option to live my life in the same level of opulence that was taken from her.

She and I were both raised to be wives of billionaires.

That opportunity was taken away from her, and I was fighting it just because I didn't choose the billionaire.

That made me feel so ungrateful and spoiled.

I didn't have to do this. I didn't have to look for a job. I could just stay at home and be a good girl to a man who I knew would never love me. But I could grow to love.

And he may not be falling over his feet to woo me, but I didn't think I'd respect him if he did. Why was I so unhappy? Was it because he made me come too hard?

The life that was being forced upon me was the one that she had expected to live, and here I was, fighting to what? Romanticize poverty?

I might have been naive to how the world worked, but even I knew there was a difference between feeling hungry because I was on a new fad diet, and feeling hungry because I couldn't afford food.

"Something like that." I smiled sadly, not wanting her to pry.

"Well, there is something to be said for our new situations."

"Oh?"

"I mean, at least our future is in our own hands now. Yes, it is going to be much harder. And we may not get the same material objects that brought us joy before. But there is something to be said about having parts of your life in your own hands. My brother no longer dictates who I see. He does not get to choose my friends, my acquaintances, or who I allow to court me. He has no say. If I decide that I want to get married, my brother will not be striking a deal to make it happen. I will never have to wonder if my husband adores me or my money. Because I don't have any," she laughed.

"How much of that do you really mean?"

"All of it. I don't know if my newfound freedom is better yet. I suppose it would be if I could land a job that would at least cover rent and basic necessities. I could learn to live without Chanel and get my perfume from samples at department stores and in magazine flyers. I can even learn how to make a simple roast chicken if I need to. But I don't know if I can learn to love a man who sees me as a contract and the means to an heir."

I sat back on the uncomfortable plastic-covered wooden bench and really looked at Emma.

The waiter came over to get her order, and she reached into her purse to count the few dollars that she had left, giving me the time to really look at her for the first time.

At the engagement party, I saw her glamor. I saw the beautiful doll with the title I envied.

When she walked into the cafe, I saw a woman struggling, but I tried to look beyond that. I saw her grace. Not the grace and poise that is taught at finishing schools, although she had that in spades as well. But there was something truly graceful about her mannerisms.

She managed to be polite, soft, and gentle, but not weak. She had managed to unknowingly make me look at my own situation in several different lights in the span of a few moments.

I went from naively determined to guilty and wondered if I was wasting an opportunity to retain a lifestyle. But now I was filled with hopeful determination.

I realized that I didn't have to be the princess locked in a tower or the pauper begging for scraps on the corner.

"Coffee's on me," I said with a smile. "Get whatever you like."

"Are you sure? I mean, I don't want to take advantage."

"No, it's absolutely fine. I'm not as wealthy as I once was, but I have a little while yet before I'm in dire straits. I'm just being preemptive and trying to find something to occupy my time. My therapist says having an occupation is a good way to keep from the grief," I lied.

She gave me a graceful smile and sat back in the chair. "Well, then, in that case, I'll take an Earl Gray latte, please."

"Coming right up." The waiter nodded, giving her heart eyes before he scurried off.

"So I also need the work for money," I clarified, not wanting her to think I saw myself as above her. "But I still have a bit of a nest egg that gives me enough wiggle room to last a few months."

"Well, if that's the case, I still recommend finding work as soon as possible. It is a madhouse out there, and it's better to be prepared. Trust me, I'm finding out the hard way. The worst position for any woman to be in is one where she doesn't have options and is forced to play a part, be it waitress or trophy."

"You said you had experience planning events?"

She was right. The worst position for a woman was in a position without options or support. Clearly, the men in our lives who were supposed to provide for us had failed. By accident or intent, it didn't matter. The fact was that we were bred to rely on them, and they'd failed us. We needed to help ourselves and each other.

"I have experience guiding event planners. That's hardly the same thing as being an event planner."

"Did you enjoy it?"

"Yes, I suppose I did. I loved watching how a party came together and how a dull, empty ballroom could transform into something truly magical. Much like Charlotte's engagement party. Though I heard her wedding was something magnificent to behold."

"It really was." I nodded. "Have you considered working for an event planner? I know a few, and I'm sure I could get you an interview."

"Really?" Her eyes lit up.

"Absolutely." I smiled.

It was the least I could do.

She had been put into a situation where she didn't have options, and she was making the best of it in a way I didn't think I could have. I had been put in a terrible situation, but I had options.

I wasn't willing to give up everything, but I wasn't willing to be Lucian Manwarring's trophy wife.

I wanted my lifestyle and my freedom, and I didn't want him to win.

Seeing me slinging hash at some greasy spoon or begging on a corner was just as bad as begging for attention or money in his bed.

If he wanted a trophy wife, I was going to make him look elsewhere.

CHAPTER 29

STELLA

"Take it all off," I said, staring into the large, round mirror with the bright pink plastic frame.

"All of it, honey? You mean like three or four inches?" the stylist asked behind me, popping his gum. His sheers were in one hand, and his other was propped up on his hip while he considered my long, luscious hair.

"Do you donate hair for kids with cancer?" I asked.

"Of course, as long as it's long enough and untreated. Have you dyed your hair before?"

"Never."

"Keratin treatments or perms of any kind?"

"No." I smiled. My stomach was tight, and my nerves were making me a little jumpy, but I was excited.

This was the moment I took my life back.

"Well, then. Your hair would be perfect, but we would have to cut it to at least here," he said, picking up a lock of hair between two fingers and bringing it just below my shoulder.

"What do you think about here?" I asked, moving his hand up to my chin.

"Honey, whoever he is, he isn't worth it. I mean, this is not the best way to mend a broken heart. You should go on a drinking spree and like fuck his best friend or cut up his clothes. All of that is fine. That is recoverable, but don't do something as permanent as chopping off all your hair for a breakup. No man is worth it. It will take years to grow all this back."

"This isn't for a breakup." I smiled. "This is shedding my old skin—the old me."

"And what is wrong with the old you? If I'm going to do a complete lifestyle makeover, I need to know that it's for the right reasons. I don't want you coming back tomorrow screaming how I destroyed your hair."

"My parents died in a horrible car crash. I was stuck in the car with them freezing for sixteen hours, and since then, I have been wallowing in a pit of depression and wine. I let other people dictate the terms of my life, and I am done. It's time for me to shed the skin of being the girl I was after the accident to the girl I am now, who is on the path to healing physically and mentally. I don't want to be the broken orphan girl anymore. I want to be the bad bitch survivor. I'm becoming fierce, more independent, and less sad. I promise you this has nothing to do with a man. Nobody has broken my heart."

"Hmmm." The stylist looked at me, tapped his shears against his lips, then moved in front of my swivel chair, looking me up and down like he was considering all of the options. "We will do an edgy asymmetrical bob, having it come forward so it's going to be higher in the back and longer in the front. What do you think?"

He moved behind me and grabbed my hair, bending it up and trying to give me an idea of what my face shape would look like with the new hairstyle.

"I like it," I said, "but I have one very important question."

"What's that, darling?"

"Would you have time to dye it as well?"

"Absolutely. What were you thinking? Maybe a nice balayage or just some face-framing highlights?"

"Pink."

"Pink highlights? Like a rose gold?" He tilted his head like he was trying to envision it.

"No, bright pink. All over."

"The new you is coming out bold, strong, and fierce." He looked at me in the mirror, meeting my gaze, and he lowered his face just above mine. "I love it."

After talking to Emma for a while, I'd ended up calling the event planner that I had always used to see if she was looking for any help.

I'd passed on Emma's information, explaining that she came from the same world I did but had had a recent lifestyle adjustment. I explained that she knew exactly what was expected at high society events and the proper way to behave and set a table.

She was also a hard worker and determined to work her way up. The event planner I used gladly took her name, and I was reminded that sometimes it wasn't what you knew. It was who you knew. And that even without my family's money, I still had something to offer.

Even if that was just sheer stubbornness.

Lucian Manwarring treated me like a trophy wife, like a good little girl, because that was what I was acting like.

That was what I was bred to be.

I wasn't so sure that was what I wanted to be anymore. Maybe if I became too much for him, too much work, too much effort, then he would drop it.

Maybe I would still have to live with him for the three years, maybe he'd still even insist on sleeping together, but maybe my sentence could be commuted to just the three years instead of till death do us part.

Ideally, I would create a look that was so far from what he wanted that he moved me into Charlotte's old room, forgot me, and left me there until I became of age. From what I'd heard, that was pretty much what he had done with his daughters. Why couldn't I get the same treatment?

When my hair was all said and done, it looked fantastic.

And just for a nice little perk, some kid going through the hardest battle that they would ever face was going to get a wig with some very long, expensive hair.

I looked at myself in the mirror, and I loved the hair.

I even loved how it made my cheekbones seem sharper, but it still wasn't right. The hair was perfect, but I looked like the backup dancer for a bubblegum pop band.

It wasn't enough. I needed more.

After giving my stylist a generous tip and leaving the Upper East Side salon with its fabulous '70s vibe and absolutely brilliant stylist, I headed somewhere a little bit more daring: the Maria Tash Broadway flagship piercing salon. It was where I'd gone to get my ears pierced, including the three piercings in the upper part of my ear that almost gave my mother a heart attack when I was thirteen.

Now I was going back and getting something far more daring.

I walked into the upscale piercing salon, praying they had a walk-in appointment available, and just my luck, they did. Some days, it felt like the entire world was on your side, and I was going to take advantage of every second of it.

I walked out of the salon an hour later with a few more ear piercings, and more importantly, a gorgeous diamond hoop in my nose. The piercings added the edge I wanted for my look.

Now the pink bob didn't look like bubblegum pop. It looked like punk rock fierceness.

The only thing left to do now was to destroy what was left of the old Stella.

Old Stella did what she was told.

She was a good girl who dressed in the finest clothes, had the nicest hair, and had a gorgeous face that was only ever decorated with the most natural makeup.

The new Stella had style and edge and took the entire world by the balls—or at least tried to. I might still have a lot to learn before I was the new Stella, but I knew one thing the new Stella would absolutely never do: she would never let a man dictate what she wore.

I headed back to the Manwarring estate, again ignoring the butler as he yelled about who knows what.

He was demanding that I stop, turn around, and explain myself as if I somehow owed him an explanation for my where-abouts. Apparently, I was a teenage girl whose whereabouts needed to be accounted for every single minute, not a grown woman who could do as she pleased.

The old Stella would have stopped and tried to be reasonable, but the new Stella was done with reasonableness.

"You are acting like a teenager throwing a temper tantrum," Hamilton said as I crossed into the bedroom that I shared with Manwarring.

At that, I stopped, turned around, looked him dead in the eye, and said something that I didn't think I had ever said to anyone before in my life.

"Go fuck yourself." I slammed the door in his face, locking it immediately.

If he wanted a teenage tantrum, then I would happily oblige.

I grabbed my phone, pulled up Spotify, found something called a 'Feminine Rage" playlist, and turned up my phone's volume as high as it could go. Immediately, a screaming guitar followed by the words *'I don't give a damn about my reputation'* began blaring from my phone, and it was just perfect.

On the side table, under some papers, was a pair of large black scissors, and they would be perfect for what I had in mind. I went to my closet and cut through all of the bullshit that old Stella had worn because it was what was expected of her.

It was pretty and feminine and delicate and gave men like Lucian Manwarring the impression that they had a right to bully, intimidate, or even touch me without my permission. Everything that reminded me of the delicate flower that I was supposed to be got shredded and then tossed out of the window.

Several Chanel and Dior dresses floated down to the streets below in shreds. One right after the other. There were visual symphonies of pale pinks, delicate greens, and baby blues, and then an absolutely unbelievable number of white, off-white, and ivory clothes.

It was like everything I owned was already washed out.

Like my wardrobe had worked so hard to be pretty and delicate but unobtrusive in any environment. I was never meant to stand out but to blend into pale watercolor paintings.

Half of my clothes matched the goddamn walls.

Hamilton was banging on the door, and I couldn't be bothered. I refused to stop my tirade of self-discovery and destruction for a butler with too much self-importance.

It was as if somehow licking Lucian Manwarring's shoes made him important enough to order me around. Well, fuck him. I had licked far more interesting parts of the man, but I didn't let that influence how I treated people.

Soon, in a moment of silence between songs, I could hear the people outside yelling or screaming, trying to get the pieces of fabric that I had thrown out the window.

I slashed through a few Birkin bags and threw them out the window when I heard a woman scream.

I peeked out and saw her grabbing the bag, clutching the torn leather. She was actually quite pretty in a pale pink dress. However, unlike mine, hers was not designer, and it was not made to fit her body.

"Hold on," I yelled down and went back to the wardrobe.

I grabbed a pale pink Kelly bag in ostrich leather and a Birkin that was in pale green alligator leather. My mother had simply loved the alligator leather and that pale green, saying that it would go with everything. But it went with absolutely nothing that I wanted to wear.

It was the epitome of the old Stella, but I recognized it was a piece of art. I would not be carrying this pretentious bag, but maybe the woman downstairs could get joy from it. Or sell it and buy a new wardrobe. I didn't care.

"Hey, up here," I called down to the girl and tossed both of the bags to her. Then I went back on my rampage. As soon as I had destroyed every piece of clothing that was some muted color, I also took care of every bag and even several pairs of shoes in pale pink and pastel blues, leaving only the blacks, browns, and a few vivid colors I genuinely loved.

My closet was practically empty.

In a closet the size of a studio apartment, which had been absolutely stuffed with bags, shoes, and clothes, what was left, what I considered acceptable, fit in one foot of hanger space.

I had four pairs of shoes left and only a single bag—an Alexander McQueen hobo bag that I had gotten as a door prize at someone's party some years ago. I loved the structure and the brass knuckles at the top with jeweled skulls.

This was the vibe of the new Stella.

The clothes were an issue, but one that I could wait out if I had to. Or I could call Charlotte and have her get me in touch with her goth cellist friend, who might like to take another former rich girl turned punk rock shopping.

Once I was finished with the clothing, I turned to the rest of the room. Technically, this room wasn't mine. I was expecting to stay with Lucian.

The question was, how much damage could I do before he kicked me out and demanded I sleep in a different room?

Hopefully, a lot.

I slashed the bed sheets, cutting through the expensive satin and the Egyptian cotton of the duvet, and even throwing around the pillows until they burst and feathers filled the entire room.

The matching antique Tiffany lamps, with their broken bulbs and shades, were tossed aside. I was even about to turn on his wardrobe when a loud thud came from the door.

Over and over it sounded, but I didn't care.

The playlist began again, and I screamed along with the rage-filled lyrics.

"I don't give a damn about my—"

Before the word reputation exited my mouth, Lucian broke down the door.

He stared at me and the destruction around.

This was it. This was my moment to prove to myself that I had what it took to see this through.

With my chin held high, I stared him down. "What do you want?"

CHAPTER 30

LUCIAN

Slowly, keeping my rage tightly under control, I walked into the bedroom to survey the damage.

Stella had been home for an hour and a half, according to Hamilton.

In that time, she had managed to destroy everything in the room.

"Get out!" I yelled, staring at Stella.

She made a move like she was going to go around me, and I stopped her. "Not you. You stay exactly where you are."

I turned behind me and saw the rest of the staff still at what remained of the doorway. "I said get out."

Immediately they all left, except for Hamilton. He stood there, giving Stella a smug smirk. He and I would have a conversation about that later.

"Now," I repeated, and it took Hamilton a good moment to realize that I was speaking to him. His face paled as he straightened, turned on his heel, and left.

If there were still a door there, I'd close it to keep him from eavesdropping.

But Stella had made that impossible.

I turned to face her and the absolute destruction of the room, as well as her new pink haircut and the addition of a diamond-encrusted hoop in her nose.

"Would you like to explain what happened here?"

"What do you think happened?"

"I think I increased your pocket money, and instead of being grateful, you threw a fit like a twelve-year-old, dying your hair, getting your nose pierced, and then destroying everything."

Feathers floating down from the ceiling fan caught my attention.

She had actually busted either the comforter or the pillows, probably both, judging by the sheer number of feathers blanketing the destruction. "Why? Don't most girls go through this rebellious phase much earlier?"

"Because I thought maybe if I weren't your perfect little trophy wife, you wouldn't want to marry me. That maybe if I ruined this perfect little girl that you decided to steal from, that maybe my father's money wouldn't be worth having to put up with me."

"Having to put up with you? Is that what you think I'm doing?"

"Isn't it? The only reason I'm here is because you want my father's money, and you thought, why not fuck his daughter at the same time. The only reason I'm here is because he died, and you saw an opportunity to add to your immense wealth."

"You think the only reason you're here is because of your father's money? I thought you were smarter than that."

I was actually a little dumbfounded and very insulted.

How could she think this was all about her father's money?

It was absolutely not the only reason she was here.

Her father could have been dead broke.

In fact, from what I'd learned about his business, I was amazed he wasn't. Of course, that was before I realized how much money was coming from shady dealings.

"Yes, and you can't have it. It's mine. I swear to god, I will take you down. I won't just be some toy you use and take out for parties while you spend my father's money. I will make you pay for everything."

She was hysterical now, screaming and stomping around the mess she had made.

"With this?" I asked, taking the stolen ledger pages out of my breast pocket.

Hamilton had given them to me when I arrived home.

The maid had found them, and he felt the proper thing was to hand them over so I could deal with the 'wailing banshee' myself.

Her eyes got wide as she saw the pages, and then she looked back at the bed like she couldn't believe they weren't still there.

A scream of rage and frustration tore from her throat as she grabbed one of the Tiffany lamps and threw it at me.

I managed to dodge the lamp, but the cord still hit my thigh.

That little infraction would be dealt with later.

At that moment, I was more concerned about what she thought she was doing here.

"Do you really think I brought you here to steal your money?" I asked.

"Why else would you want me? I have no skills, I have no experience, I have nothing but my father's wealth. I am absolutely useless."

Tears gathered at the corners of her eyes, and I didn't know how to handle this.

"The only thing I am good for, the only thing that I can do is to be a good trophy wife. Isn't that why you want me? So I can look pretty on your arm and in your bed, and you can show me off at parties to all your other old pervy friends, and brag about how you like to put me on my knees or on my back. I bet you laughed in the steam room before the match about how you planned to take me to the stables after the match and punish me for being so incompetent."

I was rarely in a situation where I did not know exactly what to do.

Put me in a boardroom, and I would dominate it.

Put me in a firing squad, and I would make every single one of those men with guns piss themselves and somehow think that I was the only one with real power. Put me in any situation where someone needed to be broken, and I broke them down to their core elements.

If there was a war to win, I won it.

But when I saw a crying woman in front of me, one that I had unintentionally hurt, I was lost.

I thought she knew.

Looking back at everything, it was clear she had no idea.

For the first time ever, I knew what it felt like to be an idiot.

I had been assuming she had the same resources, the same level of information and back channels that the other men I worked with did.

There was no way she had that, and I just didn't bother to realize there was no tongue-in-cheek with her. She didn't know anything. I had been acting like it was all some kind of torrid game. But for her, it was her life.

Fuck.

"Stella, sit down."

"No, I want to stand." She stuck her chin up in the air, making her new pink hair fall back, exposing her long neck and showing off the new piercings in her ears.

"Fine, but I am going to sit." I went to the armchairs that were covered in feathers but otherwise unharmed, dusted one off, then sat. "First, I don't give a fuck what you do to your hair. Dye it a new color every day. Get as many piercings as you want, but if you decide to get your pretty little clit pierced, it had better be a woman doing it."

Stella rolled her eyes, but I could see she was trying not to crack a smile.

She could fight it all she wanted, but she liked that I was possessive. She liked that I wanted to keep her to myself.

"Come here."

She took a few steps closer to me, but it wasn't close enough. I grabbed her arm and pulled her into my lap.

"Listen to me very closely, baby girl. I need you to hear everything I say. Is that understood?"

"Yes," she mumbled, her head bent low so her hair fell in a pink curtain, hiding her face.

"I have no interest in your father's money. I am managing it because that is what I do. I am also trying to track down some things that don't make sense in your father's books to protect you from whatever shady dealings your father may have been involved with."

"My father wasn't like you. He didn't have shady dealings," she sniffed.

"Your father was, at minimum, into some insider trading. But I think it was more, something with the Russian mafia," I explained.

She shook her head.

"I don't know for sure either way yet, and for the most part, I don't care. I'm not judging him. I am just trying to make sure that no one is going to come after you."

"But—"

"No, I said listen."

She pressed her lips together and hid in her hair again.

"Before your father died, he was working on a deal to marry you to Ziegler. Do you know who that is?"

She nodded.

"Do you know what he did to Charlotte? How he put her in danger to stage some fucking PR stunt? Used her as a human shield and got her shot?"

I hadn't wanted to believe it when I heard it.

In fact, I didn't, but when I saw the video, I banished him back to his country. The little pissant didn't listen. He tried to take my daughter again. So I ruined him. I had his creditors call in his debts, and his title was stripped. But he got to Deiderich before I could finish him.

"When your parents died while you were still in the hospital, I got a notification that Ziegler was back. He had a plan to claim you. He was going to forge the certificates and then have you institutionalized if you didn't go along with it."

"He couldn't."

I leveled a look at her that said she wasn't that stupid.

"I chased him out of the country again and took ownership before he had the chance to get back to the city."

"You stole my money to protect it?"

"You are young and in pain. He could have taken advantage of that. Where would you be? Married to a man you didn't choose, who beats you."

"You have beaten me." Her voice was timid.

"Have I? Or have I taught you the things your body can handle and how a little pain makes the pleasure so much deeper?" I brushed her hair out of her face, tucking the cotton candy locks behind her ear just so I could see her blush.

"You really don't care about the money?"

"Not a bit. I just needed in your father's books, and to keep you here to keep you safe."

"You don't want me to be just a trophy you can laugh about with your friends?"

"Stella, you were made for great things. You were meant to be mine."

CHAPTER 31

STELLA

*H*e leaned down and captured a kiss, but it was soft, gentle, almost reverent.

It was wrong.

He wasn't soft, he wasn't gentle, and that wasn't what I wanted from him.

I needed fire, passion, and heat.

I kissed him back, running my fingers through his hair as I adjusted my body to straddle his waist.

His arms wrapped around me, and his hands spread the warmth only he could give me over my back as he held my body to his.

Was this why I wanted him so much? Did my body know something that my mind didn't?

I had heard that people's instincts do not always make sense in the beginning, but they are right in the long run. Someone trusted a stranger, even though they were dirty and looked mean, and that person saved their life. Or another story of a girl refusing a date with a perfect gentleman who was in good standing with the community, just to find out later he had plans to drug and rape her. Instinct could be a powerful tool.

Could my body's response to Lucian be a case like that? My mind had been screaming at me that this was wrong, but my body knew something my brain didn't. Did something in me recognize that his motivations were not as simple or nefarious as I had assumed?

It made sense. I had always believed my father was a good man.

My mother had always told me my father was a good and honest man. But there were always things that didn't add up: late-night meetings with people who terrified me, men with scars on their faces, calloused knuckles, and dressed in head-to-toe leather.

Men that my father should not have had any reason to associate with, let alone invite into our home.

If Lucian knew about them, if he knew Zeigler was circling and ready to take my fortune and leave me bloody and broken somewhere, did this make Lucian my savior?

His fortune was just as big, if not far greater, than my father's. I wasn't naive enough to think the money meant nothing, but I absolutely could believe that it hadn't been his main reason for taking me.

If his intentions were strictly malicious, why bring me to his home?

He could have insisted I live in my parent's estate with no staff, or if he wanted to keep an eye on me, he could have had me institutionalized.

He kept me here because he wanted to. He wanted me.

Why make every sexual encounter of ours, even ones that were meant to be punishments, pleasurable for me?

If the rumors were true, most men didn't care if a woman

found pleasure in sex. Most, apparently, didn't think women were capable of feeling sexual pleasure or gratification.

Maybe I hadn't given him enough credit, or maybe he hadn't communicated properly before.

But what did I expect from a king?

Chivalry, charming conversation, and poetry were for princes and knights.

Kings did not have time for such frivolity.

He had shown me that he cared in his own way.

From the start, he'd never forced me, not really. He'd given me what my body was craving, and I'd needed it.

He made me feel alive.

He brought me pain and mixed it with pleasure so I could deal with it.

He taught me how to turn my inner turmoil into something fantastic.

Lucian Manwarring had thawed the ice around my heart and warmed my blood the only way he knew how—not by talking about it incessantly but by just doing it.

I decided to show him that I understood and could respond in kind. Maybe I'd regret it later, but something deep in my gut told me this was what I needed to do.

Deepening the kiss, letting him take over, tasting me, touching me, his hands exploring my body, I did the same.

I ran my hands from his hair down his thick neck to his firm chest, sliding my fingers under his suit jacket and feeling the broad width of his shoulders.

He had explored every inch of my body, places I didn't even know someone could explore, and it was my turn.

My fingers pulled on the tie around his neck, and his lips moved down my jaw to the sensitive place just below my ear. Every time he kissed me there, my entire body tingled, and my panties got wet.

My hips rocked on his lap, and he grabbed my waist, adjusting me so I straddled only one of his thighs, giving me delicious pressure. I couldn't see most men doing that. They wouldn't care about me getting off as long as they got off.

With one swift movement, I unthreaded his tie from his collar and threw it behind me in the rest of the ruined room, and then I pulled my shirt off, tossing it behind me, before grabbing his hands and placing them on my breasts and kissing him again.

One by one, I undid his shirt buttons and let my fingers explore and map out every inch of his chest, everything from the impossibly soft hair to the hard muscles they covered.

"What are you doing, baby girl?" he growled as I moved down his lap to give myself room to kiss down his neck to his chest.

"I want to make you feel good, sir. I want to show you how much I appreciate you protecting me from Ziegler and how grateful I am."

"Stop." He grabbed my arm and pulled me back up so I could sit just above him, looking down into his dark brown eyes that looked even darker in the fading light.

"I'm sorry. Did I do anything wrong?"

"No, baby girl, but you never have to thank me for that. If you want to please me, do it because it's what you want to do. Not out of obligation."

His words touched something deep in my heart. A man using me would never say something like that to me.

I leaned down and whispered in his ear, "I want to taste you, to explore all of you without being rushed or punished. Let me learn how to make you feel as good as I feel."

"Baby girl, you don't need to—"

"I want to, sir." I sank my teeth into my bottom lip and gave him what I hoped was a pleading look. "Please?"

"Fuck."

That was all he said before he stood, sweeping me up in his arms and leaving the room I had destroyed.

He brought me down the hall to another room, this one just as luxurious, with a large bed in the middle. He stopped only to kick the door closed and lock it.

"Do you really want to know what makes me feel good, baby girl?"

I nodded.

He threw me on the bed, making me squeal and giggle as I landed on the soft pillows.

"Feeling you come around my fingers, on my tongue, and on my cock. I love the way your tight little body squeezes me and the sweet sounds that pour out of your lips." He crawled over me, caging me in under his body. "I love the way you taste and that look you give me when you need me to satisfy you."

He grabbed the waistband of my skirt and tore it off my body, leaving me in nothing but the pink panties and bra that matched my hair.

"Take off your clothes," I said.

"No, you take them off of me. You wanted to explore me, so do it."

I lay flat on my back, looking up at him, but suddenly, I didn't feel so brave.

"Come on, baby girl, take what you want." He leaned in and whispered into my ear, "Show me that I chose the right woman to be my queen."

That was enough to send a hot spike of lust through my body. I reached up and pulled his face down to mine, taking his lips before pushing his shirt down to his shoulders.

Without breaking our kiss, he shifted his weight so I could slide the shirt off of him. Then I worked on his belt buckle.

It took me a moment to find the little latch under the buckle, but soon, I was sliding that off of him as well. Keeping my hands on the outside of his pants, I ran my fingers over the hard ridge of his cock, petting it, loving the way it felt, knowing I had done this to him.

I pushed his shoulders back, so he sat up, kneeling over me, looking down at my pink lace-covered body.

"Watch me," I said as I pulled down the cups of my bra.

"And what am I watching, baby girl?" He took his cock out and gave it a few slow strokes.

"I want to show you what you do to me," I said as my hands moved down my stomach to my panties. I pulled my legs up to a forty-five-degree angle, then spread my knees and pushed my panties to the side, running my fingers through my wet folds.

"Are you that wet just for me, baby girl?" he asked, licking his lips.

"Yes, sir."

"Take off your panties now. You are going to ride me." He stood up from the bed, taking off his undershirt and kicking off his pants and shoes.

"I want to taste you first," I whined, sliding the slip of fabric down my legs.

"Good, because you are going to ride my face first. If you want to put that hot little mouth on my cock while I do that, I'm not going to stop you."

He lay down on the bed and pulled me over him, positioning me so I was on all fours on top of him, and he wasted no time before he had his hands on my hips, guiding me to his ravenous lips.

Instantly my head swam as he devoured me, but I was distracted by the sight of his hard cock, standing proud with a bead of moisture at the very tip of the red crown.

I leaned down and licked a strip from the base of his cock all the way to the tip before tasting the salty sweetness of his precum.

It was so hard to focus with the way he was licking and sucking between my legs. Part of me just wanted to arch my hips and push back into him, giving him better access. A larger part of me wanted to give him the same pleasure he gave me.

I wrapped my lips around his hard cock and twirled my tongue around it, exploring every inch of the mushroom-like head before moving my lips down his shaft and sucking it in inch by delicious inch. I held him in the back of my throat while suppressing my gag reflex, just letting the warm, wet sucking of my mouth work over his cock.

When he slapped my ass, I ground my hips into his face and moved my lips up and down his shaft, swallowing it all.

I thought that if I could focus on the act of pleasuring him, it would stave off some of my own pleasure. At least splitting my focus should have made it take longer to be completely over-whelmed with sensation. Apparently, it had the opposite effect.

Wrapping my lips around his cock and loving each little hum from his lips against my pussy made the entire experience somehow more erotic.

"I think I'm going to come," I whimpered before giving him another lick. "I don't think I can hold it back."

His answer was to place his thumb against my asshole and trail a tight little circle over the rim, sending me straight into an intense orgasm that made me scream his name. His hands circled my waist, and he brought me down onto the bed next to him, both of us lying on our sides, with my back pressed to his chest. His hands roamed my body, letting me come down peace-fully before he took one of my thighs and brought it back over his.

"That was incredible, Stella. I was shocked the first time I made you come for me. Not that I can make you come, but how you would go from so reserved, so polished and quiet, but once you got close to coming, you turned feral. There's something primal and natural about the way you behave when you come apart. It is the sexiest thing I have ever seen."

His hands roamed my body before one hand settled on my breast and the other between my thighs, drawing small circles over my clit.

"Fuck waiting until an appropriate time. I don't want to deal with anyone thinking they have a chance in hell with you. Tell me you will be mine."

His words were growled into my ear. It was a question and a demand while his fingers played my body like an instrument.

"I—" Everything was so overwhelming.

I couldn't process what he was saying. All I knew was I was going to die if he didn't make me come again and then take me hard. The pressure building in my core was unstable, and my thighs were shaking.

My entire body felt like I was on fire. I needed him inside me. I needed him to take away the pain and give me everything he had.

"Stella, will you marry me?"

"Yes!" I screamed as I went over the edge again.

The rest of the night, we made love. It wasn't the same angry power struggle as before. It was deep, intimate, and satisfying in a way I didn't know was possible.

I woke up the next morning bright, early, and alone.

I stretched out my sore muscles and tried to remember where I was.

It took a moment for the events of the night before to trickle back into my mind. It wasn't until I became aware of an unfamiliar weight on my left hand and saw the large emerald-cut diamond set in platinum that I remembered...

I'd agreed to become Mrs. Manwarring.

CHAPTER 32

STELLA

*M*ost of my clothes were completely destroyed, so I wrapped myself in the sheet from the bed and headed back to the bedroom.

Now, of course, the entire mess that I had left was gone.

Like it had never even happened.

Even the Tiffany lampshades had been replaced.

I didn't know how I felt about that.

On one hand, I was glad nothing I had done had been completely irreparable.

On the other hand, it felt like all of that effort, all of the catharsis that came from destroying this room, was just gone.

I headed to my closet, and it was almost bare. But I was able to put together an outfit with a mid-length black skirt and a blouse that was in a gorgeous deep red.

Not the colors I usually wore, and I'd have to replace everything. But I did decide I wanted to start picking out my own clothes. Not just dressing in what had been expected of me. It was far past time for me to develop my own signature style and figure out what I wanted to say to the world when they saw me.

Thankfully, my tirade hadn't quite made it to the bathroom, so all of my cosmetics were still perfectly usable. I did something a little different with my eye makeup, trying to play off the new pink hue of my hair.

I looked at my jewelry, all of it, and didn't see anything that I really wanted to wear. I did, however, leave the engagement ring on.

A lot of things would need to be considered if I was going to keep the engagement, or still work to try and break it and run.

The fear I had before, the claustrophobic feeling of the walls moving in on me and being trapped, wasn't nearly as prevalent as it was before. But it also wasn't gone.

I took the ring off, then put it back on, taking it off and putting it back on several times before I just decided to leave it.

There was no reason to make Lucian mad until I knew one way or the other. When I was finally satisfied with my appearance, I went downstairs for breakfast.

Lucian was already sitting at the table, reading the paper with a cup of coffee in his other hand. My seat at the end of the table did not have a place setting.

Instead, my place setting was right next to his. A warm blush rose on my cheek as I realized that he had asked for the staff to move my plate next to his.

He wanted to have a more intimate breakfast than having me across the table. I liked that. I like that he wanted to be near me and talk to me during breakfast, not have to shout over the massive table.

I took my seat, and immediately Hamilton poured my coffee.

"Thank you," I said as I gratefully picked up the cup and took a sip.

"So, there is a lot to discuss," Lucian said, setting the paper down.

"Oh?"

"You have a wedding to plan," he said as he grabbed my plate and filled it.

"I wanted to talk to you about that."

"Did you change your mind already?" There was a slight edge to his voice that made me think he was expecting me to change my mind.

"No, but I have a lot to consider. And I think it is better to wait at least a little bit before we announce our engagement. There are some things that I need before I can commit to you completely."

"What's that?"

"Independence," I said.

"Married women are not independent. I will not have my wife living separately, or—"

"I am not saying I want complete independence," I said, placing my hand on his arm and calming him. I kept my voice low and slow, trying to emphasize how I was not upset. I was not starting a war. I just needed to be heard. "I want my life to mean more than just being a trophy wife."

"What do you mean?"

"First of all, I'd like not to have an allowance. I'd like at least access to my money. I have plans. Big plans. I want to be a mover and shaker in this city, a power player when it comes to policy and helping others. I plan to make some big donations with my inheritance."

I raised my chin ready for his challenge.

He chuckled. "I removed the purchase limit on that black Amex card. Spend what you like, and I already told you I don't care what you wear. I don't care what color you dye your hair next or what other piercings you get."

I raised an eyebrow. "And the donations?"

The corner of his lips lifted. "Give every fucking penny away for all I care, baby girl."

"Thank you, but it's more than that."

"Oh? What other demands does my soon-to-be wife have of me?"

"I want a life outside of this house. Meeting people. Making deals. I plan to be active on those boards, not just a checkbook."

"Be more specific," he said between clenched teeth. "Because if you think I would ever let another man—"

"No, I don't want anyone else to ever lay a finger on me," I assured him.

"Then what?" He pulled me from my chair into his lap.

I liked sitting like this, leaning my head against his shoulder, and feeling the warmth of his arms around me. Even if it made eating breakfast a little awkward, I was infinitely more comfortable like this.

I took a deep breath, needing to work up the nerve to tell him what I needed. Then, I took another long sip of coffee to give myself another minute to figure out how to express my feelings of uselessness and pointlessness.

"Of course, you realize that as my wife, you would be managing our social calendar, which includes throwing the occasional ball or gala. Those are charitable events, and throwing them can often be a full-time job."

"For some. For others, it's hiring the appropriate event planner. Most married women of our class don't work. They might sit on a few boards, and they might throw the occasional gala, but that may occupy one or two days a month. I need something more. Something more fulfilling."

"We could always just start a family right away," he said, squeezing my side.

"You have three grown children. Do you really want more?"

"I have four children. Maybe we can discuss that later. But you want something to do while I'm at work."

"I thought I knew all of your children. Luc, Olivia, and Charlotte?" I ignored his comment about something to do while he was at work. I was more curious about why I hadn't met the missing Manwarring.

Charlotte, Olivia, and I had been friends for years.

"I have another son, Thomas. We don't hear from him much. But tell me more about what you are looking for. Something more fulfilling than shopping or going to high tea?"

"I'm not saying I'm not going to shop or that I won't go to the occasional tea service, but I need more. I need a purpose in my life, something more than keeping your bed warm."

"I understand. Olivia has her magazine, and Charlotte has her cello. You need something to occupy your time, something productive."

"Exactly. Are you okay with me pursuing something like that, looking into my options, and coming up with a few ideas?"

"No," he said, setting down his coffee cup. "I don't want you to pursue anything. I have something already that'll be perfect. Are you finished with breakfast?"

"Yeah, I'm full." I had only eaten half of a Danish, some cut fruit, and a cup of coffee, but honestly, I couldn't have eaten another bite if I wanted to. I didn't even taste any of it.

"Good." He held my hand as he guided me off his lap and stood. "Hamilton, have the driver pull the car around. Stella and I are heading into the office."

"It's waiting for you at the door, sir."

Hamilton didn't even look at me, just stared disapprovingly at the ring on my finger before turning and walking away.

I wondered if the ring meant that Hamilton would actually have to treat me like a person. Judging by the scowl on his face, I doubted it.

The sun was warm the second we stepped outside, and Lucian led me to the car.

"Why are we heading into your office?" I asked as soon as he slid into the back seat next to me.

"Because I have the perfect job for you. You can put as little or as much effort into it as you like. You will have staff and people depending on you, but you will have the option to choose how busy you really are."

"That doesn't make any sense."

He lifted the back of my hand to his lips and left a kiss. "Trust me, you are going to love this."

He didn't say another word until we pulled up to the massive high-rise, and I saw a mask almost slide over his face. He was mentally preparing for whatever war the day was going to bring.

A moment before, his posture had been relaxed, his fingers intertwined with mine. But by the time I was standing next to him on the sidewalk, his posture was rigid, his expression was intimidating, and all hint of the man who had held me in his lap was gone.

I thought for a moment that he was staring down someone, but when I looked, no one was there.

It was kind of sexy. I liked knowing that people feared my man, and more importantly, the softer side of him was for my eyes only. It made those very few tender moments all the sweeter.

Moments like when he'd washed me in the shower above the stable, how he'd held me after we made love last night, and how he'd teased me at breakfast.

He straightened his tie and walked into the building.

I had to practically jog to keep up with his long strides. It wasn't until he hit the lobby that he slowed down and allowed me to walk beside him.

The lobby was covered in sleek marble and refined touches that screamed wealth and class. Even the security guards were dressed in black suits with red ties and were really only set apart by the earpieces they wore and the badges clipped to their breast pockets.

Lucian nodded to one of the guards as he escorted me past them to the elevators and hit the button for the top floor.

"Will you please tell me where we are going and what is happening?" I asked.

"Where is the fun in that?" The very corner of his mouth lifted in an almost half-smile. The second the doors opened, it was gone, and he was back to the cold, hard tyrant that I was sure all his employees knew and feared.

He marched straight into a conference room that already had a meeting going on.

Immediately, the energy shifted, and the man who was sitting at the head of the table moved and sat at the seat just to the right.

"Mr. Manwarring, I do apologize. I didn't expect you to attend this meeting. We are going over some of the finer points of the day-to-day agendas, lower-level stuff that you need not concern yourself with—"

Lucian held up a hand, and immediately, the other man stopped talking.

"I know very well what this meeting is about and everything that goes on in the day-to-day operations. Just because I may not attend the meetings doesn't mean that I don't read the minutes. In fact, Brian, there are some things we need to discuss privately in detail about what is and isn't covered in the scope of your responsibilities. Taking new business to the board without running it by me will force me to relieve you of your duties."

Brian's face paled so quickly that I was expecting him to pass out on the floor. His mouth opened and closed a few times as if trying to find the right words.

"The rest of the people in this room, however, are doing a great job staying in their lanes and making sure everything runs smoothly. Brian, however, has decreased productivity, so Mrs. Miller, if you don't mind, I think it's best if you take over these meetings so Brian can attend to his other duties."

"Yes, sir," a middle-aged woman with a severe bun pulling at her face and cat-shaped glasses said.

"I am interrupting your meeting today to make a quick announcement. This is Miss Stella Deiderich. She will be taking over the Manwarring charitable fund. If you have any questions or concerns about galas or other fundraising events, or even how your department could make an effort, or in Brian's case, save a little face, please discuss this with her. This is effective immediately. Now, please, Mrs. Miller, continue your meeting."

I waved a little before Lucian took my hand and led me out of the conference room and back to the elevator.

"What did you just do?"

"I gave you a job that will give you purpose. Now, let's go see your new office so you can get ideas on how you would like to decorate it. I suggest we start with a very large and sturdy sofa."

CHAPTER 33

LUCIAN

*I*n the less than three weeks of being in charge of the foundation, Stella had gone from quiet and observant to taking charge and exceeding any expectations I could have had for her.

I'd asked Mrs. Miller to keep an eye on her, just to let me know if she was struggling, and I would need to hire an assistant for her, on top of her current secretary.

According to Mrs. Miller, Stella was amazing and already planning the first fundraising event, meant to draw in a younger, more influential, and affluent crowd.

Apparently, she had a few ideas for more formal events that would cater to our class, but her first event was going to cater to her generation. Specifically, bringing social media awareness to all of the great things that the Manwarring Charitable Fund supported—not that I had any idea what those things were—as well as increasing overall brand awareness in the younger generation.

Mrs. Miller seemed almost giddy and excited about the idea. "You don't understand, sir. The brand has always touted

itself as a fine spirit, which it is, but it is only really being adver-
tised to the elite. It is the drink of old white men, what you
would expect to find in your grandfather's library."

"Careful," I warned. "It is currently in my library."

"Mine too," she said with a smile. "But what Stella is
managing to do with this party is make it seem like the preferred
brand of whisky for entrepreneurs, musicians, and the most
successful people of the younger generation. It's going to be a
status symbol among them as well. She is even meeting with an
award-winning mixologist to try a few signature cocktails for
the party."

"Is this your doing?" I asked.

"No, it's hers. I don't know how much of it is intentional
for the brand, or how much of it is just coincidental. She
wanted a unique venue for the party, so it's going to be held at
one of the distilleries. Since it's at the Manwarring Liquor
distilleries, it only makes sense to have drinks made from our
whiskey. She is planning what is going to be the social event of
the season for every single influencer and mover under thirty.
Not just in New York, there are people flying in for this party
from all over the world. From what I understand, everybody
on the Forbes thirty under thirty list has already RSVP'd.
There are several musicians, a few up-and-comers, and a few
names I even recognize. Not only that, but she has also set up
raffles for tickets that anyone can get with just a $10 donation.
Those raffles have already earned 1.3 million dollars in
donations."

"You're kidding," I said in disbelief.

I knew Stella was intelligent and that she would be successful
at absolutely anything she put her mind to, but this was more
than I could have ever expected.

"I don't say this lightly. I know you have made some incredible deals in your time and have grown this company into some-

thing amazing. But bringing that girl here and giving her free rein was the smartest thing you have ever done."

The rest of the day, I was beaming.

I couldn't hide how proud I was of my girl.

Mary Quinn and her bullshit were practically forgotten as I sent my assistant a text telling him to arrange a reservation for Stella and me tonight, and to make sure it was somewhere incredible.

My girl deserved to be rewarded.

She and I would go out for a nice meal, and then I intended on having her for dessert.

"I bet he just likes grabbing a handful of that pink hair while she's choking down his cock."

A loud male voice came from the executive break room by my office as I was passing by.

"Why else would he let that little whore take over the entire charitable fund? Does he even know what she's doing? I know she has no idea what she's doing."

When I turned the corner, I saw exactly who I was expecting —Brian talking shit and drinking coffee while his entire department was struggling.

Next to him were a few of the other executives, clearly just stopping in to get a cup of coffee and looking extremely uncomfortable.

One of the secretaries was clenching her teeth as she waited for her lunch to heat up in the microwave. She wasn't the kind of woman to take something like this lying down, but she was smart enough to know that confronting someone like Brian was never the right bet for a woman like her.

It would cost her job, and Brian might even be violent.

Instead, I had no doubt that she was collecting evidence to go to HR to get him fired.

Well, lucky for her, I was going to shorten that entire process.

"I mean, having the yearly charity gala at the distillery is just tacky. I know she's probably trying to be cool or hip or whatever the little bitches like her call it these days. But she has no idea what the fuck she's doing."

"How about you tell me what the fuck you're doing?" I asked, strolling into the break room.

Brian looked at me for a second, his eyes wide and the blood rushing from his face, but then the cocky little asshole smirked at me. "Just telling it like it is, boss. I think you made a mistake hiring that inexperienced socialite to run the charity. I mean, I'm sure she looks great bouncing on your cock, but is that really the type of image we want to give the charitable fund?"

"Everyone out now," I barked. Everyone, including the secretary, left the room.

Brian tried to leave with them, but I blocked his path.

"You told us to get out. Make up your mind, old man."

"Oh, you will be leaving, but we're going to have a conversation first. I'm going to teach you some fucking manners."

I grabbed him by his neck and pushed him against the wall, making sure his head hit the plaster with a satisfying thud sound. I didn't want to do any serious damage, but enough to at least hurt and shake him up a bit.

Just enough that if he decided to be a coward and sue, there was no evidence, and I could destroy him with a defamation suit.

"Get your hands off me." He struggled, pulling at my fingers. I held him tighter.

"What gives you the right to talk shit about Stella? Or about any of my employees for that matter?"

"Since when did we call whores employees? Just because it's called a blowjob doesn't actually mean there's any work ethic to it."

"I see. So you think only people who add to the company's

bottom line, who show up day in and day out and do their job effectively, deserve respect? And everyone else is just whores and sluts?"

"Exactly," he said with a satisfied grin as if I had come to accept his way of thinking and would now join him in some misogynistic douchery. "She is acting like she has a job and isn't just a pity fuck you put in an office."

"By that logic, you should be spending every single break you have on your knees in the men's room, sucking cock for a good quarterly review."

"You can't—" he stammered, and I held him against the wall, slowly cutting off his air.

"I can, and I did. Just in case it's not abundantly clear, you're fired. You can leave on your own accord, or I will have security drag you out of here by your fucking hair."

"You can't fire me for—"

"I can fire you for whatever the fuck I want. Actually, you were going to be fired at the end of the quarter anyway because you're shit at your job. But you've just given me an excuse to cut the dead weight a little early. Get the fuck out of my building." I let go of him and expected him to run off.

"No." He stood tall with that same shit-eating grin. "You can't fire me. I'm Ronan's cousin. I'm the one doing all his work on the foundation, and your little whore is just getting in my fucking way."

I had honestly forgotten I had given Brian the position he had because Ronan occasionally used the foundation to launder money.

I had been letting him do it for so long in exchange for dealing with the unions and other headaches that I had forgotten about our arrangement.

More importantly, I had forgotten that Brian was essential for that arrangement.

That didn't mean I was going to let this little pissant go around my office talking about Stella. Frankly, I would have fired him if I heard him talking like that about any of my female employees.

But the fact that it was Stella's name that was coming out of his vile little mouth, it was taking everything I had not to throw him out of the fucking window.

And this little bitch, instead of counting his blessings and running away with his tail tucked firmly between his legs, was actually trying to strong-arm me. Who the fuck did he think he was?

"I don't give a fuck who your cousin is. You are done here."

"You're going to give a fuck when he starts retaliating. You fire me, I promise you that little bitch is going to be in his crosshairs first."

"You can tell Ronan to go fuck himself. This arrangement is over."

CHAPTER 34

LUCIAN

"My, my, your new little pet seems to be keeping busy." Mary Quinn Astrid was sitting on my desk as I walked into my office first thing in the morning.

I had no idea what the fuck she was doing here, but whatever it was, I had not had enough coffee to tolerate it. I really needed to have a conversation with my assistant about allowing access to my office when I was not in.

"Leave. You have no business here," I said, refusing to look at her.

Mostly because I knew that was what Mary Quinn hated the most.

She spent so much of her time, so much of her energy, looking the way she did. Perfectly polished and poised, somehow looking like she was aging gracefully but not aging at all.

I used to think it was a feminine power she had, but after a few years, I could just see it was a desperate attempt at appearing powerful. She was no more than a manipulative shrew. All it would take was one scandal to unravel all of the influence she had.

That wasn't power. At least not the kind I coveted.

"I do actually have business to discuss with you." She stood from the top of my desk and walked towards me, not even the faintest wobble on her sky-high stilettos.

"Then you should have made an appointment with my assistant."

"No." She sauntered up to me and placed her hand on my chest as if she somehow had the right. "This is personal business. I have been made aware that you are now in possession of the Deiderich heir."

"In possession of? Do you think I keep her in a little box?"

I have never pretended to be a good person.

Mary Quinn pretended when it suited her, and I did not hold that against her. But after hearing how she treated her daughters, seeing evidence of bruises on my daughter-in-law, and hearing the stories about her drunken tirades and unprovoked violent streaks, it was abundantly clear that I needed to distance myself.

Mary Quinn was no longer an ally who came with more benefits than liabilities. She was a walking time bomb.

"Well, I don't know what else you would do with a woman that stupid. But there are a few eligible bachelors that I could point you in the direction of. I'm sure you are eager to get her out of your house."

I took a step back just out of her reach, hoping she would get the hint and not touch me again.

"And what exactly gives you the impression Stella is anything other than brilliant?" I asked.

"Well, I know she was friends with Amelia as a child, and she always seemed so simple. One-word answers never add any value to conversations. I hear the only reason she survived that hit was because she let the assassin feel her up."

"She was found by the paramedics by crawling through broken glass half frozen to the front of the car and hitting a metal flask on the roof to make a noise. She was nearly dead," I growled with narrowed eyes. "But what do you mean, assassin? It was a car crash. The driver was drunk."

Mary Quinn rolled her eyes. "It was made to look like a car accident. But I assure you it was very much intentional. Deiderich has some particularly ruthless friends that your friend Ronan doesn't want in the city, let alone this country."

"So you are saying the car accident was a hit."

Christ. The wounds from her parents' death were still fresh for Stella. I wouldn't even know how to break it to her that it wasn't a terrible accident. Next time I saw Reid, I would have him use his contacts to investigate. I was certainly not going to trust the word of Mary Quinn on the matter.

And perhaps having a mutual project would mend some of the bad blood between myself and my new son-in-law.

Recent events had changed my mind about how I wanted to deal with my children and their spouses in the future.

"If the rumors are to be believed. Just like the rumor you now control Deiderich's entire fortune and will soon be looking to get rid of the little orphan girl. Then splitting her inheritance between yourself and her new husband. I have come with a few suggestions of age-appropriate men who may be in the market for a new bride."

I could see the rumor mill was still thinking the absolute worst of me.

"No, Stella's prospects have already been secured. I do not need any assistance."

"Well, that makes sense seeing how beautifully both of your daughters' marriages turned out."

"They are both married to extremely wealthy men, who can keep them safe from conniving bitches like you. I would say that is a stunning success."

Her head flew back in a fit of false laughter. "Oh, I do enjoy this banter."

"I do not. If there is nothing else, please see yourself out."

"Come on, don't be like that." She reached out to cup my cheek.

I grabbed her wrist and pushed it away from me, making her stumble back a few feet.

She looked at me with eyes wide and full of rage. She was under the impression that no one could resist her charm. That may have been true at one time, but between time, too much Botox, and constant drinking, she was no longer what most men wanted.

She was still attractive enough. To a woman like Mary Quinn, that was the only thing she had.

Though after being with Stella and having her in my life, I didn't think I'd even look twice at Mary Quinn when she was in her prime.

"Leave now," I repeated.

"You're going to regret this," she spat.

"I can have security escort you out if you prefer." The threat was clear in my statement, and she huffed before grabbing her Chanel bag from my desk.

"Maybe I should call Ronan myself and tell him that he missed a spot on his last job. I hear he's pretty angry with you over firing his cousin Brian," she taunted.

I cornered her against the wall. "I certainly hope you didn't just fucking threaten my fiancé—because I would take that *very* personally."

Her fake eyelashes fanned over her eyes as she blinked up at me. "Of course not, Lucian. I would never."

Just like she'd never be involved in a kidnapping or that PR stunt that nearly killed Charlotte.

It was funny how Mary always seemed to be on the periphery

of tragedy but never in the mix, like a fucking spider weaving her web, watching as the flies became trapped.

It was only a matter of time before she got caught in her own web.

And I was going to make sure of it. But first, my priority was getting Stella the protection of my name so Ronan wouldn't dare touch her.

I raised an eyebrow. "We're done here. Stella is waiting for me at the distillery. See yourself out."

Mary Quinn Astrid was a problem for later.

CHAPTER 35

LUCIAN

"**W**hy are we meeting here and not in the office?" Luc asked as his town car pulled up beside mine.

"Because Stella is in there planning the party of the century, and when she is done, I am taking her to lunch," I answered, leaning on my car, enjoying the warm sun on my skin.

I rarely got time to enjoy the outdoors during the week. The only time I got any sun was when I was on the field with my team, running drills or playing polo matches.

"Okay, but why am I here? What did you need to talk about in person? I don't know if you realize, but I am a busy man."

I chuckled at his arrogance. Like father, like son.

He was a busy man, and I had raised him well.

When I was ready—and not a moment before—he would take my seat at the table and be a formidable boss. But my god could he be self-righteous, and I knew the conversation we were about to have was only going to make it worse.

"Because I wanted to talk to you somewhere I knew for a fact wasn't bugged."

"You think your office is bugged?"

"A man in my position has many enemies who would love to sneak something into my office, and since your mother-in-law managed to sneak in without me there, who knows who else could do it." I shrugged.

"What does Mary Quinn want now?" His head went back like he was already frustrated and done with the shrew. I could relate.

"Nothing of importance." I waved it off. "But she isn't why we are here. I wanted to talk to you about the measures that need to be taken to keep everyone safe as we completely sever the company's ties with the O'Murphys."

"I thought I already had." He clenched his fists by his side, as his jaw ticked.

My son was a brilliant businessman, but he needed to work on his poker face.

"Some things have recently come to light, and I am inclined to agree with you that it may be best to sever ties with the Irish mob entirely. But doing that does put us at considerable risk. Your mother-in-law also made some thinly-veiled threats against Stella."

"Would she follow through with them?"

"She followed through with the threats against Harrison's wife," I pointed out.

"True, but that's because she didn't think Edwina was good enough for Harrison. She was trying to force his hand."

"I may have insulted Mary Quinn to her face. I may have implied that she could learn from Stella's intelligence, humility, and grace."

"Oh, yeah, she's absolutely capable of going after Stella." Luc rubbed his hands over his face as he figured out what I had already known.

His mother-in-law was a problem we could no longer ignore.

She had already used my connections to do her bidding once, and cutting off the O'Murphys may make them more inclined to work for her.

"Exactly. The one thing we should never do is underestimate that woman's need for petty revenge."

Luc nodded in agreement. "When are you severing the ties?"

"Immediately. I caught one of the men Ronan had working for us bad-mouthing Stella and making accusations, and I didn't take it well. I fired him on the spot, and I may have told him to tell Ronan to go fuck himself. That he would no longer be using our distilleries, our charitable foundation, or anything else to launder money or whatever else he was using our empty warehouses for."

"Whatever else... you don't even know what they have been doing on our property?"

"My property. It isn't yours yet. And no, I preferred having plausible deniability."

Luc gave me a look that made me think he saw through my bullshit, but unlike my son, I had a good poker face. I was not about to admit that it had all gotten out of hand.

"All because some douchebag insulted Stella?" Luc crossed his arms over his chest while leaning back on the car door. "That was unusually rash of you. How long?"

"How long what?"

"How long until you announce the engagement?"

I looked at him for a few moments, debating what to tell him or what he could already know.

"Hamilton called. He is worried Stella is a bad influence on you and taking advantage of your generosity. He may have had a few choice words about your child bride."

"She is not a child." I couldn't believe he would call my son.

"Probably a wise idea, but you didn't answer my question."

"After the event she is throwing, we'll make it all official quickly. It will be a small, intimate ceremony for family only."

"I thought you always said weddings were to show the world the prize you had won and opportunities to network."

"Some are. That's not what this marriage is about. It's me and her, that's it. If she wants the big wedding, that's fine, but I don't care as long as she is mine."

Luc gave me a wide grin. "I know exactly how you feel."

"You're not going to give me shit about her age?" I had been expecting a fight, or some judgment at least.

"No, I think she is good for you."

I chose to ignore his mockery and focus on more important topics. "Have you talked to your brother lately?"

"No, not since..." He stopped for a moment and thought. "I can't remember the last time I spoke to Thomas, maybe when we bailed him out of that thing in Rome a few years ago."

Thomas had the ignoble distinction of being one of the few priests ever arrested by the freaking Vatican guard.

Even then, it wasn't him who'd reached out for help.

My son would never forgive me for the decision I forced on him ten years ago. A decision that saved his life and avoided a scandal for the family. A decision that until now, I'd refused to regret.

Secrets and regret were such quietly destructive forces on a family. I understood that now.

At the time, the Vatican had arranged for a "donation" in exchange for quieting up the whole mess. I'd paid the fines and the bribes and got him back in the Pope's good graces.

Yet another scandal avoided.

Not that Thomas would show any gratitude.

Part of me had long ago given up hope of reconnecting with my younger son, but Stella made me want to try.

"What do you think the chances are of him coming back into

the fold? Perhaps if he sees how much the family has changed? All our charitable work."

"She is throwing a party. That is hardly new," Luc pointed out.

"The party is still a few weeks out, and I hear she has already raised a few million for the Lincoln Center. I know she chose the center for Charlotte, and I suspect she is considering something for Amelia's school next. Amelia will have the funds to open a second location with free tuition in the next two years."

"If Amelia wanted to do that, I would pay for it myself, but I see your point. As we speak, Amelia's more advanced students are creating some pieces to auction at the event. Are you worried Thomas will hijack her causes and make her choose something you don't support?"

"I don't care what she raises money for. I really don't. She could put a Democrat in the white house for all I care."

"Since when have you bothered with politics? You always said red or blue doesn't matter. They both respond to green." Luc tried to hide his amusement, but he failed.

"True, but you get my point," I said, pressing my lips together, annoyed.

"I do, so what does this have to do with Thomas?"

"We were talking a while ago about what our future might hold and how she wants to work—"

"Hence the charitable foundation?"

"It's not like she doesn't have the experience throwing parties or the education," I bit out, not liking what Luc was insinuating.

He held his hands up. "I'm just making sure I am following along."

"When the topic of children came up, she mentioned that I already had three grown children. She didn't even know about your brother. She and Charlotte have been friends for years, and she had no idea he existed."

"I'm not sure Amelia does either, to be honest." Luc nodded.

"That's exactly my point. I want that to change. I think it's time he returned to the family." I took a deep breath. "I put an alert on his passport so I would always know where he was, and if he went somewhere dangerous, I could have people watch him."

"Bet he loved that."

"He doesn't know, but I know he flew into JFK this morning."

"What are we going to do?" Luc asked.

"We?"

Just as Luc opened his mouth, a loud explosion came from the distillery.

We both turned to look just in time to see several more explosions go off, starting at the front entrance and going all the way to the tasting room.

The ground shook hard enough to make Luc and I both grab onto the cars, whose alarms were now wailing as people screamed.

Before I could blink, the roof over the tasting room collapsed.

Stella was still in there.

CHAPTER 36

STELLA

"$\mathcal{I}$ think we want to have an overt Irish vibe," I said as we walked through the distillery. "I almost want to give it a pub-type feel, with different elements that really elevate it to the next level."

"I don't know how much we can really change to accommodate—"

"No," I interrupted the man giving me the tour of the distillery. "The point is I don't want to change anything. We're going to add the party venue on top of what is already here. It's something that we're going to be able to put up very quickly, probably on the day of, and then disassemble it the next day and allow everyone to get back to work with minimal, if any, interruption."

"I do like the sound of that. We do keep very strict timelines."

"I understand that completely, and the last thing I want to do is to make this harder than it has to be or to disrupt the flow of your workers. Here's what I'm thinking, and please feel free to add anything or let me know what wouldn't be feasible."

"Okay." He looked at me like he was a little distrusting of what I was saying, and I understood.

But I really did want to make this work well for everyone.

"So, I'm thinking over there, where you have all of the barrels stacked, I want to make sure none of our guests can get to those. The last thing we want is an accident. So I want to encase that area in glass, making it decor. The barrels will not be moved. We'll just put up the walls. Then it will be taken down immediately. In front of that is where I want to put the bar."

"Did you want me to build a bar?"

"No. I actually have a contractor who is already aware of the specs of the room, so as soon as I tell him where the bar is going to go, he's going to build it from wood reclaimed from old barrels. It'll be fairly simple, it'll look rustic, and the best part is that it will be built off-site, brought in, and then taken away."

"That sounds great." He really did look relieved.

"I'm thinking the dance floor is going to be where those large copper vats are. Is there anything that we need to make sure the guests can't do, like locking down any controls or valves?"

"Yes, and I will have that taken care of before you and your guests start arriving."

"Perfect." I was so excited.

All of this was coming together so beautifully.

I wanted this party to be a success, to prove to not only Lucian that I was up to the task, but to myself too. I hadn't even hired a party planner, just a caterer, and everything else was up to me.

"We do need to figure out where the DJ will be set up, and I also want to have a pedestal, somewhere Charlotte can play."

"What does she play?"

"Charlotte Manwarring. She is a cellist. She is going to play a few bar songs but edge them up a bit. It will be her and one other cellist. I also want to set up a place for Amelia Manwarring's students to auction off some of their work. We are going to make this party a full Manwarring event. Even Olivia is sending her best photographers to cover everything."

"That can be arranged. I will work with your contractor directly." The manager shook my hand. "We will make sure this is perfect. Now, why don't you follow me, and we will head to the tasting room. Your mixologist got a full tour earlier and is now working on a few signature cocktails for the event."

We walked to the back of the building, where there was a gorgeous, private tasting room.

This was going to be perfect for the VIP party, where the music would be softer, and those who wanted to talk would order bottle service with the more expensive bottles.

It was all just perfect.

I was going to make Lucian so proud of me.

We were walking down the long hallways when I heard some shouting, and the site manager excused himself to deal with whatever was happening.

I made a mental note to be sure we had plenty of security, not only because the liquor was flowing, but also because I really wanted to make sure we left the distillery in perfect shape.

The last thing I needed was a few football players to get into it with a couple of drunk rock stars.

"Miss Deiderich." Aiden, the mixologist I'd hired, gave me a warm smile. "Thank you so much for arranging the tour and tasting. I thought I knew a lot about whiskey, but I clearly needed more of an education. I learned so much."

"Please, call me Stella. And that's great. Did you get any ideas for the signature cocktails?"

"Yes, in fact, I have a few for you to try. I figured we would want three cocktails: something sweet, something more classic, and something really light and refreshing."

"That sounds perfect." I smiled and sat on the polished wooden bar stool in front of Aiden.

"First up, we have our refreshing, charred cherry whiskey lemonade."

He handed me the glass, and it looked amazing, perfectly presented with an artful garnish. It was delicious. The lemonade was tart, and the cherries were sweet and smoky but not overly heavy. This would absolutely quench my thirst after a long night on the dance floor.

"Next is the sweet. Give me one moment to make a fresh one." Aiden smiled as I sipped the lemonade.

Alison, my assistant, walked in as quickly as possible with several clipboards in her one hand and her phone held between her shoulder and ear.

I took the clipboards while she finished the call and sat down.

"Sorry it took me a moment to get back here. Some guy at the front didn't want to let me in. I had to threaten to call the police just so he would move." She rolled her eyes and took a deep breath.

"Who was that on the phone?"

"That was the contractor. He was confirming he received the blueprints. He is also working with the lighting guy and wanted me to run something by you."

"Okay."

"What do you think of having a spotlight on the cellists, but have it be an icy blue color, only while they're playing, giving a kind of cool vibe."

"Oh, I like that, actually. Reach out to Charlotte and let her know. Her friend also plays in a metal band. She might have lighting ideas that she knows work best, and find out what kind of outlets they need."

"Outlets?" Her brows furrowed.

"They are playing electric cellos, and her drummer is going to come too."

"That's great," she said just as there was more yelling outside. "Are we going to have to add him to the payroll?"

"No," I said, distracted by the shouting. "He just wants a shout-out on the party's social media. He knows several music producers are coming, and he is a drummer for hire."

"Okay." She made a note on one of the clipboards. "In the meantime, I just checked the raffle. The amount of traffic after the celebrities shared posts is unreal. Especially the Love is Blind cast. We have four RSVPs with plus one, but the entire cast shared the link. They just got the website back up, and we are now at two million dollars raised for the Lincoln Center for the Performing Arts. I also have a few luxury brands reaching out, wanting to donate trips and items for the raffle."

"Good, do it. Just make sure there are no direct competitors for Manwarring Liquors."

"Got it. It's mostly complementary stuff, like Killian perfumes, a bottle of Angel's Share, a few gourmet foods, a spa retreat, and other similar items."

"Perfect. Make sure anything we accept is added to the website and social media, and they do as well. How are we on media coverage?"

"Everyone is picking up the story, and every single magazine with a lifestyle section wants to send photographers."

"Paps can be outside, but inside access is—"

"Exclusive to Olivia," she finished for me.

"What would I do without you?" I asked.

"Host this at Chucky Cheese," she said, and we both giggled as Aiden came back with a drink for each of us.

"Ladies, here is our sweet option. A Blackberry Smash—this cocktail not only has fresh berries that taste like summer, but ginger beer to lighten it, a little elderflower liquor to cut through the sweetness, and of course, the finest whiskey. Enjoy."

The way he winked at Allison made me blush as she smiled and took a sip. This one was another homerun—perfect.

"What about the—" Alison was cut off when several loud bangs came from the distillery, and the ground underneath us shook—then another one, and this time closer.

Allison and I screamed and moved behind the heavy wooden door with Aiden.

The bangs got closer, and the ground shook until one went off right outside the door, followed by a blinding light and intense heat.

I was thrown across the room in a blast of heat...

Then everything went dark.

CHAPTER 37

LUCIAN

A high-pitched ringing echoed in my ears, loud enough to block out everything but the destruction.

I watched my distillery, the core of my business, blow up.

It wasn't until Luc grabbed me and shook me that everything came back, and I could hear people shouting, some for help and others as they tried to pull pieces of debris off of survivors.

Sirens wailed in the distance. There were going to be a lot of injuries, as most people were around what was left of the barrels and vats.

It made sense that was where the rescue teams were going to focus and try to put out the fires that were raging so they could rescue the most people.

But Stella wasn't there.

Stella wasn't anywhere near the vats.

She had been in the tasting room on the other side of the building.

Without a second thought, I took off.

Luc called after me, but I didn't stop.

I couldn't stop.

Stella needed me to protect her, and I had failed her.

I got to where the tasting room had stood. Now it was a pile of rubble and wood.

"Stella!" I called her name as I dug, pulling pieces off the pile, trying to find her.

I tried to lift a massive beam that had so much pinned under it. It was solid oak, I had picked the piece of polished wood myself, but I couldn't budge it. I used my knees, my back, everything I had, and I could only lift it a few centimeters.

Then Luc was next to me counting.

"One, two, lift," he grunted, and we both managed to pull the beam off the pile, allowing us to get to the smaller pieces under it.

We worked together frantically and silently until Luc called, "Here!"

I ran over to where he was.

He was holding a feminine hand with beige polish.

It wasn't her. I knew it wasn't.

Ever since Stella dyed her hair, she refused to wear anything beige or white, insisting that a second chance at life meant she had earned the right to color.

Still, maybe she had been with Stella.

Her new assistant? Or a friend who was helping out?

We dug her out, but the poor woman was already gone.

Luc carefully brought her to the side and called out to the paramedics who had just arrived.

I kept searching for Stella.

A fist gripped my heart tighter with each passing moment, and I was starting to realize exactly how much Stella meant to me.

I told her that I admired her, and that was true.

I had told her that I wanted her, and that was definitely true, but there was more here, and I refused to let her die without telling her what she meant to me.

Fuck that. I just refused to let her die.

She wasn't allowed to die before I did.

I forbade it.

No one knew the sting of losing a wife better than I did, and I refused to go through it again. Not now, not ever.

More rescue workers came to help dig people out, but they couldn't find anyone.

"Could she have been somewhere else?" Luc asked.

"No, she was in the tasting room, trying the signature cocktails for the party. She has to be here." I stopped to look around. The most charring was over by where the door should have been.

"Are you sure?"

"Positive. The manager sent me a text when she went in there to make sure I was here in time to take her to lunch afterward. I wanted to tell her how proud I was of her and—" The smoke and dust made my throat thick and my eyes water.

"Are you okay?" Luc asked, concern lacing his words.

"No, not until we find her and make sure she's okay." I started digging again.

Luc tried arguing that I should let the professionals do this, but they weren't as motivated as I was.

They didn't have the woman they loved under the rubble, and they weren't the ones to blame for all of this.

This was my fault.

I had lost my temper and fired Ronan's fucking douchebag of a cousin. I had said things that he would be forced to respond to, and I had taken another stream of revenue from him.

I had turned my back on the O'Murphys and then underestimated how quickly they would respond.

This was a personal attack on me.

He was sending a message that he'd helped me build all of this and could just as easily tear it down.

Stella wasn't even a target, but an innocent caught in the crossfire of a war she had no part in.

"Fuck!" I yelled as I hit the wood floor with nothing to show for it again.

I tried to calm down and think logically.

The blast had happened by the door. She was most likely by the bar. That had been the last of the bombs to go off. She may have been smart enough to get behind the heavy oak.

I looked over at where the door would have been, tried to estimate where the bar had been before the explosion to judge where to dig.

Luc was still right next to me, lifting with me, pulling away the debris, and looking for any sign.

We found a man I didn't recognize. He was badly bruised, judging by the gut-wrenching angles some of his limbs were in. He had broken several bones. But he was alive and barely conscious.

Luc yelled for the paramedics while I looked at the man. "Where is Stella?"

His eyes looked glazed. I knew he was hurt, but I was desperate.

For the first time in my life, I begged, "Please, try and think. Please, I need to find her."

"The blast sent her that way," he said, pointing in the vague direction we'd found the other girl. The other woman was much taller than Stella. Maybe if she was blown back by the blast, Stella had gone farther.

I handed the man over to the paramedics surrounding me and moved out of the way, heading over to where we'd found the other girl and scrambled to move the bricks and debris.

I gave everything I had, every ounce of determination and

strength to find her. The sun began to set, and most of the rescue teams had already departed, having no hope of any more survivors.

But I was not giving up.

Then I saw it: one of her bright pink shoes that matched her hair.

She was so excited when she found them and insisted on showing them off the second she came home from shopping with Olivia.

I remembered the way the sharp stilettos dug into my back as I made her scream my name, wearing nothing but those shoes.

"Over here," I called as I dug faster.

The dull aches disappeared into a second wind as I pushed to find her.

Finally, I pulled off a large piece of drywall to see her lying crushed in a pile of broken wood.

A small trail of blood was coming from her lips, and her skin was so pale.

I lunged for her, pulling her into my arms and holding her cold body to my chest.

"I am so sorry, baby girl. I did this. This is my fault, and I am so sorry." Tears streamed down my face, and I didn't care.

Some men in uniforms came to take her away, but I wouldn't let her go until Luc put his arms around me and pulled me away.

"Let them help her," he said over and over.

I still didn't breathe until one shouted, "I have a pulse!"

"Save her," I yelled. "Do whatever it takes, spare no expense, just save her."

One of the paramedics looked at me, her blonde hair in a high ponytail and her face and body covered in soot.

"Sir, if you want to come to the hospital with us, be ready to go the second the ambulance gets here, but stay out of our way."

"What hospital?" Luc asked, still holding me back.

They shouted something I couldn't hear, and Luc pulled me away.

"No, I want to go with her. She will be scared if she wakes up."

"There is no way you are going to stay out of their way. We are going to get there before them and make sure they know who is coming in and the best doctors are ready."

In the next second, Luc threw me in the back of the car, and we pulled out as the ambulance pulled in.

Luc got behind the wheel and drove like a madman. The ambulance ended up a few blocks behind us. Luc used their siren to help clear the way.

"We are going to make him pay for this," Luc promised.

"As soon as she is safe," I agreed. "Not until I know she is going to be okay."

"She will be," Luc said, taking another tight corner, ignoring how his back tires spun out just a little. "She is going to make it because you refused to give up on her."

"I will never give up on her. She is strong and a fighter. She has already survived so much. I will spend the rest of my life making this up to her."

We pulled up to the emergency room, and I bolted out of the car before it even came to a full stop, marching into the ER like I owned the place, because I practically did.

In seconds, I had the medical chief calling the best trauma team together.

It didn't make me feel better when I saw Stella's limp body on that gurney with the blonde paramedic straddling her hips, performing CPR.

"Do not let her die," I said under my breath, unsure if I was talking to the doctors or threatening God himself.

CHAPTER 38

LUCIAN

"We have done all we can," the doctor said as they wheeled Stella into the room I had prepared for her. "The rest is up to her. If she wakes up in the next few days, we will be able to see how much, if any permanent brain damage was done by the impact."

"If she doesn't?" I asked, knowing I didn't want to know the answer, but needing to hear it.

"Let's just do everything we can to make sure she does." The doctor patted my arm in what I assumed was meant to be a reassuring and not condescending way.

"Fine."

I wasn't going to argue with him. The man had been overseeing her surgeries personally. For him, it had been twelve hours of grueling work. For me, it had been twelve hours of hell.

Luc stayed as long as he could, and when he left, Olivia came and stayed with me for a while, and then Charlotte.

I didn't remember what we talked about if anything.

They were just there for me, and I tried to remember if I had ever just been there for them.

Not when Olivia was taken, or Charlotte was hurt.

I wasn't even there for Luc when Amelia had left him, and it nearly destroyed him.

At the time, I hadn't understood his pain.

So a girl he barely knew had rejected him—I had told him to move on and find a prettier wife. He'd looked at me like I was a monster.

What he had gone through, why Reid wouldn't leave Charlotte's room willingly, and why Harrison was willing to burn the world to the ground to get his wife back—it had taken me falling for a tenacious girl to understand that. To be reminded of an all-consuming love that I had never thought I'd ever feel again.

The doctors and nurses took a moment to hook up all the monitors and lines to Stella to monitor her vitals, and set up the room just as I'd demanded. She had a corner suite with windows, a private room with plenty of natural light, and a direct line of sight to the nurse's station.

As soon as they were done, I took a seat next to her, lacing my fingers with hers, just needing to hold her hand.

Her vitals beeped along steadily, but she still didn't have any color in her cheeks despite the transfusions.

I sat in that chair for a few hours, taking the time to look up the careers of every doctor and surgeon attending to her case. I made sure each of them was up for the task. As soon as she was awake, I would be transferring her to a room that would be set up in our home to accommodate her better and keep her safe.

Reid was in the process of putting together a team of Marines to hunt down Ronan and the others responsible for this.

Luc was handling the business, dealing with getting the party pushed back, all the news about the distillery, and making sure Manwarring Enterprises wouldn't be too affected by this.

He refused to let me help, and although I would never tell

him, I was grateful for the freedom to not think about the company.

For the first time in a very long time, I didn't give a damn about business.

My attention was consumed by Stella.

She looked so frail, lying in her hospital bed with her pink hair, a mess of tangles, and dirt still smeared under her cheeks. She had several bright bruises forming on her jaw and her shoulders. But thankfully, she'd only broken her arm and a few ribs.

One rib had punctured a lung, but that was easily repaired.

What worried the doctors was how hard she was hit in the head. Her brain was swelling with the trauma, and until it went down, they had no way to know the extent of the damage.

"Sir, visiting hours are over," a wide-set nurse said as she came in to record Stella's vitals.

"What's your point?" I asked, not letting go of her hand.

"My point, sir, is that this patient is not your family. You can see her tomorrow."

"She is my fiancée. I'm not going anywhere." I didn't even look up at her as I spoke.

"Sir, I have to insist." The nurse sounded more annoyed.

"Insist all you like, I am not moving."

"Do I need to call security?" she asked like that would do a damn thing.

"Do you know who I am?"

"You are a guest that has overstayed his welcome in my unit. Leave, or I will have you escorted out."

"I am Lucian Manwarring," I said, getting to my feet, still refusing to let go of Stella's hand.

"Is that supposed to mean something to me?" she asked in a bored tone.

"Go to the lobby and see the name printed on the plaque in

front of this hospital. I paid for this entire wing. Every brick, every single piece of equipment was paid for by a generous donation by me."

"Sir, that doesn't mean the rules don't apply to you."

"That is exactly what that means!" I roared. "I will personally tear apart this entire hospital brick by brick if you don't get the fuck out of here."

"Sir, I will call security." She put her hands on her hips like she could scold me like a small child.

"Do it, and I would love to have a conversation about how they let my daughter be kidnapped from this hospital a few months ago."

"Sir, it is not appropriate for you to be here with her. She is unconscious, and you are not her parent."

"I am the trustee of her estate," I pointed out. "In charge of all medical and financial decisions."

"She is an adult. And I thought you said she was your fiancée."

"She is. I am her trustee and her fiancé. You cannot force me to leave."

I didn't care if I was the one being unreasonable.

Screaming and shouting like a madman probably had half the security on their way to this room right now.

They would have to shoot me to get me to leave this room.

"You need to go. I don't know what kind of arrangement you have, but not here, not in my hospital."

"*My* hospital. If you have a problem with it, leave it. I love her. I am not going anywhere unless she wakes up and tells me to leave. No one is making me leave. No one."

There was a slight pulse around my hand, and I looked down to see Stella's once limp fingers curled around mine.

Her eyes opened to the beautiful golden brown I had missed so much.

"Baby girl, you're awake," I said, choking up.

"Doctors, come quick," the nurse called.

"I love you too, Lucian," Stella's voice cracked.

I placed a kiss on her forehead before whispering, "I love you so much. We have a new rule. You're never, ever allowed to leave me again."

CHAPTER 39

LUCIAN

"You know, I don't think I have ever seen you nervous," Luc joked, standing next to me at the altar.

"Fuck off," I muttered under my breath.

We were standing in my back garden on a warm, sunny July afternoon.

This was not like a first wedding, a big stuffy affair with hundreds of guests all dressed in couture and crammed in a Catholic church.

No, this was what Stella wanted.

A ceremony in nature, full of life and color. She even had me in linen pants and a shirt, just this side of formal.

"I still can't believe this is your wedding," Luc said. "After you gave me so much shit about the sculpture garden."

"Are you done?" I asked.

"If he is, can I start?" Charlotte asked as she took her place next to where Stella would be.

I pointed out, "You know, I can still remove both of you from the will."

"Go ahead. I don't need your money," Charlotte said sweetly. It was true. I hated to admit it, but she had chosen well for herself.

Back to the task at hand.

I'd wanted to get married the second Stella was out of the hospital, but she'd insisted we waited until the garden was in full bloom, giving me time to spend with her first and even start the reconciliation process with Thomas, who was supposed to be here, but I hadn't seen him.

The only guests were my children and their spouses.

The garden was full of butterflies and explosions of color, such as roses and other flowers, but I had no idea what they were called.

The string quartet went silent.

Our attention was at the end of the aisle, where Stella appeared in a gorgeous white gown with floral embroidery around her waist and down the flowing skirt. Her hair was freshly re-dyed in vivid pink, and flowers, little blue and white ones, were laced throughout.

She looked stunning. Like a fairy princess meant just for me.

Stella had recovered completely from the bombing like only she could.

She was a fighter and a survivor, and more importantly, she was mine forever.

I was prepared to spend the rest of my life proving to her how much I loved her and would cherish her always.

The ceremony was simple, with no need for pomp and circumstance.

This wasn't the show of power and wealth I had originally planned. It was just a promise to love, honor, and protect this woman for the rest of my life, a promise I intended to keep.

When the preacher said the magic words, "I now pronounce

you man and wife", I leaned in to kiss her and gave the signal for wildflower petals to be released.

They floated all around us, giving her the beautiful color and fairy tale ending I knew she would adore.

EPILOGUE

THOMAS

I could strangle that fucking Cardinal with my bare hands for forcing me into this position.

Four days ago, I was a priest in Rome, a city which never fully shed its decadent and debouched pagan past.

It was glorious.

Now, I was exiled back to this hellhole New York City and facing excommunication.

As I leaned against a tree, watching my family celebrate my estranged father's wedding, I knew precisely how the devil must have felt. The desire to destroy their false Garden of Eden just for the pleasure of seeing it burn was strong.

Then I saw her.

Mary Quinn Astrid.

The women who'd ruined my life ten years ago. That bitch.

My fingers tightened around my whisky glass, threatening to crack the crystal.

As I glared in her direction, an almost feral need to tear her life to shreds with my bare teeth rose in me.

Then my gaze landed on the perfect method of revenge. Her daughter.

To be continued...

Look for *Sinfully His* in the Late Fall 2024.

THE GILDED DECADENCE SERIES

Ruthlessly His

Gilded Decadence Series, Book One

**His family dared to challenge mine, so I am going to ruin them...
starting with stealing his bride.**

Only a cold-hearted villain would destroy an innocent bride's special
day over a business deal gone bad...

Which is why I choose this precise moment to disrupt New York High
Society's most anticipated wedding of the season.

As I am Luc Manwarring, II, billionaire heir to one of the most powerful
families in the country, no one is brave enough to stop me.

My revenge plan is deceptively simple: humiliate the groom, then
blackmail the bride's family into coercing the bride into marrying me
instead.

My ruthless calculations do not anticipate my reluctant bride having so
much fight and fire in her.

At every opportunity, she resists my dominance and control, even going
so far as trying to escape my dark plans for her.

She is only supposed to be a means to an end, an unwilling player in my
game of revenge.

But the more she challenges me, the more I begin to wonder... who is
playing who?

Savagely His

Gilded Decadence Series, Book Two

He dared to steal my bride, so it's only fair I respond by kidnapping his innocent sister.

Only a monster with no morals would kidnap a woman from her brother's wedding…

Which was precisely what I've become, a monster bent on revenge.

After all, as the billionaire Marksen DuBois, renowned for being a jilted groom, my reputation and business were in tatters.

There was nothing more dangerous than a man possessing power, boundless resources, and a vendetta.

I would torment him with increasingly degrading photos of his precious sister as I held her captive and under my complete control.

She'd have no option but to yield to my every command if she wished to shield herself and her family from further disgrace.

She was just a captured pawn to be dominated, exploited, and discarded.

Yet the more ensnared we become in my twisted game of revenge, the more my suspicions grow.

As she fiercely counters my every move, I begin to question whether I'm the true pawn… ensnared by my queen.

Brutally His

Gilded Decadence Series, Book Three

From our very first fiery encounter, I was tempted to fire my beautiful new assistant.

Right after I punished her for that defiant slap she delivered in response to my undeniably inappropriate kiss.

As Harrison Astrid, New York's formidable District Attorney, distractions were a luxury I couldn't afford.

Forming a shaky alliance with the Manwarrings and the Dubois, I was ensnared in a dangerous cat-and-mouse game.

As I strive to thwart my mother's cunning manipulations and her deadly alliance with the Irish mob.

Yet, every time I cross paths with my assistant, our mutual animosity surges into a near-savage need to control and dominate her.

I am a man who demands obedience, especially from subordinates.

Her stubbornness fuels my urge to assert my dominance, my need to show her I'm not just her boss—I'm her master.

Unfortunately the fiancé I'm to accept to play high society's charade, complicates things.

So I rein in my desire and resist the attraction between us.

Until the Irish mob targets my pretty little assistant... targets what's mine.

Now there isn't a force on earth that will keep me from tearing the city apart to find her.

Reluctantly His

Gilded Decadence Series, Book Four

First rule of being a bodyguard, don't f*ck the woman you're protecting.

And I want to break that rule so damn bad I can practically taste her.

She's innocent, sheltered, and spoiled.

As Reid Taylor, former Army sergeant and head of security for the Manwarrings, the last thing I should be doing is babysitting my boss's little sister.

I definitely shouldn't be fantasizing about pinning her down, spreading her thighs and...

It should help that she fights my protection at every turn.

Disobeying my rules. Running away from me. Talking back with that sexy, smart mouth of hers.

But it doesn't. It just makes me want her more.

I want to bend her over and claim her, hard and rough, until she begs for mercy.

That is a dangerous line I cannot cross.

She is an heiress, the precious daughter of one of the most powerful, multi-billionaire families in New York.

And I'm just her bodyguard, an employee. It would be the ultimate societal taboo.

But now her family is forcing her into an arranged marriage, and I'm not sure I'll be able to contain my rising rage at the idea of another man touching her.

Unwillingly His

Gilded Decadence Series, Book Five

The moment she slapped me, I knew I'd chosen the right bride.

To be fair, I had just stolen her entire inheritance.

As Lucian Manwarring, billionaire patriarch of the powerful Manwarring family, my word is law.

She's a beautiful and innocent heiress, raised to be the perfect society trophy wife.

Although far too young for me, that won't stop me from claiming her as my new prized possession.

What I hadn't planned on was her open defiance of me.

Far from submissive and obedient; she is stubborn, outspoken and headstrong.

She tries to escape my control and fights my plan to force her down the aisle.

I am not accustomed to being disobeyed.

While finding it mildly amusing at first, it is past time she accepts her fate.

She will be my bride even if I have to ruthlessly dominate and punish her to get what I want.

ABOUT ZOE BLAKE

Zoe Blake is the USA Today Bestselling Author of the romantic suspense saga *The Cavalieri Billionaire Legacy* inspired by her own heritage as well as her obsession with jewelry, travel, and the salacious gossip of history's most infamous families.

She delights in writing Dark Romance books filled with overly possessive billionaires, taboo scenes, and unexpected twists. She usually spends her ill-gotten gains on martinis, travels, and red lipstick. Since she can barely boil water, she's lucky enough to be married to a sexy Chef.

ALSO BY ZOE BLAKE

CAVALIERI BILLIONAIRE LEGACY

A Dark Enemies to Lovers Romance

Scandals of the Father

Cavalieri Billionaire Legacy, Book One

Being attracted to her wasn't wrong... but acting on it would be.

As the patriarch of the powerful and wealthy Cavalieri family, my choices came with consequences for everyone around me.

The roots of my ancestral, billionaire-dollar winery stretch deep into the rich, Italian soil, as does our legacy for ruthlessness and scandal.

It wasn't the fact she was half my age that made her off limits.

Nothing was off limits for me.

A wounded bird, caught in a trap not of her own making, she posed no risk to me.

My obsessive desire to possess her was the real problem.

For both of us.

But now that I've seen her, tasted her lips, I can't let her go.

Whether she likes it or not, she needs my protection.

I'm doing this for her own good, yet, she fights me at every turn.

Refusing the luxury I offer, desperately trying to escape my grasp.

I need to teach her to obey before the dark rumors of my past reach her.

Ruin her.

She cannot find out what I've done, not before I make her mine.

Sins of the Son

Cavalieri Billionaire Legacy, Book Two

She's hated me for years... now it's past time to give her a reason to.

When you are a son, and one of the heirs, to the legacy of the Cavalieri name, you need to be more vicious than your enemies.

And sometimes, the lines get blurred.

Years ago, they tried to use her as a pawn in a revenge scheme against me.

Even though I cared about her, I let them treat her as if she were nothing.

I was too arrogant and self-involved to protect her then.

But I'm here now. Ready to risk my life tracking down every single one of them.

They'll pay for what they've done as surely as I'll pay for my sins against her.

Too bad it won't be enough for her to let go of her hatred of me,

To get her to stop fighting me.

Because whether she likes it or not, I have the power, wealth, and connections to keep her by my side

And every intention of ruthlessly using all three to make her mine.

Secrets of the Brother

Cavalieri Billionaire Legacy, Book Three

We were not meant to be together... then a dark twist of fate stepped in, and we're the ones who will pay for it.

As the eldest son and heir of the Cavalieri name, I inherit a great deal more than a billion dollar empire.

I receive a legacy of secrets, lies, and scandal.

After enduring a childhood filled with malicious rumors about my father, I have fallen prey to his very same sin.

I married a woman I didn't love out of a false sense of family honor.

Now she has died under mysterious circumstances.

And I am left to play the widowed groom.

For no one can know the truth about my wife…

Especially her sister.

The only way to protect her from danger is to keep her close, and yet, her very nearness tortures me.

She is my sister in name only, but I have no right to desire her.

Not after what I have done.

It's too much to hope she would understand that it was all for her.

It's always been about her.

Only her.

I am, after all, my father's son.

And there is nothing on this earth more ruthless than a Cavalieri man in love.

Seduction of the Patriarch

Cavalieri Billionaire Legacy, Book Four

With a single gunshot, she brings the violent secrets of my buried past into the present.

She may not have pulled the trigger, but she still has blood on her hands.

And I know some very creative ways to make her pay for it.

I am as ruthless as my Cavalieri ancestors, who forged our powerful family legacy.

But no fortune is built without spilling blood.

I earn a reputation as a dangerous man to cross… and make enemies along the way.

So to protect those I love, I hand over the mantle of patriarch to my brother and move to northern Italy.

For years, I stay in the shadows…

Then a vengeful mafia syndicate attacks my family.

Now nothing will prevent me from seeking vengeance on those responsible.

And I don't give a damn who I hurt in the process... including her.

Whether it takes seduction, punishment, or both, I intend to manipulate her as a means to an end.

Yet, the more my little kitten shows her claws, the more I want to make her purr.

My plan is to coerce her into helping me topple the mafia syndicate, and then retreat into the shadows.

But if she keeps fighting me... I might just have to take her with me.

Scorn of the Betrothed

Cavalieri Billionaire Legacy, Book Five

A union forged in vengeance, bound by hate... and beneath it all, a twisted game of desire and deception.

In the heart of the Cavalieri family, I am the son destined for a loveless marriage.

The true legacy of my family, my birthright ties me to a woman I despise.

The daughter of the mafia boss who nearly ended my family.

She is my future wife, and I am her unwelcome groom.

The looming wedding is a beacon of hope for our families.

A promise of peace in a world fraught with danger and deception.

We were meant to be the bridge between two powerful legacies.

The only thing we share is a mutual hatred.

She is a prisoner to her families' ambitions, desperate for a way out.

My duty is to guard her, to ensure she doesn't escape her gilded cage.

But every moment spent with her, every spark of anger, adds fuel to the growing fire of desire between us.

We're trapped in a dangerous duel of passion and fury.

The more I try to tame her, the more she ignites me.

Hatred and desire become blurred.

Our impending marriage becomes a twisted game.

But as the wedding draws near, my suspicions grow.

My bride is not who she claims to be.

IVANOV CRIME FAMILY TRILOGY

A Dark Mafia Romance

Savage Vow

Ivanov Crime Family, Book One

Gregor & Samara's story

I took her innocence as payment.

She was far too young and naïve to be betrothed to a monster like me.

I would bring only pain and darkness into her sheltered world.

That's why she ran.

I should've just let her go…

She never asked to marry into a powerful Russian mafia family.

None of this was her choice.

Unfortunately for her, I don't care.

I own her… and after three years of searching… I've found her.

My runaway bride was about to learn disobedience has consequences…
punishing ones.

Having her in my arms and under my control had become an obsession.

Nothing was going to keep me from claiming her before the eyes of
God and man.

She's finally mine… and I'm never letting her go.

Vicious Oath

Ivanov Crime Family, Book One

Damien & Yelena's story

When I give an order, I expect it to be obeyed.

She's too smart for her own good, and it's going to get her killed.

Against my better judgement, I put her under the protection of my powerful Russian mafia family.

So imagine my anger when the little minx ran.

For three long years I've been on her trail, always one step behind.

Finding and claiming her had become an obsession.

It was getting harder to rein in my driving need to possess her... to own her.

But now the chase is over.

I've found her.

Soon she will be mine.

And I plan to make it official, even if I have to drag her kicking and screaming to the altar.

This time... there will be no escape from me.

Betrayed Honor

Ivanov Crime Family, Book One

Mikhail & Nadia's story

Her innocence was going to get her killed.

That was if I didn't get to her first.

She's the protected little sister of the powerful Ivanov Russian mafia family - the very definition of forbidden.

It's always been my job, as their Head of Security, to watch over her but never to touch.

That ends today.

She disobeyed me and put herself in danger.

It was time to take her in hand.

I'm the only one who can save her and I will fight anyone who tries to stop me, including her brothers.

Honor and loyalty be damned.

She's mine now.

RUTHLESS OBSESSION SERIES

A Dark Mafia Romance

Sweet Cruelty

Ruthless Obsession Series, Book One

Dimitri & Emma's story

It was an innocent mistake.

She knocked on the wrong door.

Mine.

If I were a better man, I would've just let her go.

But I'm not.

I'm a cruel bastard.

I ruthlessly claimed her virtue for my own.

It should have been enough.

But it wasn't.

I needed more.

Craved it.

She became my obsession.

Her sweetness and purity taunted my dark soul.

The need to possess her nearly drove me mad.

A Russian arms dealer had no business pursuing a naive librarian student.

She didn't belong in my world.

I would bring her only pain.

But it was too late…

She was mine and I was keeping her.

Sweet Depravity

Ruthless Obsession Series, Book Two

Vaska & Mary's story

The moment she opened those gorgeous red lips to tell me no, she was mine.

I was a powerful Russian arms dealer and she was an innocent schoolteacher.

If she had a choice, she'd run as far away from me as possible.

Unfortunately for her, I wasn't giving her one.

I wasn't just going to take her; I was going to take over her entire world.

Where she lived.

What she ate.

Where she worked.

All would be under my control.

Call it obsession.

Call it depravity.

I don't give a damn… as long as you call her mine.

Sweet Savagery

Ruthless Obsession Series, Book Three

Ivan & Dylan's Story

I was a savage bent on claiming her as punishment for her family's mistakes.

As a powerful Russian Arms dealer, no one steals from me and gets away with it.

She was an innocent pawn in a dangerous game.

She had no idea the package her uncle sent her from Russia contained my stolen money.

If I were a good man, I would let her return the money and leave.

If I were a gentleman, I might even let her keep some of it just for frightening her.

As I stared down at the beautiful living doll stretched out before me like a virgin sacrifice,

I thanked God for every sin and misdeed that had blackened my cold heart.

I was not a good man.

I sure as hell wasn't a gentleman… and I had no intention of letting her go.

She was mine now.

And no one takes what's mine.

Sweet Brutality

Ruthless Obsession Series, Book Four

Maxim & Carinna's story

The more she fights me, the more I want her.

It's that beautiful, sassy mouth of hers.

It makes me want to push her to her knees and dominate her, like the brutal savage I am.

As a Russian Arms dealer, I should not be ruthlessly pursuing an innocent college student like her, but that would not stop me.

A twist of fate may have brought us together, but it is my twisted obsession that will hold her captive as my own treasured possession.

She is mine now.

I dare you to try and take her from me.

Sweet Ferocity

Ruthless Obsession Series, Book Five

Luka & Katie's Story

I was a mafia mercenary only hired to find her, but now I'm going to keep her.

She is a Russian mafia princess, kidnapped to be used as a pawn in a dangerous territory war.

Saving her was my job. Keeping her safe had become my obsession.

Every move she makes, I am in the shadows, watching.

I was like a feral animal: cruel, violent, and selfishly out for my own needs. Until her.

Now, I will make her mine by any means necessary.

I am her protector, but no one is going to protect her from me.

Sweet Intensity

Ruthless Obsession Series, Book Six

Antonius & Brynn's Story

She couldn't possibly have known the danger she would be in the moment she innocently accepted the job.

She was too young for a man my age, barely in her twenties. Far too pure and untouched.

Too bad that wasn't going to stop me.

The moment I laid eyes on her, I claimed her.

She would be mine... by any means necessary.

I owned the most elite Gambling Club in Chicago, which was a secret front for my true business as a powerful crime boss for the Russian Mafia.

And she was a fragile little bird, who had just flown straight into my open jaws.

Naïve and sweet, she was a tasty morsel I couldn't resist biting.

My intense drive to dominate and control her had become an obsession.

I would ruthlessly use my superior strength and connections to take over her life.

The harder she resisted, the more feral and savage I would become.

She needed to understand… she was mine now.

Mine.

Sweet Severity

Ruthless Obsession Series, Book Seven

Macarius & Phoebe's Story

Had she crashed into any other man's car, she could have walked away—but she hit mine.

Upon seeing the bruises on her wrist, I struggled to contain my rage.

Despite her objections, I refused to allow her to leave.

Whoever hurt this innocent beauty would pay dearly.

As a Russian Mafia crime boss who owns Chicago's most elite gambling club, I have very creative and painful methods of exacting revenge.

She seems too young and naive to be out on her own in such a dangerous world.

Needing a nanny, I decided to claim her for the role.

She might resist my severe, domineering discipline, but I won't give her a choice in the matter.

She needs a protector, and I'd be damned if it were anyone but me.

Resisting the urge to claim her will test all my restraint.

It's a battle I'm bound to lose.

With each day, my obsession and jealousy intensify.

It's only a matter of time before my control snaps…and I make her mine.

Mine.

Sweet Animosity

Ruthless Obsession, Book Eight

Varlaam & Amber's Story

I never asked for an assistant, and if I had, I sure as hell wouldn't have chosen her.

With her sharp tongue and lack of discipline, what she needs is a firm hand, not a job.

The more she tests my limits, the more tempted I am to bend her over my knee.

As a Russian Mafia boss and owner of Chicago's most elite gambling club, I can't afford distractions from her antics.

Or her secrets.

For I suspect, my innocent new assistant is hiding something.

And I know just how to get to the truth.

It's high time she understands who holds the power in our relationship.

To ensure I get what I desire, I'll keep her close, controlling her every move.

Except I am no longer after information—I want her mind, body and soul.

She underestimated the stakes of our dangerous game and now owes a heavy price.

As payment I will take her freedom.

She's mine now.

Mine.

ABOUT ALTA HENSLEY

Alta Hensley is a USA TODAY Bestselling author of hot, dark and dirty romance. She is also an Amazon Top 10 bestselling author. Being a multi-published author in the romance genre, Alta is known for her dark, gritty alpha heroes, captivating love stories, hot eroticism, and engaging tales of the constant struggle between dominance and submission.

She lives in Astoria, Oregon with her husband, two daughters, and an Australian Shepherd. When she isn't walking the coastline, and drinking beer in her favorite breweries, she is writing about villains who always get their love story and happily ever after.

ALSO BY ALTA HENSLEY

HEATHENS HOLLOW SERIES

A Dark Stalker Billionaire Romance

Heathens

She invited the darkness in, so she'll have no one else to blame when I come for her.

The Hunt.

It is a sinister game of submission. She'll run. I'll chase.

And when I catch her, it will be savage. Untamed. Primal.

I will be the beast from her darkest fantasies.

I should be protecting her, but instead I've been watching her. Stalking her.

She's innocent. Forbidden. The daughter of my best friend.

But she chose this.

And even if she made a mistake, even if she wants to run, to escape, it's far too late.

She's mine now.

GODS AMONG MEN SERIES

A Dark Billionaire Romance

Villains Are Made

I know how villains are made.

I've watched their secrets rise from the ashes and emerge from the shadows.

As part of a family tree with roots so twisted, I'm strangled by their vine.

Imprisoned in a world of decadence and sin, I've seen Gods among men.

And he is one of them.

He is the villain.

He is the enemy who demands to be the lover.

He is the monster who has shown me pleasure but gives so much pain.

But something has changed…

He's different.

Darker.

Wildly possessive as his obsession with me grows to an inferno that can't be controlled.

Yes… he is the villain.

And he is the end of my beginning.

Monsters Are Hidden

The problem with secrets is they create powerful monsters.

And even more dangerous enemies.

He's the keeper of all his family's secrets, the watcher of all.

He knows what I've done, what I've risked… the deadly choice I made.

The tangled vines of his mighty family tree are strangling me.

There is no escape.

I am locked away, captive to his twisted obsession and demands.

If I run, my hell will never end.

If I stay, he will devour me.

My only choice is to dare the monster to come out into the light,

before his darkness destroys us both.

Yes… he is the monster in hiding.

And he is the end of my beginning.

Vipers Are Forbidden

It's impossible to enter a pit full of snakes and not get bit.

Until you meet me, that is.

My venom is far more toxic than the four men who have declared me
their enemy.

They seek vengeance and launch a twisted game of give and take.

I'll play in their dark world, because it's where I thrive.

I'll dance with their debauchery, for I surely know the steps.

But then I discover just how wrong I am. Their four, not only matches,
but beats, my one.

With each wicked move they make, they become my obsession.

I crave them until they consume all thought.

The temptation to give them everything they desire becomes too much.

I'm entering their world, and there is no light to guide my way. My
blindness full of lust will be my defeat.

Yes… I am the viper and am forbidden.

But they are the end of my beginning.

SPIKED ROSES BILLIONAIRE'S CLUB SERIES

A Dark Billionaires Romance

Bastards & Whiskey

I sit amongst the Presidents, Royalty, the Captains of Industry, and the wealthiest men in the world.

We own Spiked Roses—an exclusive, membership only establishment in New Orleans where money or lineage is the only way in. It is for the gentlemen who own everything and never hear the word no.

Sipping on whiskey, smoking cigars, and conducting multi-million dollar deals in our own personal playground of indulgence, there isn't anything I can't have… and that includes HER. I can also have HER if I want.

And I want.

Villains & Vodka

My life is one long fevered dream, balancing between being killed or killing.

The name Harley Crow is one to be feared.

I am an assassin.

A killer.

The villain.

I own it. I choose this life. Hell, I crave it. I hunger for it. The smell of fear makes me hard and is the very reason the blood runs through my veins.

Until I meet her…

Marlowe Masters.

Her darkness matches my own.

In my twisted world of dancing along the jagged edge of the blade…

She changes everything.

No weapon can protect me from the kind of death she will ultimately deliver.

Scoundrels & Scotch

I'll stop at nothing to own her.

I'm a collector of dolls.

All kinds of dolls.

So beautiful and sexy, they become my art.

So perfect and flawless, my art galleries are flooded by the wealthy to gaze upon my possessions with envy.

So fragile and delicate, I keep them tucked away for safety.

The dark and torrid tales of Drayton's Dolls run rampant through the rich and famous, and all but a few are true.

Normally I share my dolls for others to play with or watch on display.

But not my special doll.

No, not her.

Ivy is the most precious doll of all.

She's mine. All mine.

Devils & Rye

Forbidden fruit tastes the sweetest.

It had been years since I had seen her.

Years since I last saw those eyes with pure, raw innocence.

So much time had passed since I lusted after what I knew I should resist.

But she was so right.

And I was so wrong.

To claim her as mine was breaking the rules. Boundaries should not be broken. But temptation weakens my resolve.

With the pull of my dark desires…

I know that I can't hide from my sinful thoughts—and actions—forever.

Beasts & Bourbon

My royal blood flows black with twisted secrets.

I am a beast who wears a crown.

Heir to a modern kingdom cloaked in corruption and depravities.

The time has come to claim my princess.
An innocent hidden away from my dark world.

Till now.

Her initiation will require sacrifice and submission.

There is no escaping the chains which bind her to me.

Surrendering to my torment, as well as my protection, is her only path to survival.

In the end…
She will be forever mine.

Sinners & Gin

My power is absolute. My rules are law.

Structure.

Obedience.

Discipline.

I am in charge, and what I say goes. Black and white with no gray.

No one dares break the rules in my dark and twisted world… until her.
Until she makes me cross my own jagged lines.

She's untouched. Perfection. Pure.

Forbidden.

She tests my limits in all ways.

There is only one option left.

I will claim her as mine no matter how many rules are broken.

THANK YOU

THANK YOU.

Made in the USA
Monee, IL
22 June 2024

60334976R00174